Founder

LM Long

To my Father. who always believed I should write,
and my Mother, who never stopped pestering me to.

CONTENTS

Marta

Marta

Chapter One

Fissures of unrest threaten to overwhelm our cause here.

I skip over the puddles, the mud clinging to my feet. My steps deeply imprinted in the earth. It is not far into the jungle, patchy sunlight showcasing the green around me. The canopy still penetrable. There is no breeze to carry away the smell of a thousand defecations, so I hold my breath and jump in, my movements quick and instinctual.

Whispers of discontent float inside, their words not as guarded in this insulated space. The worried voices of older Untouchables, "food supplies are running short. . . we have to prepare ourselves. . . they will kill us first. . . is there anything the Princess can do?"

It's the last statement that sends me running for the safety of my own hut, before I can even rinse my hands upstream. My Nana used to call me beautiful before I knew the truth. Accidents are rarely beautiful, and combined with the word mistake, even less so. When it became obvious at age one my hair was a determined muddy brown, eyes even darker than my hair, and skin only slightly lighter than both, I was stripped of my royal title. I know which Princess they're referring to, they are the only ones who still call me that. The only Princess of my kind. Of course there is nothing I can do. I'm every bit as powerless as they are.

It has been over two months since we've received any supplies, and the colony can't survive without your support.

My room mate Ani is already gone when I return, her equipment bag missing from its branch on the wall. The rest of her bottles and supplies lining the shelf. My books are wrapped in their plastic sheathing and threatening to fall off one end. I pull out the slim primer I'll need later and place it on the table that serves as my desk. I reach up high to adjust the rest of my things, replacing the pen and papers I used only a few hours ago. The dress I was wearing yesterday gets thrown in the corner underneath the branches. The fabric thin and threadbare, an Untouchable will be in later to replace it with a clean one. A hanging fabric bag holds a single cracker that I consume before hanging the bag next to Ani's. Tasteless and dry, the rations dissolve quickly on my tongue. I toss my head back and inhale deeply. A bird outside our wood wall sings, a pattering of rain providing the beat for her melody.

There is not much to our hut, but it is home. The privacy a luxury, which none of the other Untouchables are allowed in their shared barracks. Untouchables are usually allowed no possessions, no space to call their own. None is expected. We are simply grateful to be spared our life.

I pull my gourd from the wall and take a quick sip of water before hooking it to my belt. I throw my album and mail tube into my satchel, the letter I've written a dozen times safely encased inside. I hurry out to catch up with Ani.

We are in desperate need of some of our most essential provisions, batteries, hypodermic needles, antibiotics.

The rain has let up some, steam now curling through the trees. The light fog obscures the path I race along, and I hear the drills before I see the soldiers. They have begun without me. I circumvent the unit I would normally join, and hurry along one of the covered walkways to Princess Julianne's hut. Julianne is the eldest of my siblings. Pale ringlets encircled her head at birth, angelic in everything but demeanor. Eleven months later came Jacob, a masculine twin. They may have been sweet once, before my birth and my mother's death. I wouldn't know.

I see Ani at the front of her line and run by without acknowledgement. It's a sea of blonde hair, punctuated by only a few brunettes. Drill is a physical representation of our minority status. If Ani's Captain notices even a flicker of disobedience she will be punished. Their cruelty is taken as an asset to our military prowess. They are nondiscriminatory in their punishments, and prejudicious in their praise. It's to be expected.

There is a large man at the end of this line, his eyes flicking back and forth- disgust, discomfort. He's surrounded on both sides by wiry Untouchables. This is the elite, the best of our defense. The military groups are formed by physical and mental prowess alone, without any regard to ones standing in the colony. If we were to go into battle, the weaker Untouchables would be on the front line, but the formations to follow would be filled with the mixed units. I know there are insurgent groups inside the Pure who disagree with this logic. They see the Untouchables as purely disposable, they think they should all be put on the front line, without any military training at all. My brother is a member of one such group. Thankfully our father, who is sharing power over the colony with my sister, disagrees with this line of thinking.

The Führer worries you have decided to cut off your aid, that you no longer believe in our purpose here. That our army may no longer be necessary.

Most of the colony try and make early morning drill, before humidity and our work can beat us into exhaustion. My satchel pounds against my hip as I run, the old leather album heavy. I carry it as a reminder of our purpose here. The brittle pages yellow with age. A picture of my great grandmother, the first to bear children, our first mother. A blurry photograph, the faces of the three children fuzzy and unrecognizable, their fathers standing proudly behind them. I've fingered the photographs, the proof that they existed, many times over the years. The men who established our Schutzgebiete, our civilization in the middle of this Amazon. The colony called Founder. I try to remember the bravery, the determination, of the diseased, shrunken men in the photographs. How it must have felt to take on such a grave mission, to be so important to the cause of mankind.

I worry something has happened to prevent you from receiving these letters.

I am almost to Julianne's when I notice a group of our smallest citizens learning basic defense maneuvers. I jump from the bridge and cross to the clearing they are practicing in, shielded by the trees. My attention is caught by two of the children who are split off from the large circle. A Pure Master has called them out from their groups. It is a grossly uneven challenge. A Pure and Untouchable child, being set against each other. The Pure child at least 50 pounds heavier and a good foot taller. Her pale hair falls in glossy sheets around her perfect facial structure. She doesn't even bother pulling it in a rag, sauntering into the middle of the ring. The scrawny mouse of an Untouchable can't be more than nine or ten, walking calmly to the center to meet her opponent. Her chestnut hair is cut short, and jagged at the ends. A punishment for talking out of turn. I wore the haircut many times when I was younger and less knowledgeable about the way things are.

The Pure child strikes first and is surprised when her fist connects with the air. Her face registers the shock for a brief moment before she turns and throws a leg up. Agile and quick to spot an opening in the Pure girl's defenses, it only takes the Untouchable a moment to duck the leg, grab hold of an arm, and bring the older girl down. The Untouchable is perched on her back, the blonde hair spread out around her, pressing the girl's face into the mud. She has a vice grip on one of her wrists, twisting it back, leaning her small body forward. I am about to cry out- I can see the pressure on the arm is too much, when the Untouchable tutor stops the contest with one word. "Elise!" She holds her own arms up, dropping the wrist immediately and jumping to her feet. The Pure master stands watching, clearly displeased. The beautiful girl is mortified to have been beaten by Elise, an Untouchable. Dirt clods cling to her hair, her face flushed and dripping with water. Rubbing her arm in pain, she rises to the jeers of her fellow competitors.

"Hasselbach!" someone yells, teasing her. The Pure girl's head bobs back, and a lob of mucus and spit slaps the side of Elise's face. It dribbles slowly down her cheek, until she reaches up to wipe it away. The beautiful girl sneers at her, daring her to do something. They stare at each other for a brief second before the girl tosses her blonde mane over her shoulder and turns back to her comrades. The Pure Master barking orders at her, muffled by the sounds around me.

The Untouchable side of the ring offers no congratulations as the tiny girl joins their ranks again. Her posture changes as she slips back into invisibility, her eyes losing their fierceness. The Tutor whispers furiously before snapping back to attention, awaiting his orders. Five little statues behind him. So young and they already realize that silence is our only defense. The only way to combat the cruelty of our situation. I push away from the scene before they can notice me, heading in the direction of my own fate.

Please respond. Please. We need you.

Lara

§

Chapter Two

A portion of music interrupts the stillness of my bedroom, "Ooh la la." Its perkiness annoys me as I reach over to hit the end button, look at the photo on the screen and realize it's my mom. I click to accept, groaning out my hello.

"Lara! Thank goodness you picked up. I found my Aunt Marion!" My mom's voice is too excited for the early hour of the morning.

"Mom," I whine. "What time is it?" I glance at the phone before screeching, "8am? Really Mom? You know I just got off the red eye from JFK."

"Sweetheart! I'm sorry, I completely forgot. I was so excited to call you because I can't believe I found her!"

"Find who?" I ask, confused since I don't have an Aunt Marion, and I think I may still be in the middle of a dream. Or a nightmare.

"Aunt Marion! My father's sister. We thought she was dead. Well I thought she must be dead because she would easily be in her late nineties and my father died so long ago. . ."

I spent the entire night serving cranky people drinks on an airplane. We had an emergency landing in Denver because a first class passenger had gas. I'm in no mood for one of my mom's stories. The faster I ask what she wants, the sooner this conversation ends, and I can go back to sleep.

"Mom, what does this have to do with me. . .at eight o'clock in the morning?"

"Oh! Honey, she's in a home, one of those Hospice deals in Yucaipa. We have to get over there today. I spoke with one of the nurses, and she's dying. I mean, Aunt Marion is dying. If I want a chance to talk to her it has to be today, and I wanted to know if you would go with me."

I contemplate this for a moment while my foggy brain begins to register the smell of bacon wafting into my bedroom. I weigh the option of snuggling back under my covers for another eight hours, in a thunderstorm no less, against feeling the weight of guilt my mom is sure to pile on me later when I don't go.

"What time do you want to leave?" I ask. Inwardly I roll my eyes at myself. "Sucker," I think.

Eventually I gather the details of when to pick her up and roll out of my bed. Throwing a robe on, I follow my nose to the kitchen. My husband, Sergio, is making breakfast. Making is not the right word. Creating. Enticing. Better, but still not right. He has worked in kitchens his whole life, his take no prisoners attitude at work quickly earning him the nickname of Sarge. I love watching him, demanding the ingredients to bend. His movements so quick and precise- every motion planned before executed. I grab a stool at the counter in front of him, a cup of chocolate appearing before me.

"Why are you up already?" he asks.

"My mother." Those two words are all he needs to hear. My mom is one of those caring and unselfish creatures to friends and strangers, but totally oblivious to the needs of her family. Well, in my case, one need- sleep.

"Well you can sleep when you're dead, mi amor," Sergio says to me.

"Well then, I hope we'll still be sleeping together," I giggle. Sergio blows me a kiss before tossing more bacon in the skillet.

"I'm happy I needed bacon for dinner tonight. I heard you talking and I threw together an omelet. Inventory's this morning or I would stay and help you eat it." He presents me with a beautiful plate, complete with a parsley leaf.

"Honey you're the best," I say between mouthfuls. "It's okay, I have to leave anyway- Mom and I are heading into Yucaipa to look up some long lost relative."

"Another one?" He gives me a warning look. "Babe, be careful. Remember what happened with Joe? That time your mom took him to look up the second half cousin twice removed by marriage?"

"Just second cousin," I tell him, laughing. It was the stuff of family legends, my mom dragging Uncle Joe into one of her family history projects a couple of years ago. It turned out we were living only an hour away from a second cousin they had known as kids. When they pulled onto his land, uninvited, he pulled a shotgun on my Uncle Joe until they left his property- no time to even explain their business.

Thankfully I was stuck on a layover in Seattle for that one.

"It's a little old lady in a nursing home," I say. "I think we'll be okay today."

"Call me when you get there anyway," he says. "You never know what those little old ladies might have in those giant handbags."

I'm reasonably certain it's industrial size Kleenex boxes and tubes of lipstick, but before I can respond he kisses my head, and is out the door.

"Mom, seriously, I'm driving as fast as I'm willing to go on two hours of sleep and a Diet Coke. She's not going to die before we get there." I picked up my mom half an hour ago, and she's been impatiently pressing me to step on the accelerator since.

"I'm anxious Honey. You know I know very little about my Dad's side of the family, not even much about my Dad. She may have some answers."

My lack of enthusiasm for spending the day at a nursing home and watching a stranger die, doesn't seem to be diminishing my mom's hope she'll find more family. Her mom lived well into her eighties, eight children, forty plus grandchildren, ten great grandchildren. I remember family reunions growing up, feeling a little lost among all the cousins- too many to remember. The last thing I think we need is *more* family. My grandfather died when my mom was young- her mom refused to talk about his death, never acknowledging any of his relations. When my grandmother died last year, the family could finally openly talk about the father they knew almost nothing about. They unearthed a few photos, the names faded, but legible on the back. They discovered an entire extended family on my grandfather's side. A family she never knew. Reading through some of my grandmother's journals gave light to another side of the story.

Her mother in law had hated her. Convinced she killed her son, they disowned the entire family. Angry letters, hurtful things said, equal blame from both parties left little room for forgiveness. My extended family made it a personal mission to find out what happened to them, with little success. Until today.

"Oh your Aunt Kathryn is already here! I knew we were late."

I'm tired and I let the passive aggressive comment slide. Not that there is room for rebuttal, my mom is halfway across the parking lot and I haven't even removed my seatbelt. I try and outrun the rain, making a dash for the front entrance. I step inside quickly and look around, praying for a pop machine and another Diet Coke. The nursing home is pleasant, as far as nursing homes go. I've only been in a few of them, when I was younger and doing volunteer work. The walls inside are a standard cream color, I hear the hum of multiple televisions in the background. Wheelchairs at the entrance, in the hallways, piled up in what I think is their rec center to the left. I wonder what it must be like to spend the last of your days parked somewhere- waiting for your next push. Pushing you toward your next meal, pushing you to your room, pushing you towards death. These waiting chairs. I shake away the morbid thoughts and step up to the front desk. Of course my mom has gone ahead without me.

"Hi, I'm looking for my Mom- she should have come in a second ago?" I ask the receptionist, a slightly overweight, very petite, platinum blond woman.

"Down the hall, to the left- room 102."

"Thank you," I tell her.

"I told her it was a waste of time though," she supplies before I can walk away. "Marion has been non-responsive for the last two days, we expect she'll be gone to the Good Lord any day now." She bows her head briefly.

"Um, thank you again," I mumble at her, wondering if that was the appropriate response for the acknowledgment of my aunts imminent departure from this life.

At room 102, I hear my mom and her sister arguing. They are barely a year apart and as different in personalities as in looks. My mom is tall, blonde- a short blunt cut. She is grounded in the present. She loves order, structure, the ways things are and are supposed to be. My aunt Kathryn. . .isn't.

"Livie, Kay and Joe do not have to fly in for this, I'm sure we can clean out the house in a weekend. Anything we find we'll report to the rest of the family. I'd hate for them to fly out for some old woman's relics. You know she probably doesn't have any money if she got stuck in this place."

My mom's voice whips back at her sister impatiently, "Of course you would say that Kath! Because I'm going to end up doing all the work. As usual! Paul and Tina can't help, she's due any day now! Are you even going to be able to go over this afternoon with me? Or do you have a psychic reading to attend?"

I enter the room before my eavesdropping becomes uncomfortable. My mom and aunt stand before me, their arguing ceasing abruptly. I take in the dimensions of the room, a large bed in the center of it, and realize immediately why they are still standing. Except for a small nightstand, the bed is the only furniture. I look around and there are no paintings, or photographs. Not even a note or card from a volunteer or nurse. Nothing to suggest my great aunt has a life inside, or outside, this hospice.

I stare at the old woman in the bed, everything about her white. Light wrinkled skin, even the age spots dotting her face pale. Stark white hair. At least she managed to avoid the cotton ball hair cut of the elderly. "Q-tips," my Dad used to call them.

"So, is she dead?" I ask, not even trying for a euphemism. She may be family, but we never knew her.

"Not yet, but Kathryn says there's no hope of her waking up. The doctors expect any time now." My mom glares a little at my aunt as she says this, but Kathryn is busy digging through her purse and doesn't notice.

I wish I could collapse into a chair, but instead I ask with a sigh, "What's next?" Kathryn looks up at me as they both realize I must have heard them from the hall.

"Well, the nurses gave us the key to her home. I think we're the only living relatives that have made any claim of her. Pretty lucky we found her when we did," my mom says.

My aunt does a little snort, as I raise an eyebrow. We both know we would have been luckier not to have found her until she was an obit in the local paper. A living dead person is nothing but trouble.

"I found it!" Kathryn says triumphantly as she pulls a hairbrush from her bag. She walks over to Marion, repositions her head, and starts combing out long strands. The hairbrush is soon filled with white hairs that have become dislodged from her scalp. A few of the strands have escaped, dancing in the air. Escape is not an option for me today. "So where are we going?" I ask my mom with a tinge of annoyance, "and where is the pop machine in this place?"

My great aunt's house is ten minutes south of the hospice. We are there before I know it, the sun finally appearing high in the sky. It bounces off the street I park on, blinding me with its ferocity. The rain has left everything sparkling with dew.

The house is completely hidden by the towering weeping willows, seeming to shimmer behind them. The calla lilies in her yard are barely in bloom, reaching their heads to the sun. Great purple irises stand at attention around them. We climb the steps to her front porch, surrounded by old fashioned marigolds. I'm struck by the scent of hyacinth, lavender. A vine of potato blossoms creep up the front entrance.

"Her gardens are so beautiful." I hear the jealousy in my mom's voice, the woman who once killed a cactus.

We meet the mailman on the way up the porch, and he hands me a tube and a small bundle of letters. It's obvious her box can't hold much more.

I pull the rest of the mail from the box, accidently unhinging it from the wall. "I wonder why her mail wasn't forwarded?" I ask, pushing the metal box into place with my elbow. I sort the junk mail to the back, some of the envelopes falling from the pile. "And so much of it," I wonder out loud.

My mom is paying no notice to me. A nervous laugh emits from her when she leans against the door and it gives way a couple of inches.

"I guess this wasn't necessary," she says, handing me the key. "We'll have to call a locksmith out today. The door is jammed on something, can you get your head in and see?"

I stuff the mail and the key in my large sling. Poking my head through the door opening, I quickly duck out again before the smell can completely overwhelm me. I hunch over on the porch, trying not to vomit. My arm reaches to my mom. "You don't want to go in there, it's, it's. . ." I can't think of a strong enough word to describe the trouble we're in. "Messy." I finish lamely.

With a laugh, my mom throws her full weight against the door and succeeds in moving it another foot. She climbs in and yells out to me, "a little dramatic there hon, it's not so bad."

I take a deep breath, and rub the temples of my head with my finger tips. From the brief glance I realize, a hoarder's house of horrors awaits us. I close my eyes and steel myself for the smell. One more breath before I follow her in.

It's only the first step, and I stumble immediately, taking out a tower of magazines. Glued together by age, or a substance I don't want to think about, the entire tower veers left as one unit. There is not enough space for it to fall altogether, instead creating a ripple effect through the room. Bombs suddenly falling from the sky, my mom flattens herself against a shelving unit. I crouch below half a kitchen table as a jar of rubber bands shatters next to me. Books cascade around the table, thunking against my feet. My mom, a few feet in front of me a minute ago, has disappeared in the resulting dirt cloud. The thumping noises stop and I decide to climb out.

My mom screams, "Be careful!" half a second too late as I step into a box. Tripping over it, I land in her arms, dizzy from the dust that stings my eyes. I cough over her shoulder, a dry hacking sound that only helps in inhaling more of the particles that float in the air. I manage to lock my knees into a semi-upright position as my mom brushes the both of us with her hands. The air lazily beginning to clear. I look up to see a figure materializing in front of us. I squint and reach to rub my eyes. My free hand searches for my moms urgently, and I feel her tense when she notices him. At first an outline, I think it's an illusion until he starts speaking.

"Where's Marion? And who the hell are you?" He's a large bald man- not muscular, but comfortable with himself and the gut that refuses to be confined by his tattered jeans and leather vest. He takes one threatening step and I notice the steel toe boots, laced up mid calf, and metal. Metal everywhere. Silver in his ears, eyes, bouncing off his jacket. His eyes are trained on us. They're a deep blue, and angry.

I'm grateful that my mom, never one to back down from confrontation, proud member of the NRA and gun enthusiast, speaks first, before my voice can betray my nervousness.

"Marion is dying, we are her family and legal owners of this home now." Her voice is solid and a little aggressive. "The more important question is, *who are you?"* She moves into a more defensive position, and I'm thankful for the self defense classes we both took after her run in with the cousin. I back up a step, stumbling over another cardboard box and waving my arms frantically to catch myself. I land hard on a small plant stand.

He hasn't noticed my fall. In fact, he looks as if his soul has been punched in the gut. Hunched over and in pain. Whoever this man is, he must have been close to my aunt. But how many years separate them? Forty, fifty? This man can't be more than forty-five years old.

My mom glances over at me before speaking again, her voice softer now, "I'm sorry, was my aunt close to you? Did you know her well?"

He turns his back to us, and I see him stuff a tube in his shirt. "I have to go," he says, before disappearing behind a pile of papers. We hear a back door slam shut before we can react.

I quickly pull my cell phone from my purse and whisper, "should I call the police?"

My mom is brushing the dirt from her thighs. "I think he's gone now, and it wouldn't do us much good to get the authorities involved."

"Did you see him take that tube?"

She glances at me, motioning to the ground. "Yes, but look at the floor- there's got to be a hundred of them. I doubt the one he took really matters to us."

"It's a place to start anyway," I say, looking down the little pathways created by walls of stuff.

Three hours into the afternoon and barely a dent has been made in our assault on the house. I'm on my fourth Diet Coke, the tubes have all been opened and the contents placed in a large Tupperware bin. Papers, pictures, letters, that's the gold, the inheritance, my mom is looking for. Anything that we think should get further inquiry is set in the bin. Everything else is thrown on the back porch, headed for the garbage dump.

"Have you been looking at some of this stuff Mom? This house is a time capsule of media."

"I can't believe how much there is to sort through. I never imagined this. We'll have to come back this weekend with some of your cousins and a dumpster." The first crack in her confidence shows in this statement. The only evidence of any family we've found is the letters contained in those tubes, and they don't seem to be related to us- the signature of Princess Julianne must be a joke of some sort. The old fashioned writing too difficult to decipher, they've gone in the bin to be inspected later.

"I'm sorry Mom, there's hope that something will be here- it looks like she kept every newspaper from the early 1930's and up."

Sifting through a box of papers, I hold one up to her. "How can she keep a phone bill from 1967 and not have a couple of photo albums from her childhood?"

"Not to mention all of these odds and ends." She grabs a large mason jar filled with thumbtacks. "The jar is lovely." It's an almost turquoise color. She holds it up to catch some sunlight through the dirty window and it glows.

"Okay," my mom says, dumping the thumbtacks and placing the jar in the bin, "we'll close up. I'm glad we found a locksmith to come out for us today. The new locks should keep out any unwanted visitors."

I stand up to stretch. "Except the mice," I say, wrinkling my nose. We've already unearthed a few skeletons- leaving them for one of my cousins to scoop up.

My mom's bravery only extends so far.

Marta

➤➤→

Chapter Three

A guard is outside of Jul's hut as I approach. He makes a motion to block my entrance without ever looking at me. I examine his features closely and realize he's new. "I'm here to see Julianne," I call at him, staying out of arms reach in case he's one to strike before speaking.

He looks down his nose at me. "I'm aware of who you are, and why you're here. *Princess* Julianne has asked for me to guard her door until she is ready to receive visitors. She was very clear that included you."

His back stiffens as he locks his eyes forward, over my head.

I blush in anger. Jul does this occasionally, asserts her power over me, tries to remind me of who I am.

As if I needed reminding.

At eighteen, Julianne was old enough to select a husband and begin writing the letters. I overheard her once, talking about her "male duties." The fake laughs all around her. She thought she was being original.

"Fine," I say to him, mimicking his tone. "I have other errands to attend too this morning. Tell the *Princess* her letters will be waiting in my room."

I smirk at the guard and begin to turn away when I hear my sister, "Mar-turd!" Her voice has an unpleasant lyrical quality to it. The vowels high and nasal. "You know I'm only joking with you, come back immediately. You know I hate that filthy encampment, and I can't trust any of these soldiers to retrieve the letter for me."

I cringe. As children we had seen the same tutors. Pure enchanted by her looks or power, caring very little if she learned anything at all. I would hide in the corners, my sister's plaything, gleaning what information I could from them. By the time we were ten, I was doing all of her schoolwork in the upper classes, while she flirted with the Pure Masters. When I was moved out of the Royal barracks at twelve, Julianne would seek me out to write her speeches, her proclamations. She was much more interested in her many admirers than in the business of running the colony. It was the same at eighteen. She sent me the rough drafts of those first letters to our Patron. The waste of paper still hurts me. Her spelling and grammar were shocking, but even worse was the tone of the letter itself. The conceit, the selfish demands. No news of the colony, no pleading for vital resources. It took a month of constant flattery, subtle hints. Then a week of not so subtle hints and a conference with my Uncle Dale. Eventually she released her hold on the writing of the letters, but still had final review and signature of them. Perhaps it was for the best. I quickly agreed to her terms, our arrangement a closely guarded secret among the Untouchables. Jul retained the admiration of her Pure peers, and I was able to relay the needs of our community to the outside world.

"Marta! Did you hear me! Come back here!"

I turn on my heel and see her framed in the doorway. Lips stained bright red, eyes lined in a dark paint. Much too thick, it gives her the appearance of an owl. Her beaky nose adding to the illusion. She is dressed in a ridiculous assortment of materials, a dizzying array of colors. Bits of taffeta and lace tucked in here and there. Her blonde hair is in a bouffant style, and shining. Stray hairs refuse to be confined in the up-do, copious amounts of grease forcing them in place. I stifle a laugh at her, barely keeping my composure as she slightly pouts in my direction.

"Come in here!" she demands. "You know the letter needs to leave first thing tomorrow."

I stand still, teasing her. It's petty I know, but really the only ammunition I have.

"I'm not going to apologize- if that's what you want," she says haughtily, turning and flouncing back into her hut.

I'm left with little choice but to follow, casting aside the beads and netting hanging from the doorway. My foot catches on a low-table inside and I lunge forward, collapsing into a pile of pillows. Cushions spread across the flooring and piled high in the corners. She is the only one in the camp to have this luxury, there's not enough fabric to make this possible for anyone else. At least not enough fabric Jul is willing to share with anyone else. Thankfully she is staring into a mirror on her wall and missed my entrance. I adjust my position on the floor to look more casual, as she turns around to reach for my package. I hand over the white mail tube, which she casually flings into the back room. I doubt she'll even read the letter before she signs it.

If she signs it, she's been known to forget.

"You haven't complimented my hair, and it's the latest thing. The last box was lined in magazine clippings, I didn't find them until today." Fluffing it with her fingers, she lands on the pillow next to me in a seductive pose, her rear end high in the hair, lips pursed out and eyebrows wiggling. I'm the only woman in the camp that can't be punished for finding little humor in my sister's antics. I reward her with a grimace before launching into my prepared appeal.

"Our water supply has been tampered with again, the children are dropping little pellets that fizz and pop into the rain buckets. It would be funny if the water didn't taste so awful afterwards, and Samuel has stopped complaining of stomach pains. He'll be over to fix your roof. . ."

Her face has taken on a dreamy quality.

"Jul?"

"Marta," she says, as she stares off into the distance. "Have you ever thought about what it would be like to have a pet?"

I'm momentarily confused by this question. "Like the small snakes the boys catch?"

"Oh Marta, you can be so silly sometimes. A pet. Like a dog. A tiny little pooch I could feed scraps to and carry around the colony with me in my knapsack." She's so excited by the idea she's practically in my lap, her eyes shining. "Oh! Think of it Marta, I could even put my ribbons around her neck. She'd be the cutest thing!"

I think this is a poor time to point out there are many people in the Untouchable encampments who would kill for those same scraps she's thinking of tossing to an imaginary plaything. I don't even want to humor her today.

"I don't think she could ship us a dog Jul. We've never received anything alive before."

With an exasperated sigh she says, "do you ever feel so, so tired of it all." This last phrase uttered with a sweep of her arm across the room.

From my vantage point, I see the draperies hanging from the ceiling, artwork on the walls. With the exception of the tent our father occupies, her wood and clay hut is visually no different outside than the seventy-nine others in our colony. The interior however, is completely unlike the rest of the sparse residences. The more lavish of the Pure have newspaper clippings framed, usually a chair or a table covered in fabric. Tools for their trade, small toys for their children. Jul's room is filled with things. Boxes, figurines, newspapers, magazines, spilling from every surface. There's even a rag rug underfoot that was my mothers. I like to lay on the floor and trace the patterns with my fingertips. It is said the locals in the nearest village Manacapuru, sell the rugs for kisses. Judging from my unexpected arrival, I would say my mother was quite free with her kisses.

Dwelling on my mother, I nearly miss the naked Untouchable suddenly entering from the back room. He saunters in without even a glance at me, and Jul erupts into giggles. She must have planned for this, knowing it would embarrass me. Thoughts of my mother vanish from my head, my cheeks burning. The man grabs a manuscript from the teetering pile, sitting in a chair across from me. He opens the book haphazardly, his eyes unfocused, his fingers swiping at the pages. I know he can't read. I jump up to leave when Jul grabs my arm.

"C'mon, Marta it's a joke. Martin doesn't mind."

I inhale deeply. How would she know if he even minded? Untouchables have no opinions, no chance of expressing disapproval to the whims of our Pure Masters. I send a look of pity in his direction, but he is oblivious to me, my discomfort, my compassion. Exactly how Jul planned it, he's a good actor- I hope she'll spare him after I walk out.

"I have to go Jul. Please remember to sign the letter, and I wouldn't let the Führer see the little game you're playing. You'll lose your pet." I try to nod stoically in Martin's direction.

It's an empty threat and she knows it, our father would never take anything away from Jul that offered her pleasure. She's giggling, at me I assume, or my advice, as I attempt to casually walk out the door. My nails digging into my palm, I'm trembling with indignation by the time I'm out of earshot. I sprint the last hundred feet to the undergrowth, taking refuge behind a tree. Clutching the trunk, I inhale slowly, exhale. Leaf-cutter ants crawl near my hand in a single line. They are a funny sight, hidden beneath the green leaves on their backs. The forest floor moving in a synchronized dance. The green leaves, the tree bark, seem far too heavy a load, but they manage it effortlessly. Some call them Sauba Ants, or wee-wees. Tiny things, they are a constant nuisance to the colony, decimating entire groves of trees before we were sent the knowledge of how to fight back. I pluck the leaf off one of them, another thing to be grateful to our Patron for. I'll need to report this swarm to Derrik.

Collecting the ant waste is one of the tasks of the Untouchables, it's the only thing keeping them away from our food supplies. I move my hand away before they can bite me, and take more deep breaths. Eins, Zwei, Drei, I count them in German, trying not to hyperventilate.

The air is heavy today. Oppressive. My skin is covered in wet- precipitation, perspiration. I stretch my fingers, unclench them from their fists, and walk back to one of the wooden pathways. I've seen this kind of humiliation before, and I've given up trying to understand my sister and her games. She hasn't selected her mate yet, and her companions have long since been given work in the colony. Everyone is expected to work, the jobs of the Pure are less labor intensive and don't begin until age sixteen, but then, everyone works. My sister passed sixteen over four years ago. She does not work- not allowed to work. Flirting, lolling about, thinking up menial tasks for her admirers and servants- that is the work of our Princess. One more month before she is expected to give her final decision on her husband. Three requirements. Blond hair, blue eyes, light skin. The Pure encampment is filled with boys, and men, who will make her a suitable match. Our father has been patient, one month to go and she'll have to find someone new to tease. It can't come soon enough.

A glance at the sky tells me drill is over, the colony headed to work. Women will be walking down this path soon, water buckets on their heads. I have to move. The feeling of flight welling up in me, I want to leave. *I could leave here*, I know I could. One stretch and I start loping strides in my Uncle Dale's direction.

The colony is split into two factions. The Untouchables live on the North side of a stream, two large stilted barracks extend out from a dirt path. A separate barrack behind them the Pure never visit, it's filled with the young and the elderly. Ani and I are in the hut closest to the bridge which serves as our connection to the Pure. There are three more huts near ours that are unoccupied. In my great grandfather's day, they held other Untouchables who were allowed special duties. When there weren't as many Pure to compensate for the responsibilities of the colony. They've been empty for years, the walls crumbling. They now serve as an impromptu gathering place in inclement weather.

I race through the Pure encampment which is closer to the beach, on the South side. Wooden pathways criss cross through the huts, through the jungle. It is dangerous on the paths, but more dangerous to step off of them. The jungle floor is alive, and it is said if you stand still long enough, you will be consumed by new growth. If the trees don't get you, the insects will. I'm always careful running through any old growth in the jungle, the bees can be especially deadly.

Most of the Pure rarely venture past the safety of the colony, but my uncle lives in a tall stilted hut on the beach. It will take a couple of hours of jogging to reach him. Close to the water, he says it's an excellent lookout point, since we're only ever approached in that direction. A tribe of Untouchables is spread out behind our colony and in the direction of the mountainous jungle. A shaky truce has existed since the beginning, protecting us from their arrows, and them from our guns. Shrunken heads hang from posts which mark our boundaries. A reminder to the both of us. It works, a tribal Untouchable hasn't been seen in at least two generations.

I'm sipping my water when something plops on the path next to me. *Excrement.* Monkeys in the trees high above me. A stick nearly collides with my head, and I clip the gourd to my hip and start running. They grow bored of me quickly when I don't react to their game, the bombs missing me by inches. The wooden path is easy to spot through the constant fog. Someone has already been through here this morning, the branches roughly chopped away. A ray of light breaks through the darkness in front of me. The forest thinning, I scan the beach for intruders, but there are no soldiers here.

I think my uncle lives out here because he's not comfortable in the colony. As the second son of my grandmother, he should be head of our military while his brother controls the camp. My uncle finds the military as brutal as the encroaching jungles around us, so the Führer took control of the soldiers. He built this hut for my uncle and made up a reason for him to be here. My Uncle Dale rarely leaves it now except to advise my father on various colony matters, and maintain the mechanical and electrical operations of the colony.

I have my letters to keep me busy, my uncle has his own duties. I am an Untouchable and he is Pure, but we are both out of step in our world.

The ladder is down when I approach his hut, and I hear arguing inside. My brother's voice is easy to recognize, loud, harsh, angry.

"I think I should be allowed to go! They trust me with the secrets, but not with this- it's ridiculous. I am no longer a child!" A pounding noise shakes the dust into the air above my head. He must be stomping his foot, exactly as a child would do.

I hear my Uncle Dale's voice next, melodic, quiet, and soothing.

"You have to understand you're Royalty, no one thinks you are incapable. Royalty is simply not allowed to go. Not since your mother's time." I can only imagine the pointed look my uncle is giving my brother, while trying not to roll his eyes.

Officially our mother disappeared because of the shame she brought on the colony, but when I was younger and my brother felt like being cruel, he would tell me the truth of the incident. My mother was killed, and I was given to the Untouchables because of her sins. Because of her mistake. I was still considered royalty, even without the title, and a female at that, so I was spared.

"It's not only too dangerous, but the colony is afraid you may become contaminated," he continues.

The ladder is not hard to climb, and he finishes this statement as my head peeks over the base of the platform. They both turn to me at the same time. Perfect timing to make his point clear.

"Marta, how nice of you to visit today- your brother and I are in disagreement, and perhaps you can act as intermediary, hmmm?" my uncle chuckles a little at this. My brother scowling.

My status may be a joke to my Uncle Dale, but no one else in the colony would find this kind of humor funny.

"I'm not sure I would be the best to mediate a discussion between you and Jacob," I say, pushing myself to my feet, and trying to force a laugh. My brother's scowl deepens. I wish my uncle wouldn't rile him up.

"As if we needed your opinion on the matter," Jacob says. "If I want to head out of the colony tomorrow, who is there to stop me?" He defiantly looks back at my uncle, who has retreated to the far side of the room. He is pouring fresh water from a pitcher into a cup made of bark. A second cup sits on a table, which is leaning slightly to the left on three legs. Electrical gadgets compensate for the missing fourth. Things we have no use for in the colony, something called a toaster, and an A-track player. I scan the rest of his hut, junk of every shape and size in every corner. Some things are identifiable, the old generator, a few lanterns with broken glass-plates, something my uncle calls a telephone. Most is not. It appears messy, but I know my uncle could find any part, in seconds, if asked.

I look back at my brother, shrug my shoulders, act nonchalant as I say, "I think if you wanted to go, you should be able to go."

My uncle sets the pitcher down to stare at me in disbelief. I don't typically agree with my brother. On anything.

"A good idea even," I assert.

Jacob's eyebrows pinch together, "You want something? That's it, right?" Two steps forward and his finger is in my face, his voice sing-song, teasing me. "What could Mar-turd possibly want?" He uses my nickname much more forcefully than Jul does. She treats me like a pet, while Jacob thinks I'm a poisonous insect in need of squashing.

His face inches from my own, I take a step back and feel a spike in my neck. The wall behind me is covered in animal horns. Wire as thick as my finger wrapped around some of them, and delicate strands, thinner than my hair, on others. The brightly colored wires are my favorites. I love to pull the coils off the horns, unraveling a little of the wire. I grip the ends and toss the spiels out the window, watching the wire bounce and spin all the way down.

"I really don't want anything Jacob." I keep my head down, cowed. This would normally pacify him.

"Oh, stop acting like a scared mouse." He turns his back to me and struts over to my Uncle Dale's chair, one of my favorite pieces of furniture in the colony. One of our Grandfathers spent years carving it. It was used as a place of honor for the reigning Führer to sit during meetings and such, but my Father's girth eventually created a crack down the back. It's barely noticeable, but the chair was still discarded for its imperfection. My uncle managed to squirrel it away before it was sacrificed to a bonfire. Jacob sits in it, caressing the arms. A smirk on his face.

"You think you can go. Right? If our Father allows me, maybe I can bend the rules for you too?" A big sigh as he takes the cup of water my uncle offers him. "The only problem is Father will never allow me to go. Royalty. Him and Uncle had gone a dozen times by the time they were my age. How does he expect me to rule if I've never even been beyond the waters?"

I cock my head to the side as my uncle approaches me. "Well, maybe if Uncle were to intervene?" I say, taking my water and batting my eyelashes at him, thrusting out my bottom lip. An exaggerated appeal I know will work.

A real frown from my Uncle Dale, as he taps the wooden cup with his fingertips. Once a month a party leaves for the nearest village, a four day journey round trip. Two Pure selected by my father are allowed to go. They're ancient Pure men, usually trusted family members, guards. Last month the party returned empty handed. Canned food, supplies they had- but no mail. Princess Julianne was the only one truly angry at them. The boxes always contain beads and baubles, rubber bands in funny shapes, hair pins and bows. Things that are utterly useless to the colony scattered amongst the things we need. Jul loves the stuff, raiding the boxes as soon as they come in to decorate her rooms and herself.

There was a time when we could request specialty supplies we couldn't get in Manacapuru. I even managed to smuggle in supplies for the Untouchable encampment, since I was usually on hand to take away the things Jul had no use for. My Father rarely cared what was contained in the boxes. The long white mail tubes that came in were his responsibility. Filled with small rectangles of hard, shiny plastic, and wads of colorful paper. Nothing of any true value from what I could see. It has been over four months since our last request was completely fulfilled. Two months since a box even arrived. Our surplus is running dangerously low of the ointments and medicines, bandages, mosquito netting, and nylon tarpaulins we need. In the Untouchable encampment at least, I'm the one to blame for it.

"I think I'll go and have a talk with your father," my uncle says determinedly. "Perhaps it is time you were to go into the village. Time for you to learn a few things." He glances at my brother, dropping his shoulders and nodding his head in resolution. He doesn't look up when he addresses his next remarks to me.

"I won't pretend not to understand why you came here today Marta, but I know it is absolutely impossible to apply to him on your behalf. You will never be allowed to go, and you will never be allowed to leave this village. Be grateful you can still write the letters. Be grateful he hasn't taken that away from you too."

He drops out the doorway, easily sliding down the ladder. I watch him until he jogs out of sight, hidden in the jungle depths.

A painful shove in my back sends me airborne out the door. I flip on to my side before landing hard in the soft sand. I've managed to keep my arms out from under my body, but my hip is in pain. My brother is laughing, high above me. I should have never turned my back on him, *Schadenfreude*. I know better. I shakily sit up and breathe in deeply. No ribs are broken. I have to get moving before he decides to inflict worse. I may be a better fighter, but I'm no match for him. I would never be allowed to win. On my feet, I follow my uncle's path into the jungle.

Chapter Four

The Führer occupies the largest structure in the center of the Pure encampment, the other huts revolving around his. Six walkways that branch off, like spokes on a wheel. It's impossible to approach his home without passing through the center accommodations, the guard's huts, the tightest circle. Two guards positioned on each walkway. There's only one guard I know of that will let me through without comment, and I have to trust his neighbor will be looking the other way as I slide by.

It's a hard run back. I favor my right side, limping slightly. I don't know how far behind Jacob is, and the terror keeps me moving forward. I break through the green barrier right at the edge of the colony. I sit for a minute on a rock near one of the walkways, evening out my breaths, a cramp seizing my left calf.

I stand up to walk it off, grimace in pain as I make my way into the Colony. Most of the Pure must be at lunch or working inside their huts. I'm grateful no one notices me for once. My calf and ankle are on fire, my hip is aching, and I'm walking straight into the center of the lion's den. My anxiety is at its peak when I approach the inner circle. My eyes fill with moisture when I realize Henrik is with James today.

Henrik was four when my mother was killed, and still remembers her laugh. James is his older brother, and was my mother's personal bodyguard, closer to her than my father ever was. I am told all the men were in love with her, even the Untouchable ones. I used to pester Henrik for stories of her, her beauty legendary. The ones he couldn't collect from James, or others in the colony, he would make up. I naively believed all of them, until I grew old enough to know better, and begin hating her.

My feet tap loudly against the wood as I walk through the two guard huts. They both turn at once and bob their heads in acknowledgement. Henrik's eyes take in my appearance. He can't hide his concern, but he would never put me in danger by speaking. He mouths silently, "What's wrong?"

I point at my hip and grimace dramatically, before smiling at him and shrugging.

He guides me with his eyes toward a loose tent flap that conceals a small opening into my father's quarters. The Führer uses thick waterproof fabric in place of the clay and wood walls which form the rest of our huts. They never melt in the rain and need less repair. I don't often spy on my father, the petty squabbles of the Pure encampment boring to me, the lovemaking with his whores disgusting.

I pull myself up to the structure and slip through the flap. I have to swallow the cry of pain when the wood rubs against my hip. I scan the inside of the tent and inhale deeply, holding the breath. I will myself silent, before crawling toward the corner closest to me. There are large animal cages back here I can hide in, concealed under pillows and fabric. I found them when I was younger, trying to hide from my brother and his pack of "friends." They thought it was funny he had an Untouchable for a sister. Two generations ago the colony kept animals for the poachers who visited. Eventually the predatory animals learned to stay away from our colony. The poachers had to go further down the river, and deeper into the jungle for their prey. The cages remain, all but forgotten.

I carefully remove the pin for the door and slide in, adjusting the fabric above. I tuck my legs underneath me and test myself for more bruises, enjoying the few minutes of silence. I run my fingers through my hair, trying to pull out the knots. Henrik looked so handsome today; I didn't know he was assigned to guard the Führer's huts. I wonder when it happened, the weeks since we last talked filled with responsibilities. I haven't been able to steal some time for him. Voices approach, my Uncle Dale moving into this room, just as I had hoped. My other senses sharpen in the darkness and I hear two, no, three men with him. My sister Jul enters next, I can hear her teasing voice. Strange for Jul to be here, but not unprecedented, the meetings usually bore her. One of the men plops on my crate. He must be taking advantage of the open flap, because all at once I'm surrounded in stench, thick and warm. I recoil into myself, trying hard not to gag. He continues to flirt with my sister, enjoying her attentions I'm sure. My eyes are watering when there is movement above me. The sound of half a dozen people jumping to their feet, the Führer has entered the room.

"Sit," he commands. A heavy thud above me as the man sits.

"Full report." Always efficient, the Führer is only verbose when speaking with the colony.

"Marie reports three births this week. All seem to be Pure, I think we may have finally weeded out the bad stock." The man reporting can't help but add this, a smugness to his voice. I know this to be true, my roommate Ani said there hasn't been an Untouchable birth in almost three years. Marie is the Pure midwife and Shaman; Ani is one of her students. None of the Pure students wanted to be responsible for concocting the potions and treatments the Untouchables need to remain childless. Marie decided it was necessary to train an Untouchable in her ways. Ani was chosen.

I remember that baby- still wet with afterbirth, Ani running through the encampment for the barracks. I was only fourteen, still adjusting to my new quarters and new responsibilities. Ani walked into our hut soaked from the waist down, shivering. It had been dry season, the river low. She had run straight through the water, avoiding the wood bridge. I helped her undress and searched her for leeches. Then found one of my warm furs to wrap around her. I covered for her in drill- pretended to be her in the line up. They didn't know the difference. Her desperation for the baby, terrified someone would lay hands on her and kill it before she got to safety.

The sound of tinkling bells drowns out the man's voice. Heidi, the Führer's new wife, must be serving refreshments. Her every step accompanied by music, her ankles wrapped in tiny bells. It's a punishment inflicted on her through no fault of her own. A preventative measure, so she can't escape. The

Führer's voice bites through the noise, Heidi's feet shuffling away from my crate. The commander has finished his report.

"Good, I've heard a lot of discussion about who should get the mail this month. I'm not easily swayed by the arguments, but Thomas is getting on in years and the journey is hard on him. I've chosen Henrik this month, along with my son Jacob. Dale is right, it is time for him to take on more responsibility. Marta will join them."

I hear an immediate shockwave hit the room. Grateful for the general exclamation of surprise, it masks my own gasp of shock. I will be joining them, an Untouchable, a Royal. My wish. Granted.

The only person not offering objection is my sister Jul. I hear her giggles, muffled, and it occurs to me this is her doing. One of her jokes, she can't have realized I actually wanted to go. It couldn't have been my uncle. I don't know how he could have intervened, and I hear him protesting loudest of all.

"John, sending an Untouchable sets a bad precedent. You can't believe this is a good idea. We don't want a rebellion on our hands when they realize there's a way to leave."

"And go where exactly Dale? The village? And then what? They have no money, no weaponry, no food of their own. They're stupid Dale. They can't read or write. Leave?!" the Führer's laugh echoes through the hut. "Go ahead, let them! See how long they survive out there."

My uncle falls silent with the rest of the group, and then I hear my sister clear her throat.

"Oh yes," the Führer says. I hear everyone rise from their seats, "Julianne has made her choice. We will announce it at Session tonight. Dale, follow me, the rest of you are dismissed."

I hear them file out behind the Führer. Jul still laughing, teasing- her target no longer interested in amusing her. He must sense he is not her choice. I sit completely still, listening. A loud growl alerts me to the fact that I'm hungry, skipping lunch to be here. I count to one hundred in German, and then English, to be sure it is safe. Another rumble from my stomach and I'm in motion, my uncle will be searching for me soon. To share the news. Peeking out from behind the fabric, I slide my body through the tent flap, silently jumping down. Careful to put my weight on only one foot. James is still here, gesturing for me to move past him. I dart out and see Henrik speaking with a general, their backs to me, their voices low. Silently I head for the shadows of the huts. There are Pure men and women sitting on the stoops, fanning themselves, little beads of sweat dripping steadily. The late afternoon sun is disappearing behind the trees. It will be drill again soon, and I see a few women in line at the seamstress hut. She owns the only sewing machine, a singer, operated by a pedal. Swearing angrily in German, her fingers are flying fast over a pair of uniform shorts. There is a red welt across her palm, a demerit for poor workmanship. I slink off the path and through another set of huts before I am spotted. *"Hässlich!"* a female barks. Haven't I been called ugly since birth? It shouldn't bother me now. I turn toward my attacker and am immediately recognized. A girl, maybe a few months older, on the walkway next to me- dark blue eyes, dirty blonde hair, tan skin. She is lucky to be in her position, easily mistaken for one of us, if not for her clothing. Newer, no patches. She backs away, defensive. There are no insults from me today, my brain foggy and tired. I wave her off, annoyed at myself, enough with the hiding. I straighten out my spine and jump back on the walkway. Marching through the rest of the Pure encampment, I pass groups of woman balancing their water, arms filled with fabric. I don't even acknowledge them as I step nimbly over the bridge, to home.

"Ani!" I yell, tripping up the steps to our hut. "You're not going to believe. . ." My throat closes tightly, the words waiting to be heard. My uncle is already here, sitting in the only chair. He is thumbing through one of my books, feet on the desk. A quick glance at my shelf and I notice the First Primer missing. It is required reading for the younger Pure, and I have been using it secretly to teach some of the Untouchables. Annika is nervously fluttering about. She is arranging her bottles and supplies, fingers pulling at her dress and buttons, polishing her belt buckle. Little uncomfortable movements, she doesn't like my uncle here. He slams the book shut to look up at me. I am more disheveled than usual- sweaty and red from crouching in the crate, a bruise forming on one of my calves from my fall. My hair has frizzed out again, and I don't think I've removed all the twigs which have caught in it. I look directly at him.

"I'm going to the village." The shakiness of my voice betrays my excitement, and he doesn't even ask how I know. Maybe his presence here was enough to alert me.

"Yes, I've been sent to tell you. Your brother will be accompanying you." His fingertips dig into his forehead, rubbing the spots where the gray is condensed most. "What I want to know is, why? Why are you so hellbent on going? There is nothing for you there. Your mother lost her life visiting that godforsaken village, and it's dangerous. Dangerous for the colony, and dangerous for you."

I can't tell him the real reason. That I want answers. I want to know what happened to the nameless men in the photographs, the ones who helped establish Founder, before disappearing from our history. Where are their families, their colonies? I could be shot for questions like these, forbidden topics, even between my uncle and I- usually so open about everything. I'm evasive in my answer, trite.

"Doesn't everyone want to go? The danger being part of the fun?" His eyes focus intently on me. He is suspicious now. I am cautious, overly so. The danger would not be fun for me. I realize I've made a mistake.

"I mean, I want to see the village. The stores, our allies, the cannibals. I want to see the mail, where it comes from." I shrug my shoulders and he relaxes his gaze. He shoots a quick glance at Ani, who is busy crushing some herbs for tea. She appears to be ignoring us, but the way her shoulders are tense, her head tilted to the side, she is listening intently.

"Meet them in the morning, before drill, on the beach." His face softens, his eyes looking straight into mine. "Stay away from your brother. There's something funny going on between him and your father, something I don't understand. It's more than preparing him for leadership. Your brother's appearance this morning, and then how easily your father agreed to him going. Be careful, and Marta. . ."

"Yes?" I ask.

He taps the desk lightly, his eyes furrowed.

"I hope to see you soon. That's all." I feel confused by his words, his tone not exactly matching the sentiment. Like he's questioning me.

His tapping ceases abruptly and he stands, tucking the chair back into the desk. "I'll take this with me," he says, holding out the book. My primer in his hands as he walks out the door.

I cross over to Ani, the pupils of her eyes large and watery.

"When he picked up that book. . .I almost lost it." I notice the tea leaves are ground much too fine.

"My uncle can be kind, he's not like my father. He's just sending me a message." I pull her into a hug to steady her shaking.

"Not to educate us," she says.

"Right," I murmer.

Lara

§

Chapter Five

"Honey, I'm home!" I yell out to the empty house, I know Sergio is still at the restaurant, working dinner service. Pretending someone's home is my way of shaking the willies out of my system. The aloneness of an empty house at night scares me. It comes from having so many cousins around constantly. I grew up on a farm, and even though I was an only child, there was an ever revolving door of family living with us, sharing my bathroom, taking up space. Now privacy has changed from luxuriousness to just loneliness.

I flip the television on for some camaraderie and begin shedding my clothes as I make my way to our single bathroom. Turning the shower on, I don't even bother waiting for the water to heat up. Stepping straight into the jet stream, a whip of cold rips through me. The shock waking me up more effectively than all the caffeine I've consumed today. I wash my hair twice before satisfied that the grime is gone. I bundle myself into my bathrobe and pad out to the kitchen. Sergio has left me dinner in the refrigerator, a heart is taped to the outside. I rip the paper off, giving it a kiss and setting the food in the microwave. Deciding he deserves a thank you text, I pull my bag off the counter to search for my phone and come up with a bundle of letters instead.

"Oh crap!" I had dropped my mom off on the way home, helping her carry in the bin from Marion's house, but I had forgotten to hand her all the recent mail. Deciding to text her as well, I dig my phone out from the depths of my bag. The microwave beeps in the middle of my text to Sarge.

The plate is steaming when I pull it from the microwave. I breathe in the smell of oregano, rosemary, and basil. Sergio and I met on a plane, three years ago. I was six months out of high school, my dad had just died. I wasn't ready for college and wanted a change. When I saw the ad for flight attendants, I took a chance and landed the job.

He was in the seat next to me on the way to Dallas for training. He had purchased a home in Redlands, my hometown. He was older, more experienced.

I fell in love immediately.

We flirted the whole trip, and when we landed, he had my number.

I eat my lasagna and text my mom to let her know I have the mail. She immediately responds. I need to sort through the junk for the possibility of a social security check, and bank statements. The sooner the family has a handle on her finances, the sooner they'll be able to know what to do for her. I groan inwardly because my date with Conan is put on hold, so I can sort through a comatose woman's mail.

A half an hour later, my empty dinner plate sits on the dining room table next to three piles of paper. Despite my complete exhaustion, the excitement of doing something a little illegal and completely nosey, has gotten to me. The grocery ads and obvious credit card solicitations, have gone straight into the recycling bin. Marion has some strange looking correspondences, and in sorting they've naturally fallen into three distinct piles. Strange, stranger, and normal.

I begin with the strange pile first, handwritten envelopes, some with doodling on the outside. There's a little over twenty of these, and I soon I realize they're not letters as much as. . . .fan mail. To my aunt? Scanning through them quickly, they're all exactly the same in content. Some postmarked from prisons, the rest from towns and cities familiar, unfamiliar, out of the country. Even one in Spanish- all the same. Loving, gushing, admiration for my aunt and the "cause," whatever that might be. I throw most of them in the recycling bin, saving one to show my mom in the morning. For a woman sitting in a hospice entirely devoid of personal expression, no visitors, and empty walls, these notes are so weird. Where are these friends?

I start in on the normal looking pile. Bills by the look of them, the electricity bill first, overpaid by quite a bit. I've never known anyone to overpay their electrical bill. Bill comes in and we pay it- why overpay? At least mom and I won't have to worry about the electricity going off any time soon. The water, garbage, all overpaid by hundreds of dollars. The next bill I drop in shock. It's not a bill. A money order for two thousand dollars floats from my fingers to the floor. I search the envelope for something else, but there's no letter, no note, just a notation on the check- "Founder-Master Race." It's filled out to Marion. I reach for the next envelope and it's three hundred dollars in cash, wrapped in white notebook paper. Again, no indication of what it's for. I start tearing through them quickly and all the envelopes in this pile are the same. Money orders and Cashier checks for only a few dollars, and many more containing thousands of dollars. All filled out to Marion, all with the notation, "Founder- Master Race." I quickly calculate over twenty-five thousand dollars. Spread across my dining room table it's more money than I've ever held. More money than I've ever even seen. I look at the clock on my wall and consider calling to wake up my mom. Twelve thirty-five. Sergio should be home soon, and I'm not sure what she could do about it tonight anyway. I gather the money together into one of the larger padded envelopes, and place it next to the letter I'm saving.

My hands trembling from the shock, the adrenaline, the caffeine, the late hour, I pull a letter from the pile I've labeled as the strangest. These letters come from the same type of white mailing tubes we found on the floor, except the tubes were stuffed in the mailbox. Ten pages of the cramped, old-fashioned handwriting. Long sloping cursive letters almost illegible, signed Princess Julianne at the bottom of each page. I try deciphering a few words before my eyes go blurry. "Jungle, and supplies?" Not ready to tackle this project yet, I stand up stretching.

The front door bell begins buzzing.

My heart jumps, it's close to one in the morning. Who would be at my door? It can't be Sarge, he would use the garage. The front door buzzes again, more insistent, and I timidly approach it.

"Sarge?" I call out.

There is only silence. I back away a few steps, my hands shaking involuntarily, my heart rate accelerating. Walking over to the counter and my phone, I wonder if I'm imagining the door buzzing. Wonder if my ears are playing tricks on me. I've had little sleep in over forty-eight hours now, maybe I'm overreacting to nothing. I pick up the phone and stare at the screen blankly, when I hear the garage suddenly roll open. I let out a breath I didn't even realize I was holding. Sarge springing through the kitchen door.

I'm so glad to see him, I burst out, "Babe, I. . ."

He doesn't even see me as he makes a dash for the living room. He flings the front door open, an orange glow illuminating his silhouette. I look past him and see flames on our porch. *Flames! A fire on my front porch*! A spark jumps and catches the living room curtains, which are instantly consumed. The flames criss crossing the ceiling before I can even react. Sergio turns toward me, grabs me- snaps me into the present.

"Lara! Dial 911. Grab your purse, the pictures! Get out!"

He runs for the back bedroom, and I know he's getting our safe box. I take a minute to shove my feet into work pumps I have kicked under the kitchen table. I sweep the papers on the table into my bag. Grab the wedding picture from our side table. A platter from my counter, wax fruit and all. I pull a calendar off the wall. I don't weigh my choices, as I try to salvage what I can. Stuffing items into my purse as the air turns black around me. I'm losing my sight when I realize my phone is still in my hand. It takes me three tries to dial 911, and by the time I do Sergio is back- pushing me to our back patio door, into the yard, and then turning on the hose. I am screaming into the phone at a woman who clearly doesn't understand me. The only fact I can hold on to, are the flames now licking at the back windows.

"Fire!" I yell into my phone. "Fire!" I am sobbing out my address, over and over again until I finally hear the scream of the fire engine. I drop my phone in my pocket and desperately reach for Sergio. He has given up the hose and drags me into the far corner of the yard. Our side fence collapses, water arcs high into the air. Two men come through the gaping hole, giant in their yellow suits. Their faces red and wet. Indistinguishable to me, I see their lips moving, instructions I think? I can't hear them over the water and fire. The fire! I'm surrounded by yellow. We walk through the fence, shielded from my home. I mourn the loss of my hydrangea bush as one of the blossoms disappears underneath a heavy black boot. We keep walking to the sidewalk, and then to the street where my neighbors have gathered to stare. My sobs have been reduced to hiccups, and I suddenly feel embarrassed, in my robe and heels- with my purse around my shoulder. A wax apple still in my hand. Sergio in his work whites, carrying our lock box. It's all so unreal, my neighbors pressing in on me with words of comfort, questions I can't answer. Old Tom from across the street, in character pajamas. Meg from next door in a negligee and pearls.

I suddenly have the mad desire to laugh. I grasp my husband's hand again and look up into his face. There are tears there. The fire reflected in his eyes. My world, our world, burning.

An hour later.

That's all it took, an hour for my home to become a blackened shell. *Up in smoke*, what an appropriate saying.

The firefighters are efficient, and soon they have another call, another emergency. They're packed up and gone. A toilet and a tub, the only items recognizable in the blackness that is left. My neighbor's houses on either side, untouched- perfect in their normalcy. The police show up as soon as they realize it's arson. A fire inspector shortly thereafter. My husband telling his story over and over again. "He pushed the garage opener as he was pulling up the driveway. Watched as someone dropped something on the porch and ran. He thought it was a prank. Sometimes the teenagers toilet papered our home, or smashed a pumpkin or two, harmless pranks. We live in a safe neighborhood. Grudge? Money problems? I can't believe it would be arson. He didn't see what they were driving." I sit in the back of a police cruiser, a heavy wool blanket over my shoulders. Meg has brought me a bottle of water, and I'm slowly trying to sip it, trying to keep it in my stomach. The inspector spent almost no time with me, realizing almost immediately that I have nothing to say, no good information. I can't even tell him clearly if I heard the door bell ring.

My mom appears around four in the morning. Sergio must have called her. I see him running around, stopping to thank firefighters, police. Offering comforting words to our neighbors and friends. I hide in the car, ducking behind the steel bars of the cruiser. I pretend to be asleep, and my mom arrives as the sun begins shining over the rooftops, pulling me from semiconsciousness. She forces me to face this thing.

"Lara, we need to go now. The police are leaving. You're coming with me."

I drop the heavy blanket and follow her. My feet are so heavy, my bag is so heavy. I collapse into the back of my mom's sedan, where the sobs begin again. Loud choking sobs. Sounds I don't recognize coming from myself. Sergio is next to me, his own tears silent.

"It's okay, it's okay, it's okay," he says.

"It will never be okay. Never." I choke out. "What are we going to do?"

"We're headed to your moms, I've already called out for the week. We have to work on the insurance. . . it *will* be okay. You'll see," he says, his voice hoarse. I feel a sense of guilt for the loss of his voice. I have made him face all of this alone. Forced him to be strong, because I wanted to wallow in weakness. I wipe my own tears away.

"We'll get through this." I say, firmly, willing myself to believe. "You're right. It will be okay, we'll get through this."

It is so early that there are only a few cars on the road. I numbly watch them zip by. My mom lives in a gated retirement "village." My father would have hated this place, the perfect lawns and cream colored fronts. Every house a carbon copy of the next one. It's why she lives here now. The farm felt too big without him, and when I was gone, she realized she couldn't face her home alone. She sold the ranch, her possessions moved to storage, and bought suburbia. A land where no memories could assault her.

The gate opens just as we pull up. The security guard waving out to my mom. She rolls her window down to motion him over. They love her here, the spitfire who brings them treats. Miquel is on duty today, and he runs over to the side of the car before we can pull through.

"Miquel, I have your magazines!" She pokes my father's car magazines out to him. His subscription paid for another three years.

"Thanks Ms. Butler! You're up early today- we've had some trouble this morning." He takes the magazines and leans easily against the side of the car.

"Trouble, really? My daughter too- they had a fire," she responds.

"A fire! Oh no! Senorita, I hope you are okay?" He only stops speaking long enough to glance at me. Obviously caring more about his own gossip. "Someone tried to jump the wall here about an hour ago- can you believe it?"

My mom's grip on the steering wheel tightens, her knuckles turning white. "Did you catch him?"

"No, the dogs scared him away. The police just left. I wish I had been on duty, I would have caught him for sure!"

A car pulls in behind us and gives a friendly sort of honk. "Okay, hold your horses," Miquel mutters under his breath. "Well, I'll see you later, Ms. Butler. You have a good day and take care of yourselves. Thanks for the magazines!" He quickly jogs back to the security booth, as we pull through the gate.

I walk in the front door of my mom's house and head straight for the master shower. Closing the bathroom door behind me, I shed my robe and drop my purse. Collapsing on the tub floor I let the shower run over me, the soot, the grunge, slipping down the drain. I turn the tap up on high- as high as I can stand the hot water, until I feel like I'm burning too. A knock on the door and I hear a muffled shout. I get up quickly and turn on the cold water, shampoo my hair. I try to make my actions quick, I've indulged in enough self pity for the morning. Grabbing a fluffy towel off the shelf, I shake out my hair. When I enter my mom's bedroom, I see she has laid out a set of pajamas for me, and a note in her shaky handwriting. "Sleep," is all it says. I wonder briefly where Sergio has gone, since I'm sure it was his voice I heard, but decide to heed my mothers advice. Climbing under her covers, I'm asleep in seconds.

It is dark when I wake up disorientated, in a slight panic before I realize I'm in my mom's room, in her bed and her pajamas. The covers next to me rumpled, the pillow indented. The fire suddenly comes to the forefront of my consciousness, and it seems like a dream. A nightmare someone else has experienced. There are emphatic voices coming from the next room. Authoritative voices. My mom trying to shush them. I'm awake now, but still tired. I slept too long and too late into the afternoon. Or is it evening? My purse is still under the nightstand where I threw it this morning, so I dig out my phone. *Three-thirty.* I groan and decide to get up. Kicking my bag under the bed, I vaguely remember there's something important in there, and I don't want anyone snooping before I can look. I grab a robe from the hook on the wall, slip into a spare pair of slippers.

Padding out to the hall the voices become louder. No one is shouting, it's my Aunt Kathryn, trying to be heard over general hubbub.

I see Uncle Paul first, a frown on his face. I enter the room and my Aunt Tina is also here, her belly round and dropping. My mom and Sergio are perched on a chair across from them. It takes me a moment before I realize there's also a stranger in our midst. A uniformed police officer is taking notes as everyone speaks at once. His uniform is wrinkled, the shirt untucked. *Not exactly a professional, is he?* I zero in on my mom who pats the seat next to her, which I take, gratefully. She hands me a soda water, before I can join the conversation.

"Okay everyone, Lara is awake- we need to fill her in on what's happened."

The officer gets to his feet, "I'm wrapping up now anyway. If I think of anything else I'll give you a call. I'll need your daughter to come down to the station when she's feeling up to it, and answer a few questions," he says, looking at me. His eyes are a pale blue gray.

I shrug my shoulders, not caring one way or another. I look for my husband and see concern in his eyes, his hair rumpled from sleep. His face needs a shave. He must have joined me in bed this afternoon, and I didn't even realize it.

"Alright," he says, heaving the familiar green Tupperware bin over his shoulder, the one we so carefully filled yesterday, "we'll talk soon." The officer sees himself out, and no one speaks before the door slams shut behind him. I turn to my mom.

"Lara, there was another fire," she says.

I jump up and spill my soda. "What? Where?"

"Sweetheart!" She pulls me back into a sitting position. "At Marion's. There was a fire at Marion's this morning. The message was on my phone when we got home. Sergio and I drove out there, but it was too late. The house, the gardens, everything is gone. It's even worse than your fire-because there was so much accelerate. At least that's what the fire inspector thinks, all those papers and things in her home. It was too late before they even got there, arson again. They could tell almost immediately, the neighbors said they woke to a crashing noise. Most likely a bottle going through the front window."

I look at her in disbelief and don't know what to say. My head turns to my Uncle Paul as he begins to speak.

"And Marion is dead. Died this morning, natural causes, Kathryn was with her at the end."

My hand reaches for my mom's and I can only think to comfort her a little. "Mom, I'm so sorry. You were so close to finding something. It is all so, so overwhelming."

She pats my hand, "I know. The police think there's a link between the fires, and possibly the attempted break in last night. The investigator had to take my tupperware container for evidence."

A loud rapping noise startles us, and my mom hops up. She peers out the peep hole and jumps back with a little shriek. Slowly opening the door, we are silent when two police officers enter the room and introduce themselves. They're here to ask us some questions about the fire.

My mom is the first to comprehend, her eyes rolling back in her head. There is no one to catch her when she crumples to the floor.

Chapter Six

It is hours later when they finally leave. "No, we didn't ask to see his badge. Why would we have questioned him? He knew all about the fires, and it was very professional. He took all the evidence; we didn't rescue anything else from Marion's. She had no personal possessions at the hospital. We know nothing about her." I keep my mouth shut unless asked a direct question. They both seem suspicious of me, until my mom informs them I'm still in shock. It mollifies them a little. I remember the letters, the checks, but I don't want to say anything to them. I'm terrified they'll take it away as evidence too, and my trust in the system is a little rocky at the moment. They hand us business cards, and try to be sympathetic. Trite phrases I'm sure they say to everyone. One last look at me before they're out the door. My relatives following them shortly. My mom disappears into her bedroom, and I head for a stool at the kitchen counter- Sergio already at the stove, finding comfort in what he loves doing best.

My mom reappears a few minutes later, a large photo album in her hands. She silently slips it to me, and I carefully open its ancient cover. A smell wafts from the pages, stale cigarette smoke and old perfume. The edges of the pictures are yellowed, and I pull the first one from its sticky, plastic sheathing. It's my grandfather as a small child, "John 1942" penciled on the back. He is standing in someones backyard, bushes almost consuming the background.

"I have to tell you something, both of you," I say, looking up from the photo album. Sergio slides something in the oven and then leans on the counter to look at me. I slide the album back to my mom and jump off the stool. "Wait a minute, and I'll show you." I drop to the floor of my mom's room and dig under the bed until I retrieve my purse. I run back to the both of them and dump the contents unceremoniously on the counter. The glass on our wedding frame shatters, a banana falls to the floor. I poke through the refuse until I find the padded envelope, pulling out the pages of the "princess" letter, now crumpled and even more illegible. I hand everything to my mom and she stares at me in disbelief. A smile crossing her face for the first time today.

"Why didn't you tell the police?" She asks, but I can tell she's not serious. I ignore the question and tell her to open the padded one first.

"I think that's what's causing all the trouble, I didn't want them to see it until we could discuss it first." Sergio crosses over from the kitchen to lean over her shoulder. She pulls out the first check and gives a gasp of surprise. I see it's one of the money orders for the largest amount, twelve thousand dollars. Sergio grabs it out of her shaking hand.

"This is crazy! A check for Twelve. Thousand. Dollars?! Unreal." He turns to me, "Honey, why didn't you say anything before this?"

"There wasn't time, with the fire, and then I forgot and only remembered when those two cops showed up. There's more though."

"More than this?" My mom asks. "It's like cash money." She pulls out the next few money orders, and then dumps them all on the counter at once.

"It's a little over twenty five thousand dollars," I tell her. "Look at the notations on them, that's what I can't figure out, maybe we could google it? And there's these," I hand her the letter.

"A letter from the tubes that were all over the floor! Amazing. This one is dated recently, but look at the writing style. So old-fashioned- like my mother's used to be."

"You can read it?" I ask my mom. "It was giving me a headache."

"It will help to have a magnifying glass, but yes, I think I can read them." She reaches for her laptop.

I head for her desk to fish out a magnifying glass, and Sergio walks back to the kitchen.

"I think we should take all of this to the police station," he says, gesturing to the pile. "As soon as possible. Now. I don't like this. Whoever that fake cop was, whoever burned our house, those guys are serious. I don't think we should be messing with this." He puts on an oven mitt before pulling a pizza out of the oven, mozzarella dripping over the crust. My stomach rumbles.

My mom answers him before I can, "It can't hurt to take a look. . .before we take this to the police." My mom's excitement is palatable. No way we are handing this over yet. She wants answers, even if the letters don't contain information about her father, or his family. There's still a mystery here, one in which people are willing to do some major destruction for. Kill even. Sometime in the last hour my sorrow has turned to rage, and it needs a target. The house I loved the minute I saw it. The house we were planning on raising our future children in. The house we honeymooned in to save cash. Our home, gone. I'm as anxious as she is.

"Got it," my mom says, pulling up a search engine on her computer. "Founder, master race." I see her type the words in, before she announces, "Madison Grant, the nations most influential racist."

"Racist?" I echo, "like fascist, white supremacy stuff?"

"Exactly," my mom states. "Listen, he started the whole blond-haired, blue-eyed Nordics as a "master race" thing. He thought the state's should eliminate "inferior races" who were of no value to communities. He even convinced Congress to enact immigration restriction legislation in the 1920's that led many states to ban interracial marriage, and sterilize thousands of "unworthy" citizens."

I let this sink in for a minute, America creating laws like that. The possibility people may still think like that. I think of racism as being something that happens on an individual basis, in the long since past.

"So these are racists, right? Sending checks to Aunt Marion? But why?"

"I don't know, there's nothing like this in our family. White Supremacists?" She involuntarily glances at Sergio, who is looking straight at me. He begins to laugh.

"Should I get out now? It's a little late, don't you think?" He plops a slice of pizza in front of me and I start to giggle.

Horrified at myself, I slap a hand over my mouth. I can't believe I've found humor in the situation.

Little jabs at Sergio- jokes about working in the kitchens- he's Latino after all. My uncles call him a short line cook, even though he's professionally trained, works in a Michelin Star Restaurant. Jokes, a way to razz him, that's how we show love in our family, like Paul's bald spot- and my cousin Elaine's nose. Both points of contention for them, and an endless source of amusement for the rest of us.

"I didn't even know people still thought like this. I mean the occasional slur you hear about. The unchecked language creating a media frenzy. Crazy people in other countries, but here? In America? White Supremacists? It's like something from Jerry Springer."

"It used to be common honey, I mean even when I was growing up it was still "us," and "them." It's easy to change behavior and actions. More difficult is the thought process, the perception. We live in California, so it's easier to forget. Too many cultures blending together; easy to forget you're a majority in this country, when you live in the minority."

A line from one of the fan letters, "What trials you must go through, living amongst them after all you've already endured. How I admire you for your strength." The checks, master race, Founder. Words gleaned from the letters in the tubes, "supplies" and "jungle." The postmark in Portuguese. I piece it together and reach for the letters.

"Mom," I say. "I think these may be important." I don't even wait for her to try and read them, pulling the magnifying glass off the counter and bending down to squint at the words. I skim sentences I think are gossip, different health problems ailing members of their "colony." The last paragraph is the most interesting, and I concentrate on the words there.

Fissures of unrest threaten to overwhelm our cause here. It has been over two months since we've received any supplies, and the colony can't survive without your support. We are in desperate need of our most essential provisions, batteries, hypodermic needles, antibiotics. The Führer worries you have decided to cut off your aid, that you no longer believe in our purpose here. That our army may no longer be necessary. I worry something has happened to prevent you from receiving these letters. Please respond. Please. We need you.

Um Beijo! The Aryan Princess to Cannibals.

This paragraph sends my heart racing, and I take large gulps of air. Close my eyes. My mom is alarmed, tugging the magnifying glass from my hand. The letter slips from my fingers, drifting to the counter. A gasp from her as she starts to read.

"What does this mean?" she asks.

I open my eyes before I answer, the bits and pieces clicking into place. I pull out the photograph of my grandfather again, examine it closely. *It could be.* "I think I know exactly what it means. . .there's a white supremacist camp somewhere in the Brazilian jungle. Marion was, or is, their leader." We stare at each other, my mom's eyes filled with confusion; my ears buzzing with the possibility.

"Ridiculous," Sergio states.

I jump, nearly falling off the stool. I forgot he was even here.

"This is nonsense." He marches out from behind the counter and picks up the letter. Waves it in the air, "How could an entire group of people survive in the Brazilian jungle- white supremacists for that matter, and there's not even a hint of it in the news? It's impossible, *completamente imposible.* This is probably some game Marion was playing with a pen pal."

"But Sarge- the checks? How do you explain those?" I'm exasperated he dismisses my theory so immediately, when everything fits so perfectly.

"I don't know, but I think it's time we get to the police station. Both of you finish your pizza, while I clean up. We're leaving as soon as possible. Maybe if we get rid of this stuff, you guys will come to your senses and we can move on."

My temper flares, *move on!?* How can he not see it? It all adds up.

We're glaring at each other when my mom speaks, "I think the checks, not the letters."

We both look at her.

"My father. . .The checks go to the police. Not the letters." Her mouth is set in a tight line, and I remember she's hurting too. That my house wasn't the only one to burn today.

"Oh Mom, I'm sorry, of course you can keep the letters." I send a heated look at Sergio, daring him to disagree with me.

"Fine, the checks- you keep the letters. But I don't want to hear anymore about secret colonies, and white supremacy. I think Marion was just a nice old lady with eccentric friends and false ideals. A lot of old folks are like that."

I exit the stool and give Sergio a hug. "Sure honey- and there really is a pot of gold at the end of the rainbow." I smile up into his face before kissing his nose. "Let me get some clothes on and we'll go."

It's past nine when we head out to the police station. Sergio has the lock box with him, placing the checks in there while I was getting dressed. He has already contacted the detective in charge of our case. My mom has brought her laptop- to do more research, despite Sergio's protests. I've stuffed the letters back into my purse, and as an afterthought took my mother's photo album. It has been a while since I've looked through it, and I might have some time at the station. We're all wide awake, Sergio and I from our naps, my mom because the excitement of the day has still not worn off of her. I am dressed in one of her pantsuits, a coral pink affair with pearl buttons. It reminds me of my flight attendant uniform, the polyester chaffing my thighs. It goes well with my salvaged pumps. My mom has a light lavender one on. She's paired it with flats. Sergio gives me a slightly horrified look at the two of us together, before hugging her.

"I can see where Lara gets her looks from," he says, winking. She giggles, before grabbing her matching handbag.

It is January and unseasonably colder than usual when we pull out of the garage. There is a thin coat of frost beginning to work on my mom's lawn. The retirement community is quiet, most of its residents already in bed, or passed out in front of buzzing televisions. The security gate rolls by the window, my mom giving a little wave to the guard. A different one this time, Keldrick- a large black man who loves my mom's lemon bars. I'm partial to them myself.

We turn left at Westland, then a right. The opposite direction we should be going in. I'm about to say something to Sergio when I notice him nervously watching the rear-view mirror. A look in the mirror, face to the front, back to the mirror. Two right turns and we're back on track, the police station just two more blocks. The light in front of us is red, when Sergio suddenly swerves on to the 10 freeway. I grab the dash in front of me, my mom giving a little yelp from the back.

"What's wrong?" I ask him.

"I don't want to sound paranoid, especially after snapping at the both of you, but I think we're being followed."

My heart drops and every spy movie I've ever seen flashes through my head. Sergio pulls off the freeway again and races through a green light, swerving left. I try to keep my eyes forward but I can't help it; whipping my head around to see the car behind us. My mom dives to the side of her seat, as a blue Suburban smashes into the back of us. The jolt propels us through the next intersection and into cross-traffic. Sergio mutters something unintelligible in Spanish as he pushes the accelerator down. "I did not learn to drive in Guadalajara without picking up a few things." He swerves behind a car which nearly sideswipes us, before turning us back into our lane. I don't know what has happened to the rear end of my mom's car- there appears to be no damage on the Suburban. He is several cars behind us, ducking in and

71

out of traffic. A few sparks fly up from our bumper area and I'm afraid there's been gunfire.

"Honey! Gunshots!" I yell, peeking over the back seat again.

"No," he says loudly. "It's the bumper dragging on the pavement."

"Um, that's reassuring," I mumble sarcastically, but he doesn't hear me. He's focused on keeping us in our own lane of traffic.

I glance over my shoulder and see my mom in a prone position across the back seat. I decide it might be best to slide down in my own seat, and my knees knock against the dashboard.

We take the next on-ramp but don't exit the freeway- racing around the cloverleaf and spitting back into another intersection. Sergio taking the turn much faster than this olds-mobile has ever even been driven in its lifetime. My seatbelt digs into my stomach as my body tries to slip across the bench seat. We fly under a bridge and are suddenly back on another on-ramp, and then the freeway, going northbound. The next off-ramp, then a right turn. I dare to look behind us and don't see the Suburban.

"Sergio, the University of Redlands! Turn right! Here! Now!" I scream at him. The car jumps as we hit two speed bumps and lose the rear end of the car. He makes the turn in time to park us in front of the station.

"Out, out!" Sergio yells, unlocking the doors and diving out of the car. We're running for the front entrance and Sergio hits the glass door first, impatiently banging his fists. The door inches open at the same time my mom and I reach it. Through the opening and exhausted, I collapse on the first empty, orange-plastic chair I see. My mom hasn't even made it that far- she is hunched over a water fountain at the entrance. One hand in the spray, one hand on her chest gasping for air. Sergio is in charge, not even out of breath, running down our story to the officer at the desk. Another officer listening races past him to look outside, but I know he won't find them. We lost the Suburban at the last turn. We are safe for now.

They pull each of in for questioning separately, Sergio first. Twenty minutes later my mom opens up her laptop, for lack of something better to do. I breathe in the crowd around me, homeless women, young children, an expensive looking man. There's a rattling noise at my wrist and I look down to notice the person next to me is chained to the seat. I think it's a man at first, with a full mustache, until I notice the pleather skirt and rattlesnake heels. He is staring at me. "Nice shoes," I say, and he rewards me with a toothless grin. I quickly look away, pretending to be preoccupied with something in my purse.

My fingers brush against the photo album before finding the white tube, empty of its letter. I pull the tube out and scratch at the mailing label, working on it until it peels off. Taking out the album I flip to the back, where my mom has pasted the letter. The label goes on the opposite page, "Manacapuru," it says. I put pressure on the pages and then the whole thing is shoved back in my purse.

Just in time.

"Sylvia?" An officer calls out to the crowd, focusing in on my mom and I. My mom hands me her laptop and smooths the nonexistent wrinkles from her pants, following the officer to the back. I quickly google Manacapuru and it pops up immediately. The earliest flight is to Rio di Janeiro, connecting to the Eduardo Gomes International Airport. Then a six hour boat ride from Manaus. Manacapuru is a huge city in Brazil, a modern city. I wonder briefly where the actual supremacist village could be hiding. Three days of travel, at least, to get some answers. The mailing label's address, all we have to go on. I don't consider the danger. I know we would be in more danger staying here. A different country, a change of scene, a place to hide. The last place these Aryan brothers would expect us to go. I work it over and over in my mind. How to tell my mom, how to ask Sergio.

How I will keep this information from the police that are waiting to question me.

A female officer interrupts my thoughts, my mom at her side. "The police went to check on the house while we were here," my mom says. Her eyes brim over with tears.

"It has been ransacked," says the officer. She's not much older than me, and too cute to be police. *Too perky.*

"An absolute mess, we have a unit closing it up now if you'd like to go over and take a look. I think they're almost finished with this phase of the investigation." She glances around before shielding her mouth with her hand, and whispering, "we believe it's a scare tactic, if the people responsible really wanted you dead, well. . ."

Then we'd be dead. I finish the sentence for her in my head.

"We can bring you in for questioning another day," she says, a little more loudly to me. Her face softens as she speaks to my mom, "I would recommend you guys finding a safe place to stay tonight and get some rest. Do you need our help? Do you have anywhere you can go?"

I stand up to pull my mom into a hug. I know exactly where we can go, but I wouldn't exactly call it safe.

Marta

➤➤→

Chapter Seven

It is late afternoon when I find myself on the Pure dining hall steps.

"Ow!" the girl next to me exclaims. I've accidentally elbowed her in the side trying to jostle closer to the front.

"Sorry," I mumble, but she's already been pushed further back and doesn't hear me.

The dining hall is fully enclosed on three sides by a thick mesh screen. A row of fire canisters line the open back for cooking, and there are small refrigerators connected to a generator my Uncle Dale is in charge of maintaining. I'm nearly to the front of the line when the Pure kitchen attendant makes a motion for us to enter. He scuttles away quickly before he can be swept up in the incoming horde of us. There are a few Untouchables inside already, scrubbing at the pots and pans stacked in groupings near large water barrels. We scavenge for the leftovers. There's plenty left at the buffet today, more than enough to feed the forty people here. No defecation to the food either- the Pure are in a good mood.

Perhaps the news that the Princess has finally chosen a mate has spread.

There is always little time to eat. Most of the citizens grab small packets of food before running down the steps and back to the barracks. The children will need to be fed and put to sleep before Session. I decide to take a seat at one of the low tables, and Ani joins me, along with a younger man Derrik. Excepting the clean up crew, we are the only Untouchables to stay.

"I wonder what it would be like to have hot food?" Ani begins.

"Or more than a spoonful of pudding?" I respond.

"How about grain that isn't mush?" Derrik adds.

"And meat that isn't tough." Ani finishes.

It's a game we play at every meal time, we live on the leftovers of the Pure, unless I manage to smuggle food from the boxes. There's food to be found in the jungle, but fruit and nuts don't exactly add weight to our frames. Extra meat goes to those who can't make it to the dining hall in their specified times. The children, the elderly, the Untouchables who work the gardens, do the laundry. Servants to my father and sister. We keep the food and supplies stashed in metal boxes under the overhang behind my hut. Since it has been over four months since the last box has arrived, many of them have had to do with what meat and bread we can scavenge from the dining hall. With no way to preserve the fresh food- by the time it reaches their mouths it is usually cold, molding, or worst of all, crawling with insects.

"Ani tells me you're going with the party tomorrow, to get the mail," Derrik says, aound a mouthful of grey beef.

I give Ani a dark look, this was supposed to be announced tomorrow. When I would be long gone and unavailable to answer nosey questions.

"Yes," I answer him, hoping my curt reply will end the discussion.

"I can't believe the Führer would allow it, an Untouchable leaving the colony. Besides the occasional disappearance, this has never happened before. One of us, *leaving*." His voice has an awestruck quality to it, jealousy mingled with fear.

"I don't think you're coming back," Ani says, shaking her head slightly.

"What do you mean?" I ask, choking on a chunk of meat that has lodged itself in my throat. Derrik hands me the water, before thumping me on the back.

"Exactly what I said, I don't think you're coming back. We haven't heard anything about the war in ages. It could be over. They could have lost. I think that's why our packages have stopped."

My mouth drops open in astonishment, water dribbling down my chin. Heresy, I've never heard anyone in the colony speak like this before. The war? Over?

"Interesting view," Derrik supplies, "but what if she doesn't come back because her brother has plans to kill her."

"What!?" I exclaim, while I whip my head around, scanning the dining room. What if someone overheard him?

Ani's lip twitches, she's trying to conceal a smile. Derrik is stoic. They could both be punished for their bravado.

"Why would my brother kill me?" I ask, genuinely curious to know their theory, even if it's a joke. It's rare anyone is killed in the colony, every person is needed, even the Untouchables. Punishment or humiliation, is much more likely.

They both flinch, their eyes disbelieving, as if I would ever question such a thing as my family wanting to get rid of me. Permanently.

"You have to know they see you as a threat to their supremacy, Marta," Ani tells me. "I can't believe you never realized."

"Me?! A threat? How?" Skepticism lines my voice, until I remember my Uncle Dale's advice, "be careful." It does add weight to her theory.

"Even the Pure have noticed how much influence you have over your sister, and Jacob commands little respect. You need to be careful," Ani says, echoing my uncle.

"I can't believe you would want to leave," Derrik interrupts. "It's so dangerous for us out there. Why would you want to take that risk?"

"She doesn't want to leave," Ani says. "Right, Marta? The Führer has commanded it. Anyone would be crazy to want to leave here. It's the only place we know we're safe."

"Safer," Derrik says quietly. His eyes dart above my head before glancing down at the table, clearing the silverware in one sweep of his arm. "We'll pick the bananas tomorrow; it was good talking with you both, but I had better get going." Derrik's words seem disjointed from the conversation until I take a brief look behind me. A Pure guard has entered the dining tent from the back steps, probably to assess the cleanup.

Ani plasters a wide smile on her face before standing up with him. "I have to speak with Marie. I'll walk out with you," she says, grabbing my plate before I can object.

The water barrels in front of me are still filled with dishes, the Untouchables scrubbing furiously. I sit frozen, thinking the conversation over in my head. The guard's heavy steps behind me, a prickly sensation crawling up my back. Fear. How am I a threat, when I live in such terror?

"There you are." My heart contracts at the familiar voice, the warmth in my chest chasing the cold anxiety away. I swing my legs out from under the table and turn my body around to face him. No wonder Ani was smiling, it's Henrik.

"I thought you might be in the dining hall," he says. "I only have a couple of minutes before second drill begins."

I hop up from my seat, and veer sideways, the sting of my ankle surprising me.

"Dale already told me we're meeting in the morning, at the beach," I grunt, moving my weight to the other foot.

"It's not that." Henrik looks concerned but doesn't reach for me. "I wanted to warn you, something funny is going on with your brother. The general you saw me speaking with earlier, Thomas. He told me the Führer had already granted him permission to go on the mail run, days ago. Then, this morning, he was called in to speak with the Führer and told he wouldn't be going this time."

"That's it?" I frown. "There's nothing unusual about that. The Führer changes his mind all the time."

"Not like that, not about the mail run. Ever since your mother. . . .I'm sorry," he finishes lamely.

I shake my head, gesturing to him. "But you'll be there. My brother would never do anything with one of the Führer's guard present." The pride thickens my voice when I say this, *the Führer's* guard. I smile at him. "I'm not worried."

Henrik steps closer, taking my hand, and a tingle tickles my fingertips. I shiver from the pleasure of his touch. His eyes bore right through me, so blue. A pool of water, I'm sinking. Our hands clutched, the warmth creeping up my arm. He shouldn't be touching me so, we shouldn't be playing at this. He wants to say something, the words half formed on his tongue. I lean forward, hoping, waiting. Words I don't know if I'm ready to hear. Our bodies nearly touch, and I am on tiptoe, our faces inches apart. My ankle screams at the extra strain, but I can feel his breath on my own lips, the balm to my pain. He cocks his head to the side, his eyes flicking to a corner behind me. A noise there, distracting him. I wince, rolling back on the balls of my feet. The moment gone.

"I was. . .worried about you this morning." His free hand caresses my hair, and I lean into his touch. I allow this feeling to wash over me. I turn my brain off as his hand moves to the crook of my neck, my shoulder. It rests on my chest, and he feels my heart beats, rapidly accelerating, while the rest of me melts. I count twenty before his hand drops to his side and I can open my eyes.

"I won't be able to speak as, familiar, as we have been, on the trip," he says, lifting my hand to his face, and then, thinking better of it, loosening his grip. My arm falls limply back to my side. Do I imagine the longing look in his eyes, before turning away from me? I grip the corner of my table as he marches toward the door.

Back to where he belongs.

There's a flash of movement to my left. A little head peeking out from behind the buffet tables.

"Elise?" I ask, unsure. She stands up, and I can see I'm right. It's the girl from the match this morning. In a few steps I'm in front of her, and she's even smaller than I initially thought. Her hair covered in a rag, trying to conceal its length. A trick I've tried many times before, but rarely works. The little tendrils force themselves out from beneath the fabric. Her face is dirty, she must have come striaght from children's drill. It's hard to gauge her age, but she's younger than nine or ten. Eight maybe.

"They wouldn't really kill you? Would they?" she asks. Her lip is quivering, not a trace of the hostility I saw this morning. She appears vulnerable now.

I close my eyes and sigh loudly, "you overheard that, huh?" I kneel down to her level, try to smile reassuringly. "I saw you this morning, take down that girl."

"Amalia," she says.

"Was that her name?" I ask.

She bounces her head.

"It was an excellent move," I tell her.

I'm rewarded with a big grin. She's missing her two front teeth. "I love to fight," she says with a slight whistle. "It makes me feel so, so powerful, for just a minute, you know?"

And I do know. Powerful. I truly smile back at her then. "Between the two of us, I don't think he could take me." I mouth the words, "my brother," at her and she erupts into giggles.

"I don't think so either," she says conspiratorially. She places her hands on her hips and says seriously, "remember, it's all about the element of surprise."

I give her an exaggerated wink, and then shoo her along. It's getting late and her caretakers might be worried. There's a Session to attend.

The Führer is incredibly charismatic, his excitement building up the crowd- his rages increasing the fervor. It's one of the few times I love to watch him, manipulating emotions. The passion in his voice, effulgent. Each day here is much the same, the menial tasks performed over and over, punctuated by birth or insignificant squabbles. Sometimes an act of violence from the people, or the jungle. The Führer's speeches are the pageant, the entertainment, usually accompanied by a performance of music. Session is not mandatory, but everyone attends.

I hobble back to my hut to use the latrine. Ani is there when I arrive, laying out on her hammock. She looks pale, her arms folded behind her head, relaxed.

"You don't seem too torn up about my imminent death," I tell her, wrapping my ankle in a long strip of fabric.

"I've come to terms with it long ago," she half smiles at me. "I wish there was a way you didn't have to go. I'm afraid for you, Marta."

I can't tell her I want to go, and so I tell her a truth instead. "I'm afraid for me too."

"I was being serious earlier, not about the war of course, but about your brother. You need to be careful." Beads of sweat appear around her hairline, her pupils growing larger. "I would have told you before, but there's never a good time to talk."

Loud voices and a scraping noise outside tell me now is not the time either. Intending to pack my things for tomorrow, I look around the room and realize there's nothing for me to bring. I wouldn't trust my books, papers, or writing utensils to the journey. I would never remove the album from its place here. I doubt Henrik, or my brother, will allow me the time to primp, so my comb is out. I won't need the gourd of water, or the packets of food. In the end, I decide on nothing, and Ani and I join the group heading for the fire ring.

We stay away from the clearing, hiding within the trees and bushes. Most of the Pure are already seated, the prime spots near the fire, closest to the Führer, already filled. The fire is merely ceremonious, the light and smoke it emits more valuable than the warmth it's providing. The night has chased away the sun's heat, but the sweltering humidity remains.

I'm grateful we're not allowed near, that the Untouchables are spread far enough apart to allow movement. We've stripped some of the plants of their leaves on our walk over and with our makeshift fans flapping, for once we are the lucky ones. The fans provide a breeze, and a way to keep the bugs away. The Pure are shoulder to shoulder, muttering and complaining.

My sister Jul enters and sashays to her chair, taking the time to walk around the fire ring so everyone can admire her. A different outfit from this morning, she is covered, barely, in a sparkly material. Her large breasts threatening to fall out the top, the fabric stretched much too tight over her rear end. "Ende," I hear the whisper drift from somewhere. The raucous laughter barely contained next to me. I hear the murmurs of agreement, "die Dirne," and "das Luder." One of us? One of them? It doesn't matter, I tense up. Condescending, rude, cruel even, but Julianne is not a slut. Our mothers mistake and consequences planted too firmly in her mind. I want to defend her, but it's a ridiculous thought. I would cause an unnecessary scene. She takes her seat, lifting one leg slowly to cross over the other, licking her lips.

Everyone jumps to attention as the Führer approaches, even those of us huddled in the shadows, the ones he couldn't possibly see, stand. He takes the three stairs to his seat, his eyes sweeping across the expanse, commanding the rest of us to sit. Henrik and James take their position behind him on the podium. The Untouchables slipping back into the darkness, their fans quiet now. The Pure readjust themselves to better advantage, before squatting down on the logs.

"My comrades! You are welcome tonight! I will make it short since there is an early journey to prepare for tomorrow. My trusted guard Henrik will be attending to the mail, and I have decided since I am getting on in years," a pause while he waits for protests. They're half a second too late and he has already continued, his voice an octave higher. "Since I am getting on in years," he squints into the crowd, "and my son Jacob will soon come into the dictatorship. I will have him join the expedition." I'm not surprised he doesn't mention me leaving tomorrow. I wonder if Ani and Derrik are right. Do I become another disappearance?

He continues, "We have come to a critical time in history. There are heathens around us who threaten our heritage. There are those in this world who would see the Aryan race extinguished. Who believe we are the evil ones, the ones who threaten their culture, their traditions." He sneers at us. "The traditions of those cursed by a loving God do not concern us. Their subjugation to a superior race is the only thing they should be concerned about. We are the chosen people. We are the ones who are scientifically and spiritually designed to control this world. We are winning the war outside of this jungle. The quality of our race is in this circle." Cheers erupt from the Pure. "We must not become discouraged, our Patrons are dependent on the procreation of our women. They rely on us to provide them with warriors for the final strike. They prepare the world for us."

The statements echoed by the Pure, chanting, cheering until it becomes one voice, one sound. "Aryan blood." I drop back another foot until my back is resting against a tree. I grasp at it, my palms pressing against the smooth bark, anchoring me here. I'm leaving the colony tomorrow, to go to a village outside of Manacapuru. We are told the village is a safe haven, heavily protected from the outside world. There have always been rumors of Untouchable snatchers though. Poachers who have burned whole colonies for Untouchable slaves to sell on the black market. It is why we don't leave, the war, the poachers. We are safe here. I remember Derrik's whisper. *Safer here.*

The chanting dies down and the Führer smiles at Julianne. Holding his hand out for her to join him on the podium. She stands and I realize her dress has snuck up her thighs. It is no longer covering her back side. I lean forward as if to help her, but from here I can only watch. She's about to turn up the stairs when the Führer's wife Heidi, catches her by the wrist. She is hastily whispering in her ear. Julianne flushes, adjusting herself to the snickers of the crowd. Pushing Heidi roughly away, Julianne loses balance, stumbling up the steps. The Führer has turned red, flushing from anger he barks to the crowd. "Julianne will make an announcement." He sits back down solidly, and everyone is immediately silent.

Julianne is not used to having the attention of the entire colony so focused on her. It unhinges her, causes a crack in her veneer. Smoothing out her dress, she thrusts out her chest, batting her eyes down at the crowd. There is discomfort in the movements, normally she would be enjoying the attention, but she feels the restlessness of the crowd, the animosity.

"Yes, an announcement. My announcement." This restores her composure, and she straightens her back. Jutting her chin high in the air. "Thank you Father, I have decided on my mate. *My husband.*" A giggle erupts from her as she seems to look directly at me. Tossing her hair over her shoulder she turns to Henrik, offering him her hand.

The air goes out of me.

I decided to take a swim once, in the river. It had barely finished raining, my body caught in the swift current; I was pulled under. There was no time for the last breath, surprised by the force at which it caught me. I exhaled right before my face disappeared under the water. Pushing my legs as hard as they could go, willing myself to break the surface so I could take that breath. The edge of darkness, the panic. The pain deep in my chest. Ripping my heart apart. I am back in that place. Henrik taking her hand. No choice. Events I can't control, pulling me under. Julianne turning to him- pressing her body against his. Ani is here, gripping my arms, in my ear, willing me to breathe. The crowd cheers, pleased with her choice. I can inhale. I can exhale.

"Did everyone know?" there is an edge of panic to my voice. Her lips search for his, an arm slipped around his waist. "Did everyone know. . .I loved him?"

"No, no I only guessed. I wasn't even sure if you knew." Ani is trying to be reassuring, but I can only release myself from her. Wrap my arms around my chest. Hold myself together.

"We'll go; I'll lead you." She pulls me along, other hands joining her as she moves toward the bridge. Helping me along, petting my hair, my arm, whispering comforting words in my ear. Their compassion breaks me down, the tears slowly, silently rolling down my face. I trip on the step up to our hut and fall to my knees, choking on my fury. My body convulses as the dry heaves take me, the pressure finally releasing. My dinner sprayed out on the floor. I collapse in it, vomit, tears, and snot. Sobbing.

"Marta. . .Marta!" Ani is inches from my ear, "you have to get up now, we have to rinse you off. Pull yourself together. You have to be strong now."

She pulls me to my feet, and I feel so weak. A gourd of water dumped over my head. She helps me strip down, pulls a new dress over my head, guides me to my hammock. I hear her sweeping, clearing the evidence. I close my eyes and pray for a different tomorrow.

Chapter Eight

I wake to the reality of the next morning, my heartbreak better than any herb Ani could give me for sleep. I am groggy, on the edge of a nightmare. The pain is tangible. I can feel it stabbing at me, but I find it's manageable. Good even. It reminds me of why I'm leaving today, why I must get out. My feet drop to the floor and I get moving. My cracker has already arrived, but I'm not hungry. I decide to leave it for Ani. She has scrubbed our floor clean in the night, there is no evidence of my weakness. I hobble to the latrine and wash my face in the stream here. It feels puffy, my eyes are swollen. My hip is tender and bruised. I'm poking at it when I remember my fall, a lifetime ago. Only yesterday, my brother, the warning, the announcement. I don't even return to the hut, and dawdle for a few minutes at the bridge, the water rushing high underneath. Huge fish lazily following the current. I stretch my legs on the wooden slats, tugging each foot in turn and then testing the weight on my ankle. I think I can run; I reach my arms over my head and pull at my elbow. Feel the muscles strain.

The moon is bright, the clouds not yet formed. I won't need my flashlight, or even have to wait for the sun to peek out. A quick scan of the jungle and I spot an opening into the shadowy darkness. A hole that must have been cut last night. I grab my walking stick, testing the sharpened point with the tip of my finger. When I pull my hand away a tiny pinprick of blood remains. I clench my fist around the shaft, and start to run.

The vines crisscross above me, some as thin as my arm, others thicker the Führer's waistline. I pick my way carefully over a dead tree, a strangler fig has sucked the life from its bowels. Her long, snake-like limbs wrapped around the trunk, cutting it off from the essential nutrients it needs to survive. My senses are sharp as I run, aware of the movement above me, animals who never let their feet touch the mossy ground. Flashes of color all around, the birds and flowers providing an ever shifting picture of beauty. Snakes curled around the trunks of trees, usually asleep.

My stick all the protection I need.

The beach is empty when I arrive, the sun barely rising. The sky is alight with the dawn, and I decide to lay on the small patch of warm sand, listening to the waves lap at the rocks. Coral pinks, hazy purples, floating on the blue backdrop. For a moment I allow my imagination to run free, and pretend I am far from here, with Henrik maybe, and our children. I am building our home in the clouds when a giggle rips across the beach. Impossible dreams. I sit up, my hand on my forehead, pressing against my skull. She is never up this early, but I see them, Henrik stiff and upright, walking toward me through the trees. There's my mail tube in his hand, and Jul is hanging on his arm, her free hand fluttering over him. Adjusting his collar, smoothing his hair, rubbing his back. She runs to approach me, happiness radiating from her.

"Oh Marta! I'm so glad you're here first! I have something to give you." This is not what I expected, and I'm sure my face betrays me. My mouth opens in astonishment, and my eyes burn with hatred. I push my hands against my knees to stand, Henrik not acknowledging me in any way. She is reaching for his pocket, kissing him on the cheek. A paper flutters out, it's a picture, torn from a magazine. I adjust my features into one of indifference.

"The dog, Marta." She hands me the scrap.

I study it carefully. A thin girl, thinner than anyone in the Untouchable camps, in another sparkly dress. Sequins I think they're called, the word floating into my consciousness from one of my many conversations with Jul. Her hair is everywhere, more hair than I've ever seen on a person. The head disproportionately larger than her body, and altogether ridiculous. In her arms is a dog, a toy really, an accessory maybe. It's all so confusing.

"Yes, it's a dog," I tell her, trying to hand back the paper.

"No, Marta!" She is laughing now, speaking slowly so I can understand. "You will get this dog for me, in Manacapuru."

88

"The village?" I echo back at her.

"Yes, *the* village. This princess has a dog, and I want one too." She is pouting at me, a hand on one hip.

"You want me to bring back, this dog, for you," I say, pointing at the magazine picture.

"Yes. Good. We understand each other. I have to go back to bed. Honestly I can't believe I even came all the way over here, but I couldn't trust Henrik to deliver such a serious, important, message. She is teasing him, pinching his butt as she says this and securing a small reaction. A slight shake of his head and a grimace, his eyes closed tight.

"It's why I had the Führer put you on the mail run. Who else could I trust?" She laughs to herself again, whispering something in Henrik's ear. He shakes his head at her and she slaps him lightly. Sticking her tongue out as she storms off, a silky wave of fabric floating behind her.

He finally meets my eyes, my own hurt reflected there. Sad and beaten, my heart aches for him. I open my mouth to say something, anything to him, but he holds a hand up to stop me. His fingers are splayed wide, his palm white. I close my mouth tightly, and he grimaces before turning away and running after her.

I push the breath out through clenched teeth. My brother has arrived down the beach, loud and obnoxious. There are men with him, carrying large bundles in their arms. Jacob's voice condescendingly authoritative, ordering them to load the supplies. It's something they've done a dozen times before without his help. The boat is bobbing in an inlet created by the rising water. We're lucky it's rainy season, or it'd be another day of hiking to the water. This tributary to the river only available six months of the year. Guns and ammunition, food and supplies are loaded. Extra gasoline for the motor.

I do not move to help. I am like a stone, hard, silent, watching. Gripping the paper in my hand.

Henrik returns to the beach, but he makes no motion to fetch me. Jumping aboard the boat and busying himself with the task at hand. I glance down at my own hands and notice

I've involuntarily shred the paper into long strips. I tear them even smaller as Jacob begins yelling at me, telling me they're ready to go. The pieces float to the ground, and I make myself take a step, and then another one, and another one, until I have crossed the expanse. Hands easily encircle my waist, lifting me in the air, tossing me aboard. I pull my legs into my chest and bury my head in my knees.

We are on our way before I even realize it. The boat skimming the water, wind whipping across my face. It reawakens my soul. There is never wind like this in the jungle. There is a life, a heartbeat to the trees, always movement, the landscape persistently shifting. Eternal, endless, depressing rain sometimes. But wildness? No, not like this. Tearing at my hair, it envelops me with its lack of restraint. I am laying across the very front of the boat, my head above the crook where the sides meet. The bow, I think my brother called it.

I love the waves, the occasional break in the brown water, the bow thrust high in the air, and then crashing down. A spray of water across my face. I'm delighted by it all, and I can't help but laugh. Henrik is at the controls, Jacob pestering him with questions. I have no idea what they're talking about because Henrik's face is impassive. Jacob is angry about something, furious even. I can see he is shouting, wiping his face with the back of his hand. He is spitting on himself! I laugh loudly into the wind and it carries my voice away. Henrik and Jacob are too far back for me to eavesdrop and I don't care. I'm alone up here, free and happy.

It is easy to see the sun out on the river. Around midday the heat becomes unbearable and we stop for lunch. Henrik drops the anchor in a small inlet, and I am fascinated by some of the creatures swimming in the river. Jacob and Henrik have disappeared below deck, so I take the opportunity to relieve myself over the side. It's awkward, but I manage without making too much of a mess. I move to the other side and lean over as far as I dare, to get a closer look at the water below me.

"I thought I told you to be careful," Henrik says. He startles me, and I almost tumble over the side before catching myself. "Did you forget? Your brother would love to see you in the water."

A hot flush creeps up my neck, and I turn away from him, but not before he has taken a seat next to me. He hands me a canteen of food. The metal is cool, but when I pop open the lid, steam releases. Food is an unexpected gesture from him, I assumed I wouldn't be eating anything hot on this journey.

"Where's Jacob?" I ask, unwrapping my fork.

Henrik nods to the back of the boat. "He's trying to fish, thinks he can find something we haven't eaten a thousand times before. I didn't have the heart to tell him it's of no use. Besides, I wanted to see how you were holding up."

I feel the heat rush to my face, and I concentrate on the floor boards. I know he means more than this boat ride. Julianne's deception, and his own for that matter. My anger has turned into a sort of weariness and embarrassment. We would never have been allowed to be together. I don't know how to answer his question correctly.

"You don't have to say anything," he says. "I know. There's just, nothing I can do about it." I'm grateful he *doesn't* do anything, like pat my back for instance, before heading back to the controls. I unwrap some canvas from one of the boxes and spread it out on the boat floor. The canteen of food remains untouched as I uncurl my fingers around my fork, no longer hungry. I wrap everything up before laying on my side, the rocking luring me into sleep.

Hours later a yell awakens me, and. . .gunfire? I try to bolt up, but there is no room to move.

"What are you? Dumm?" Jacob is whispering harshly in my ear, his body pressed against mine, his hand covering my mouth. I try to wiggle from his grip, but I'm trapped against a large wooden box. He smiles at the terror in my eyes, pressing his hand even harder against my face, covering my nose. There is movement to the side of me, and I think he is reaching for his knife, when another shout echoes off the water. Momentarily distracted, I bite down on one of his fingers, hard.

He recoils and I bring my feet up swiftly to push his body away. He tries reaching for me again, but I am prepared for the attack. Curling up into a defensive position, my elbows aimed for his head. His body relaxes on the floor, a gleam in his eye as he repeats his insult. "Dumm."

"I'm not stupid," I respond, translating his poor German. "What's going on?" I ask, trying to keep my voice low and steady. His attack has unnerved me more than I want him to know. He is nursing his finger. "Pirates," he answers.

"Poachers?" I ask because I'm not sure what language he's speaking.

"No, Pi-rates." He says enunciating every syllable. "But yes, basically the same thing as Poachers. Henrik says we should be safe, since we're going in the wrong direction to be of any interest to them. We need to stay down, just in case. They're firing warning shots into the air."

The other boat is getting closer to us, and my body turns ice cold. I stare up at the sky. It has turned a deep pink color, purple licking at its edges. The clouds floating lazily across the backdrop, the sun is a blood red. I begin shaking at the thought of being kidnapped by strange men. My worst fears about leaving the colony, realized. The engine noise is getting closer and our boat has come to a stop, thrashing about in the water. Jacob is whispering to me, "Whatever happens, stay down. Henrik will try to get us out of here."

I think about this. Cowering while Henrik fights for our lives. This may work for Jacob, but it's not what I've been trained for. I'm strong, a good shot with a rifle. I think I can get a gun before anyone notices me. Determined, I start inching toward the boxes of ammunition. Jacob doesn't notice, he has moved to the right of the bow and is staring intently at Henrik's feet.

The other boat is right next to ours now, I can hear the crew shouting to one another, shouting to Henrik.

"Thomas?" Someone yells, and then a string of rapid Portuguese I can't follow.

"Thomas está dormindo abaixo," Henrik lies smoothly. "Será que ele lhe deve dinheiro?"

A round of laughter from the other boat, more Portuguese than I can understand. Another round of laughter before a shout of broken English. "No, not money, a drink. Tell him he works you too hard while he sleeps. To come and find me when he is next in Manaus."

"I will," Henrik responds, lifting his arm in a wave of goodbye. I have retrieved my gun as the voices begin fading into the distance. Where is Manaus? And how does Thomas even know these Pirates? I'm about to ask, when Henrik is talking to us both.

"You can sit up now, they're gone. You can put the gun back Marta." He is chuckling a little. "There was never any real danger, I recognized their boat right away. It's better they think there's only a few of us living on the river, so we don't seem like a threat to their livelihood. I had to scare Jacob to keep him down, he doesn't obey orders well."

Jacob is scowling at him, stomping to the back of the boat. Henrik has made him look like a fool.

"They think we're pirates too?" I say, figuring it out.

"Of course they do, Thomas cultivated the lie long ago. I'm his son, learning the trade. Occasionally we split our "spoils" with them, things from the boxes we don't technically need. It helps to have allies on the river, it can be dangerous." He makes a face at me, sticking out his tongue, obviously trying to lighten the mood a bit. I stick my tongue back at him before replacing the gun in its container.

My canteen of food is still at my feet, most likely cold by now, but I'm so hungry I pick it up anyway and dig in. I've eaten much worse. I pull the canvas on to my lap, covering my legs. The night has grown cooler than I'm used too.

"I think Jacob and I should get a few hours of sleep. We don't want to approach Manacapuru until the morning." His brow furrows in concentration, thinking about the pirates, or maybe other unknown dangers I'm unaware of. "You had a long nap Marta. Do you want to take first watch?"

I nod my assent to him and he steers us into another inlet, dropping anchor. Walking back to Jacob, I see them whispering. Henrik is apologizing, both of them heading down to the cabin of the boat. Henrik's head reappears.

"Come and get me if you see anything, even an animal. Don't try and shoot them yourself." He chuckles again and disappears.

I find a lukewarm water bottle in the compartment I'm sitting on. I chug it in one long drink and then sit back to listen to the sounds of the approaching night. I clear my mind, focusing on the river, the jungle. Waiting for unfamiliar noises. The sun is almost fully down. The twilight overtaking the last rays of light, filtering through the clouds. The jungle becomes more alive at night, the noises louder, when there's no eyesight to compensate for your hearing. There is a woman screaming to my right- terrifyingly loud. Howler monkeys. I would recognize their unholy screams from anywhere, their voices filled my nightmares as a child. I scan the trees but can't catch sight of one. They won't descend low enough to be bothersome, and their voices fade into the background as the sky grows darker. A flock of birds in flight, wings of gold glittering in the night sky. The evening passes slowly, and I swat at the mosquitos. For every one I manage to kill, two more appear. I turn it into a game and soon their bodies litter the deck. I light a candle that keeps the rest of them at bay.

I've had too much sleep, my senses hyperaware. I'm not tired, and it's only when Henrik rouses himself that I give up the watch. Normally I would welcome the chance to have the time with him. Alone. But Julianne's proposal has made things awkward between us, and he doesn't attempt conversation with me again. He starts the engine of the boat, pulling us slowly back on to the rushing river. Concentrates on moving us to the center of the wide expanse. Soon the shoreline disappears and I stretch out on the deck, cover myself in netting, pretend to sleep.

I wake up disorientated and much too hot. Sticky and uncomfortable, I root in the boxes for another water bottle, trying to figure out a way to relieve myself in private. Standing up I spot the landing ahead of us, colorful boats wobbling in the water, tethered to the land. Short and squat buildings, gray at the end of a long pier. There's a man standing on the dock, binoculars in hand, waving to us. Henrik aims right for him, yelling, even though there's no way he could hear us yet. "Matt!" We slow down as we approach, carefully navigating through the other boats. I see the man clearly now, maybe a few years older than me. His hair is a dirty blonde color and his eyes are blue. One of us, I think. Well, one of them at least. I'm surprised when he assesses me with a large lopsided grin. His hair falls into one eye when he grabs one of the tow lines. I'm blushing when he reaches a hand down to me. I instinctively grab it, and notice we have the same skin tone. Still considered white, but actually a golden brown color. We are perennially tan, even in Monsoon season under the canopy, when we only see the sun in dappled rays. He hoists me up unto the deck. I'm unsteady and he grips me around the waist. "Whoaa there, you'll want to wait a minute, get your land legs back." I notice his English is heavily accented, and I answer him in the mother language, trying to impress him.

"Ich werde in Ordnung sein."

He looks at me quizzically. "Don't speak English, huh?" He reaches down to pull up Jacob next, who is scowling at me. Embarrassed by me.

"No, she doesn't," he says, daring me to disagree with him.

"I do too," I say boldly. "I thought everyone knew German, the mother tongue. I'm fine," I translate for him.

"Well don't that beat all." He laughs at me, "German? You won't find many people around these parts speaking German. Portuguese, yes. German, no. You'd have to go west to find their settlements. Follow me."

Henrik climbs out of the boat on his own, helping another man wrap the ropes around a wooden pole securing us to the dock. He speaks sharply to him before running after Matt. Jacob reaches back into the boat for his gun, and follows him at a slight distance. I quickly reach in and grab one of the other weapons, throw it into a backpack with one of the canteens. I don't know if I'll be coming back to the boat and I don't want to risk it. I sprint to take up the rear of the party as Jacob turns back to me and mouths, "You'll pay for that." I give him a smile, not without a good fight I won't.

There's a group of men sitting near the dock on white plastic chairs. Laughing, talking to one another, they wave at Matt as he walks by. Untouchables, dark men, with black eyes. I want to ask Matt why they're not working, why he's so friendly with them, but I'm too far back and the questions seem rude somehow. I'm passing the group when one of them whistles, high and sharp. They're leering at me, and I blush. I know there are still Untouchables left in this world, in labor and work camps. Countries that haven't been conquered and continue in the obstinate belief that Aryan blood isn't sacred. Haven't I heard this over and over from the Führer during his Sessions? I've seen the lab reports our Patron has sent. I'm ashamed of my own genetic patterns which label me an Untouchable, my blood not as strong as those of my Aryan brother and sister. Henrik hears the whistle, waits for me, grasping my hand. "Hold on to me," he whispers, "they won't do anything, just being friendly." I want to ask him what he means when we're entering another building. A sign on the door labels this a store. I take two steps inside and stop in shock. Every wall, shelving in between, piled high with things.

It is overwhelming. I can see Jacob is equally impressed, but trying not to show it. Keeping his face impassive, he walks to a low counter where Henrik is already with Matt. They are speaking with a dark haired man behind the counter, another Untouchable. No one is paying attention to me so I begin fingering the closest cans. Peaches, cherries, apples, green beans. I recognize a few of them from the boxes which arrive each month. So many more I don't recognize, couldn't even fathom. Shiny packages draw my attention, "chips." I crinkle the wrappers, enjoying the sounds they make.

"She can open up one of those if she wants," I hear Matt tell Henrik. "I'll put it on your account."

I don't wait for the disapproval of Jacob, I rip the package open with my teeth. An unfamiliar smell assaulting my nostrils. Onions? I take a chip from the package and put it on my tongue. Crunchy ecstasy. Beyond delicious, I put another one on my tongue and let the flavor fill my mouth.

"We have strict instructions on what we can bring back." Henrik is at my side, his whisper tickling my ear. "Pure blood, Pure minds, Pure bodies." Warmth spreads down through my limbs at his touch. "The cheesy ones are my favorite though."

He hands me another bag before returning to Matt and the man. I finish off the onion chips, licking the wrapper. Deciding to save the cheesy ones for later, I drop the bag in my backpack. I continue down the aisle, my fingertips bouncing off the jars and cans until I reach a wall of bottles behind glass. Pulling open one of the doors, a blast of cold air hits me. It's so refreshing that I stand shivering, until the chill becomes painful. I realize they are refrigerators, much larger than anything we have back at the colony. "Coca- Cola," I read on one of them, dropping this in my bag as well. I'm reading the colorful labels when a shelf of magazines catches my attention. Dozens of newspapers and books, men and women of every shape and size on their covers. Some of them are laughing, their hands entwined. In disbelief I grab at one, tear through it, an Untouchable and Pure kissing on the cover. Every page, filled with women like Julianne's clippings.

But these women are not Pure, with skin of every shade I can imagine, from the color of sticky dark dirt to glowing white, paler than any Pure child in Founder. I'm trying to comprehend this abomination. Their arms and limbs encircling one another, smiling. Drinking and eating together. Collapsing on the floor in a heap, I pull another magazine off the rack and begin reading. Clothing, shopping, shoes, handbags. I throw this one down and decide on a newspaper instead. Our Patron sends us these in every box, news of the ongoing war in every word, the same information over and over. The Reich continues to grow stronger, the rest of the world will eventually succumb. Pockets of rebels still fighting, the world still at war.

There's election coverage in this one. Information about the President of the United States, a country we have long since conquered. Our Patron is from there, somewhere called California. Why would they have a president? The Reich would demand allegiance to a Führer or Leiter. I scan the headline until I find the Presidents name. "Barack Obama." *Strange name.* There's a picture on page two. I don't bother to read the rest of the article, flipping to the next page, I'm only interested in the photo. This will make things right, the President will be make this right. Maybe they do things differently in America. I find the photo and drop the newspaper, pages fluttering to the floor. It is impossible. Absolutely impossible. The President of the United States is dark. I read the word in Portuguese. "Negroe." Translate to German, "Schwarz." In English, "Black." There are heavy steps behind me, and I glance up. Jacob. "So now you know." He takes in the papers on the floor, the magazines, sneering at me before saying, "The war is over, and we lost."

Chapter Nine

I have lost the ability to speak. It is too much information at one time and I am unable to comprehend it, let alone ask questions. Henrik pulls me from the ground. Leads me away. Matt guides us to a hotel, a sprawling megastructure of buildings, manicured gardens, he's unaware my illusions have been shattered and chatters incessantly on the walk. I have seen pictures of large buildings, but could never have dreamed of entering one myself. It's so beautiful, the floors sparkling, the furniture plush. I run my hand across one of the walls and feel the smooth texture. I try to process the idea that I could be free here. If I leave, if I can escape, I could be equal in this world. I could live in such comfort. There would be no more hiding for me.

I am guided to a room on the second level, with indoor plumbing and overhead electrical lighting. Comfortable chairs and a large bed invade most of the space. Linens everywhere, the windows, the lamps, the bed, even in the bathroom. My head is still spinning, but I am captivated by the bathroom, the toilet gleaming white. I stop my tour to push down its handle, delighted when the water disappears from the bowl, reappearing. I shut the door and relieve myself. Flush the toilet. It's so fun, I can't help but do it again, and then again, and again, until Henrik calls for me to come out.

He is alone, standing near my window. I allow myself to stare at him for a minute, this man I was never allowed to have. He could be mine here. In this place, we could be together. My head feels light, and blackness creeps at the edge of my vision. I collapse into the bed, sink into it, so I can regain my balance and composure. I've never imagined something so soft and comfortable. Better than any of Julianne's pillows. I feel the texture with the palm of my hand, tracing the lines of thread. The silence grows uncomfortable, and I wonder if we can ever be truly relaxed with each other again. He could have prepared me for this, he could have said *something*. Henrik opens his mouth and I know, this is the time for explanations. This is when he'll reveal his secrets.

"I was against you knowing, but the Führer has wanted this for a while. Julianne's request making it easy to send you."

More betrayal. My heart contracts. How is it possible to continue loving someone, when he would deny me such beautiful truth? The war is over.

"I'm trying to understand," I say, "about the cause, about the Reich. That the President of the United States is black. There were Untouchables, kissing, the Pure. Is my whole life a lie?"

"Not your whole life, maybe just. . .parts of it. I know it feels like exciting news." Folding his arms, he turns away from me, staring into the jungle that is tapping at my window.

"When did it end? How long have we known?" I'm eager to know all the details, eager to accept this new reality.

His back is rigid, but I can tell he's smiling. The way he tosses his head back, ever so slightly.

"Since the beginning. We've never not known. The princesses and the colony were a backup plan. In case the war went bad, we would still fulfill the dream. The Aryan dream of a beautiful nation. When the first three children were old enough to be told, they decided to keep it a secret among royals. Easier to rule this way, if everyone believes there's a cause worth fighting for and that others are fighting for. A cause worth hiding from, and that others are hiding from." He pauses, "then there's the money," he says, turning towards me.

"Money?" I've heard the Führer use this term before and have never paid much attention to it.

"Yes, money, currency. It's what we use to pay for all of this." He sweeps his arm around in a wide arc. "People outside of the colony, in other countries all over the world, work for money, and they use it to provide themselves with things, stuff. They don't have Patrons sending them boxes of necessities, or benefactors giving them wads of cash and credit cards. We could never maintain a colony our size if there were not people all over the world who believe in our cause, protect our secrets, give us our livelihood."

"So there are more of us? Right? We're not the only ones?" This strikes me as important, to know we're not alone.

"Not as many as you have been led to believe. I know of one colony in Sweden, and one in Vietnam. Not nearly as large as ours, and with different Patrons. It would be too overwhelming for the Patrons to take on more than one colony." He says all of this so casually, and every word so shocking to me. My entire life, a sham.

"The Untouchables?" I ask.

He has the decency to look ashamed. "There are no Untouchables out here. At least not in any of the developed countries of the world. Everyone is equal, skin color, eye color, all of that doesn't matter. Unfortunately, your father is right about one thing. The Untouchables would never survive in this world, uneducated, poor. They would be at the mercy of predators much worse than anything in the jungle."

My blood boils, "So why not educate them? Why not tell the world of our existence- let us live as equals?!?" I yell the last line at the top of my voice, rattling the window.

"Are you listening to me?" he roars. Then taking a breath, he steadies himself on the back of a chair. "The money. How would we live? Our Patrons send us everything we need because we are an Aryan nation, an Aryan force ready to strike." He pounds his fist into the wall. "If we were to give it up, how long do you think the money would last? How long do you think we would survive?"

I think about the bounty of food in the jungle, the medicines Ani compiles from plants. Are *we* so dependent? I bite my lip as Henrik continues. "The Pure are content as long as they believe they are a chosen people, lording over the Untouchable class. The Untouchables may not be happy, they may live as second-class citizens, but they are safe. Can you think of a single Untouchable killing?"

"The threat of death has always been implied, Henrik," I say vehemently.

"But no one has been *killed*, Marta. Not in a very long time."

I have no reaction. I simply can't believe it. That we would be living in terror, starving, working ourselves to death, to be safe. That he could suggest my mother is still alive somewhere.

Henrik's eyes soften. "Understand Marta, I would never do anything to hurt you. This is what is right for us. This is where we belong."

My eyes blink rapidly, a crease forming in my forehead. "Why do we belong there? Why, Henrik? Why can't we leave?"

His body tenses. His mouth opens and closes again. I see the thoughts flash across his features, how much to tell me, how much to conceal. I don't want to hear his lies, so I ask another question instead.

"Who else knows this? Why would the Führer want me to know this?"

"Only a few of us know the truth. The Führer obviously, Thomas, Dale. . ."

"My Uncle Dale knows," I interrupt him, "and he never told me?"

He takes a seat in the only chair. "Of course he knows, you forget he did the mail runs with your father long ago."

"But Jul doesn't know," I say, thinking over our conversations in my head.

"No Jul doesn't know, and she must never know. She, more than anyone, would want to leave. We can't let that happen."

"You haven't answered *why*."

"Why you are being told now?" he asks.

"Yes."

"Did you ever wonder why our colony is named Founder?"

"What?" I ask. This is not what I expected him to say, I've never questioned the name of the colony. I've always assumed it was because we were the first of its kind. Possibly even the first colony formed. The founders of a new revolution.

"It wasn't always called so, "Founder." For a long time we were called Zweite Kolonie. Second colony."

I nod my head at this, trying not to look surprised.

"In the fifties our name was changed to reflect a new genetic study called the founder effect. Our Patron began calling us that in her letters, and sent us the research."

"Genetics?" I ask him, I know the term, it's the reason we are led to believe our blood is not as good as those of the Aryan race.

"Genetics, or genes, are difficult to explain. They're basically tiny fragments in our bodies, that make us who we are. They predetermine things like our eye color, hair color, skin color, even things like illnesses, and our intelligence.

"I know what they are," I tell him.

He raises an eyebrow at me, before continuing as if I haven't interrupted him. "Well, the founder effect says when a population of people begins small, like with our three princesses, the genetic pool is small. The more tightly controlled we make the genetic pool, the less variation there is."

"That's why there are so many less Untouchables now? Because we are being genetically weeded out?"

"Exactly right," he says, relief in his voice. I'm catching on quickly. "So you see, in a few more generations we won't even have a population of Untouchables. The entire colony will be Pure, and we'll have weeded out the defective genes." He says this proudly, smiling at me. He doesn't realize I'm one of those *defective* genes who needs weeding.

A big sigh from him, "our problem is right now. The Führer feels a rebellion coming on. The Untouchables becoming bolder. He hasn't done much about it yet, still believing they are too afraid of the outside world to launch an attack. There are also too few of them to overwhelm our forces. There's no chance they would win in a fight, but he's afraid they will try, and lose. He doesn't want any casualties, and regardless of what he says otherwise, he doesn't want anyone to escape."

"Are you trying to tell me my father," I spit out the word, "*cares* about our well being? When we're being genetically *weeded*? I won't believe it."

Henrik jumps to his feet then, throwing his arms out wide. "Maybe it is a little far fetched to use the word "cares," but in his own selfish interest he does care about the survival of the colony."

"The money you mean. He cares, about the money."

"Yes, of course about the money. The money is only one part of it though. Marta, if someone were to escape and go public, we would lose everything. Everything! Do you understand? Most of us would be shunned by the rest of the world. We would be considered crazy, ostracized, maybe even prosecuted. You don't understand that word."

"Then why wait Henrik?" I yell. "Why not kill me now?!"

"Stop being dumm," he says, as he begins pacing the floor, arms locked behind him, head bowed low. "We would be locked up. Forever maybe. Marta, you don't know what it's like out in the rest of the world, and your father thought it might be easier to convince you if you were allowed to see for yourself."

"Convinced me of what?" I ask.

He stops moving long enough to stare right through me. "Convince you to keep our secrets, to stay in the colony, to stem the rebellion."

Henrik leads me to a room downstairs. A woman is here clearing the dishes, her blonde hair wrapped tightly around her head. Henrik walks over to her speaking softy. She leaves and he motions for me to sit down.

"She's going to bring us lunch and then Matt will be here to meet up with us."

"Where is he now? And where is Jacob?" I ask.

"They should be down at the dock now, loading up the supplies. While we were talking, Matt has been showing him the same images you will see a little later."

"So Jacob knew about the war?"

"Your father thought it was best to tell him before we left. I meant what I said though, you have to be careful, especially now that you know the secrets. I'm not sure Jacob is trustworthy, that he won't spill our secrets to that group of his. It's not only the Untouchables planning a rebellion, your uncle has warned you about Jacob's group. Their animosity toward the Untouchables. The Führer is hoping what violence can't do, maybe friendship, trust even, can.

"And what is that?" I ask.

He looks surprised at me, "Bring you together. The Führer wants an alliance between the two of you."

I snort at him as the woman brings out two sandwiches and sets them in front of us. I'm startled to feel a hand run through my hair, but when I look up she is gone. I shake my head, thinking I must have imagined the pressure on my scalp.

Henrik thinks I'm shaking my head at him. "It will have to happen, you two will have to get along," he says.

The thought Jacob and I could ever get along, let alone become allies, friends! It's laughable. I dig in to my lunch with abandon, the sandwiches icy cold and delicious. A glass of fizzy drink appears before me and I'm surprised when froth tickles my nose. I drink it quickly and a large belch escapes. I cover my mouth, mortified, but Henrik is laughing. There is a deep laugh behind me as well, full of amusement at my expense. Matt has arrived.

"How did Jacob take it?" Henrik asks him, getting up from the table.

"Better than I expected I guess. He looked bored, said his father prepped him for this over a month ago. It was a little unnatural, but I showed him the list you gave me. He asked to see more and I left him to do his thing. It's not hard to navigate the computer with some instruction. He'll probably have cleared out by now."

"Good, it's Marta's turn." They both look at me expectantly, but I'm at a loss of what to say.

"Thank you?" I respond.

Henrik rolls his eyes. "Your lead," he tells Matt.

Two hours later I am sitting front of a screen being lit up with images. Moving pictures, video, they call it. At first I kept touching the glass, fascinated by the motion and sound. Trying to reach inside. Matt got frustrated and forbid me from touching the screen again, apparently he couldn't type with my fingers constantly in the way. Henrik yells out a word and Matt clicks a new screen, each one different, and each one horribly, horribly wrong. I can't believe these are real people, doing such things to each other, but there they are, on the screen. Regular people, not even royalty. There's no excuse for their behavior.

I see random acts of violence, fires, shootings. A crowd cheering as men are trampled to death by animals. Bulls, Matt calls them. Sexually promiscuous women and children, used as entertainment. A girl's shirt falls to her knees, exposing her breasts. There is uproarious laughter even while she tries to cover herself. We are whipped in disobedience, shamed every day for our existence, spit on, mocked, sometimes kicked or pushed. Bullied is what these people would call it, easy to avoid if you're quiet and unobtrusive. Even the Pure receive punishments occasionally, if they go too far. The Führer is the exception to this rule, the one exception. Most consider it an honor to serve him, in whatever capacity he needs. None of this random brutal savagery is allowed. This open perverse sexuality. I'm not sure what I imagined the war to be. It certainly wasn't this.

Matt explains America, the land of the free, and the theory behind capitalism. He calls it the land of commercialism, materialism. The images scare me with their brightness. Ten times worse than Julianne. The things they have, overwhelming. Lavish homes I can't believe are real, fast cars and sleek airplanes, boats larger than houses. Then there are the people. Gleaming white teeth, giant heads, malnourished and orange skinned. Some of them have bits of metal protruding from their body parts, designs colored all over their body. It hurts my eyes to look at them. I rub the smooth cream cotton of my dress and feel the plain buttons that line the front of it. I tuck my feet under my chair, to hide my worn, leather sandals. Henrik is right, how would we survive in such a world?

Our time is finally up, the cafe closing, we've been here for hours and my head is dizzy with the images. I know there will be nightmares tonight. Henrik is saying goodbye to Matt, telling him what time to expect us in the morning. Matt is heading back down to the dock to help Jacob load the rest of the supplies, to make sure he arrives safely back to the hotel.

We head back, Henrik following me to my room. Stopping at my door, he fumbles with my key.

I put my hand on his arm, "I still don't understand. Why did you show me all of this? What do you want me to do?"

He turns the key and opens the door, gesturing me inside. I walk past him and he shuts it behind me.

"I tried to escape, the second time I ever came here. You likely don't remember, you were so young, over four years ago." He is lost in his own thoughts and I don't know how to tell him; I do remember. They had been gone for over two weeks, the Führer furious, he was about to send out a scouting party. It was the first time I realized how much I cared for Henrik, how much I missed him teasing me. When he returned there was no Session to explain the missing days, everything returning back to normal. I pestered Henrik for details but there was only a standard reply, the same one Thomas officially gave the Führer. "They were lost, cannibals set upon them, and they managed to escape." It never seemed accurate to me. They returned with all of the supplies, the boat still intact, neither one of them even seemed injured! My curiosity eventually caused Henrik to speak harshly to me, and it became one of those forbidden topics I was not allowed to speak of.

Henrik takes a deep breath and continues, "I left as soon as my feet hit the dock, no explanation to Thomas, I headed straight to Matt's father Eli. He was in charge of the "education process" before Matt took over. He was surprised at my request, but not unwilling to help me. I was given some money, better clothes, and then smuggled on to a caravan headed to Manaus." He stops, looking at me carefully, I can see there are tears in his eyes. "It was terrible there, I was completely unprepared for such a life. The noise alone, the filth, the people pressing against me, hands pawning me constantly, begging for something- when I had nothing! I spent most of my nights hidden behind barrels, scrounging for food. I didn't know how to use the money and so lost it to a scoundrel almost immediately. I would have died, if I had not met up with some of Thomas' friends."

"The same friends we saw on the water," I realize.

"Yes, they recognized a familiarity with me, a resemblance to Thomas. He was there, in Manaus, and they took me to him. Told me a story that was similar to my own. Thomas had tried to escape years before, joined in their escapades before he wanted to venture out on his own. It was a lie of course, he returned back to the Colony. The Führer forgiving him immediately because of the wealth of new information, because he offered a new kind of protection from these Pirate predators. Thomas understood what I was going through, helped me make up a story to tell the Colony. Apparently we all have moments of weakness." He laughs, a low chuckle that can't quite cover the sadness in his voice. He takes my hand in his. "You're another kind of weakness." He caresses my cheek with his free hand, running his fingers through my hair. I'm angry at him, but can't resist being pulled in, his arms slide around my waist. My head on his chest, feeling his breaths, listening to his heart beat. "I'll understand if you want to run, but I'll make sure to find you. Eventually Jacob will rule the camp, someone will have to take control of the Untouchables. An alliance will be necessary, or we'll lose it all."

I turn my face upwards to his, "So you want me to go back to camp, make nice with my brother, pretend all of this never happened? How am I supposed to do that? Lie to Ani? Impossible!" I break away from him, but he clutches my hand before I can get far.

"Not impossible, hard. Remember I've been doing it. For years." I look straight into his eyes, and see the sadness, regret, but more than that, a hardness. He believes in what he is doing. Believes that he is right, with every fibre of his being. How can I have such assuredness, just from his words? He pulls me in again, our faces practically touching. I whisper to him, "I wish. . ."

Our cheeks meet, and he grunts as I reach my arms around his neck, pull him tighter to me. The tears force themselves from my eyes, dripping down my nose. He feels them on his face and pushes me back. Two hands in front of him, creating more space between us. "I know, I wish it too. But there is no other way. It has to be like this." He grasps blindly for the door behind him. Gripping the handle, he doesn't take his eyes off of me. "I will give you time to think. We leave in the morning."

I manage to meet his eyes one more time, before he walks out, shutting the door behind him.

Chapter Ten

I walk, pacing the fifteen foot space in front of my bed. Back and forth, Elise's face, a child prostitute. Back and forth, Ani's skills as a gifted healer, a joke, a witch doctor. Back and forth, Henrik, dirty and homeless, his blue eyes dead. Back and forth, Thomas the pirate. Back and forth, words I've never heard before, racing through my head. Racism, condemnation, persecution. Back and forth, freedom. I stop. Freedom.

I walk to the window where Henrik was standing this morning. Watching the rain forest, the color, the greens teeming with energy. It pulsates, moves, a living entity. A bird flies low, under the canopy, soaring through the rays of light that pierce the dark. A sloth asleep high in a tree, her young in a vice grip around her waist. Is there really freedom out there? Or another kind of bondage, worse than the one I would be leaving behind? How would I live? I am not always happy, but I am protected, shielded from the outside world. Safe. The word Henrik used working itself over and over in my mind. Can I keep everyone safe? Anxiety slowly spreads through me, and even in the suffocating humidity of this room, I begin to shiver. I realize that I am more scared out here, than I am back home in the Colony. Could I have a life without Henrik? I strip off my clothes and get into bed. Turn off the lamp beside my head. My decision is made. I will protect our secret. I will return with Henrik. I force myself to sleep.

It is morning, no horn pulling me from unconsciousness today. I return to the beautiful bathroom and fiddle with the knobs of the bathtub. I practically change my mind when I turn on the water. An icy cool spray envelops me. I sigh in pleasure. There is no cold in the jungle, just different degrees of warm. Sticky, moist, sometimes insufferable heat. There can be coolness, and relief, but nothing like this. This is cold, and it's beautiful. There are bottles of shampoo and soap in front of me. I dump the entire bottle in my hair, scrub until my fingers are wrinkled and raw. I want to be clean. Stepping out of the shower, I find myself in a large mirror. There are only a few of these in the camps, and nothing as big as this one. Jul would go crazy with envy if she knew of it. There is an angry blue and green mark across my hip that is still tender from where I fell. I flex my ankle and it feels fine. I pull my hair back from my face, stare into my eyes. If I am equal to the Pure, does that also make me beautiful? Henrik must think so, or why else would he love me? I run my fingers through the strands before tying it in a braid.

I don't want to return to the stuffiness of my bedroom, but I know they will be waiting for me downstairs. I inhale the scent of the towels before snuggling into them. I am never dry, but the moisture works its way off of me so I can slip my dress back on. I slide my feet into my sandals, and then rub the ointments into my skin, shoulder my backpack. There is no one waiting at my door by the time I'm ready, so I decide to find my own way. My stomach rumbles loudly when my nostrils register the aroma of frying meat. I fling open a door downstairs and food, delicious, mouthwatering food, is piled up on a table across the room. There are several people serving themselves and I have to remind myself that we are all the same here. I do not have to wait to eat. I follow the lead of the person closest to me. Grab a plate, some silverware. I have to stop myself from eating directly off the serving spoon, hot eggs, roasted vegetables, cold fruit, grilled meat. My plate is overflowing and I can't seem to stop. There is a chuckle from behind me, familiar, but not Henrik or Jacob. I turn, and a banana falls from the crook of my elbow. Matt bending over to retrieve it.

"Hungry this morning?" he laughs, gripping my free arm and directing me to a seat. "Let me get your drink, you don't have enough hands," his laughter is contagious and I find myself giggling.

I dig into my eggs and by the time he returns they are almost gone. Dropping my banana and a cold bottle of water on the table, he sits in the other seat at the table. Picking up his fork he begins eating his own, only slightly smaller, portion of food.

I concentrate on my plate. He's the first stranger I've ever met, and I don't know what to say to him.

"You're the first girl they've brought here in a long time," he mumbles, his mouth full of food.

"Excuse me?" I ask.

"The first girl," he repeats, "they've brought," another pause to swallow, "in a long time."

"Yes. . .ummm. . . I know," I respond, stuttering and blushing furiously.

"I'm wondering why, is all." He speaks between bites. "I mean, I know they want to educate you about everything, bring you up to speed about what's going on in the world. I remember when that Thomas fellow first brought Henrik out, he nearly had a heart attack right there in the internet cafe. Now they're educating *Prince* Jacob. There's always just two of 'em." He traps me in his gaze and I can't pull myself away. Staring into his eyes, I wonder if I could tell him. Spill my secrets to this man. He glances back down, says into his muffin. "So where do you come in on all this?"

I can't look at him now, so my eyes focus on everything else, his flannel shirt. The tan and callused hands. The light reflecting off my water bottle. I finally settle on telling him the truth.

"I don't know what to say."

He gives me another probing look, "maybe it's better not to say anything?"

I am noncommittal in my reaction. I'm not sure if he means this. Is it a trick to make me feel more at ease with him? To let my guard down?

"I do have a question of my own though," I finally say, "even though maybe it's not fair to ask since I couldn't answer yours?"

He grins, and leans far back in his chair, kicking his feet out in front of him and resting his hands behind his head. "Me? I'm an open book. Ask me anything."

I smile, "It's not about you. It's about. . .well, my mother. You mentioned the girls that used to come here? One of them was my mother. She used to come here before I was born, and pick up the mail sometimes."

His mouth drops open, gaping at me. He is frozen in shock. It's a strange reaction, and I'm about to say something when I notice his chair teetering, his weight unbalanced on the back two legs. His arms drop at the same time his chair crashes down. The fall is awkward and he lands squarely on his left arm. I jump up to help him, when I feel a hand lock into my shoulder. Henrik.

"It's time to go," he says. "If you're coming."

He reaches a hand down and pulls Matt to his feet in one swift motion. Matt retreats a few steps from us, rubbing his shoulder, still gaping at me. The dining room has gone silent, the workers in the kitchen peeking out to see what the commotion is about.

Henrik glances around the dining room and holds a hand out for Matt to shake. "Thank you for everything. I will see you in a month." His dismissal is obvious, as is his stress on the word I. Did he hear our conversation? Matt shakes his hand and Henrik looks to me, lifts his eyebrows.

"Yes, yes," I breath to let the annoyance clear itself from my voice, "of course I'm coming."

The diners have continued their breakfast, there is no spectacle to gawk at. The kitchen workers have also returned to their business- except the woman who served us lunch yesterday. Her wavy blond hair hangs to her waist, her face is serious. She is standing in the doorway of the kitchen, staring. One last look at Matt, still rooted in his spot, and I follow Henrik back to the boat.

Lara

§

Chapter Eleven

I settle in for a long sleep. The flight to Rio from Los Angeles is a little over eight hours. Our sleep patterns are off, and thank goodness. Easier adjustment when we get to Brazil if we're already on their time. I pull the hairband from its ponytail and shake my hair out, I can already feel the jet lag. The sluggishness in my thoughts. The numbing, tight headache. I wonder if I should have let more of our family know what was going on. Where we were going. The police are watching the homes, afraid someone may be targeting our family. Mom made a quick phone call to Paul to let him know we were headed somewhere safe, her home had been broken into, and something was wrong. He was worried and offered to come over. I heard her putting him off, telling him we had to leave, we'd be in touch soon. It was better if he didn't know.

She sounded very convincing.

I was surprised my mom and Sergio had kept the letters to themselves. The checks and the fan mail went to the police- but neither of them offered up the letters, or our theory about Aryan involvement. My mom holding on to the belief we could still find information about her father, through Marion's communications. I think they didn't want to sound crazy. Or things were already so crazy they didn't want to add fuel to the fire. I was happy we could keep something though, something tangible to hold on to.

I had whispered my plan to them in the back of a squad SUV. The officer's radio drowning out any noise we made. My mom was the only one to protest. Sergio willing to go along with it, wanting to get us somewhere safe, believing we wouldn't find anything. My mom terrified we would. We took one walk around her house, picking at the shattered remains of a lifetime. A picture of herself as a baby, sitting on her father's knee. The frame cracked; the glass shattered. She held that photograph for a long time as we bustled around her, salvaging what we could. She stood still and silent, in the middle of all that chaos, until finally deciding that I was right, that we needed to go. I made a phone call into work to check on our flights and get us on standby. Most people don't realize how incredibly easy travel is for a flight attendant and their family. The international taxes pulled from my next paycheck. Sergio had our lockbox with the passports, visas to Brazil intact. My mom's passport was hidden in her underwear drawer, the three year old visa to Brazil tucked inside. Sergio and I had plans to attend Carnival last year, before I was called into work. The antimalarial drugs were another phone call, this time to our doctors, and ready in less than an hour. Our vaccines all up to date. We took my dad's old truck which hadn't been driven in over two years. Sergio called the detective and told him about visiting an aunt in Chicago. He arranged a half hearted police escort to the airport. There was a brief moment of panic at the check-in desk, when we were getting ready to board the plane.

Were we seriously doing this?

I have always been impulsive, my job enabling my behavior. Sergio and my mom are much more grounded, they make decisions much more carefully. To jump on a plane, suddenly and without plans, they must really believe this trip is important. I only hope we can find my mom's answers in Brazil. I'm not sure I'm ready to face a village of psychotics, but I am ready to escape the reality of my own situation here. I don't want to face the charred remains of our house, the pity from my coworkers. I want answers, and this has to be the best way to get them.

The next flight was barely half full and we made standby without any issues, one of the perks of flying on a Wednesday. Waiting to board, I jumped at every white man that walked past us. Suspiciously staring down any of them who gave me more than a passing glance. Sergio noticed and gripped my hand to reassure me, "there's security here," he whispered. I'm sure he thought he was putting me at ease. I had watched too many security training videos to feel really confident that we weren't being followed. It wasn't until we were on the plane, and I was in my element, that I could breathe again.

I don't recognize any of the flight attendants, although I've flown with the captain before. I'm happy about this, I can avoid the familiarity that comes from working for the airline. I'll be one of the nameless masses today. I decide to turn my brain off and concentrate on the hum of the engines. We reach cruising altitude and my mom slides into the row next to us. It is completely empty, so she compiles a makeshift bed out of extra pillows and blankets. Stretching out across all five seats she buckles herself in. Sergio puts his seat back into the reclining position, stretches his legs in front of himself. He is in the window seat and props his pillow up against the wall, resting against it. He begins snoring almost immediately. We will be safe, the rest of my family will be safe, and I need to sleep now too. Pulling up the armrest I snuggle into the side of Sergio and close my eyes.

A dinging noise awakens me and I automatically reach for the call button. My seat belt keeps me confined to the sitting position as my conscious mind reminds me I am not in uniform, this is someone else's job today. I wipe the drool off my face, pick the crust out of my eyes. The windows of the plane are still closed, a glance at Sergio's watch tells me we have a little over an hour left of flight time. We have slept through lunch service, but the drink cart is making a final round in front of me. I take a cup of water for myself, and have them place one in front of my mom and Sergio. I decide to make a trip to the lavatory before they wake up. In the bathroom I splash water on my face and try to run through the past two days in my head. I am in the air all the time, so this is not so different for me. Even on my days off, Sarge and I try to fly here and there. Lunch in Seattle at Pikes Market, an overnight trip to Sausalito in San Francisco. Last years balloon festival in Albuquerque. Broadway. We've done the Europe thing, visited family in Mexico several times, but this is different. Crazy even. To hop on a plane with no reservations in place, no luggage, not even a solid plan in mind. At least Sergio's Spanish should get us through some of the rough patches, it's not so very different from the Portuguese we'll need to navigate Brazil.

I leave the bathroom and head back to my seat, my mom and Sergio awake now, drinking their water. Looking as groggy as I feel. An announcement we'll be landing in 30 minutes. They make a beeline for the lavatories. I reach in the seat pocket in front of me for the inflight magazine, hoping to find a layout for our airport. We only have forty-five minutes to try and make our next flight.

I think most airline employees love airports. Every terminal is like being home again, the design may be different, but they're all organized exactly the same way. The hum of the people, the announcements over the scratchy intercom, the large windows looking out to the runway. We leave the plane and I feel immediately comfortable, breathing in the regenerated air, pushing through the tourists and locals. They let me take the lead and I guide them through the maze of security. We won't have to clear customs until Manaus, and our gate isn't far. We arrive in plenty of time before boarding, the agent handing us our passes immediately.

"The flight's not full?" I whisper to her.

"Not at all." She answers in perfect English, "it's not tourist season yet, still too rainy." She smiles at me, "you'll even get a meal on the flight." I slip her a box of chocolates, the international sign of gratitude, and find Sergio and my mom. They have returned from one of the duty free stores near the gate, bags filled with toiletries and gum, a wad of cash in my mom's hand. Sergio is on the phone, chattering with an insurance agent. We sit in a series of seats and my mom starts pulling things out of their packages and replacing them in a canvas sling she has purchased. "I love Brazil" stitched across the front, it's the height of tourist kitsch.

"Really, Mom? Really?" I make a face and hold the bag at arms length.

"It's the best they had, unless you want the Christo silkscreened one?" She raises one eyebrow at me, and I put both hands up in defeat, dropping the bag back in her lap.

"I think this should be enough soap and shampoo for a while. I bought them out of bug repellent," she says, dividing up the socks and tubes of toothpaste. "I think we might need this." She hands me a thick book and a map. "Look it over on the flight to Manaus, I'm going to ask the agent if she knows the best way to get to Manacapuru." With all of the supplies now packed, she tucks the cardboard containers back into the plastic bag, heading to the garbage can closest to us, before making her way to the gate agent.

I turn the book over and see it's an Amazonia travel guide. I open to a page at random and notice a beautiful frog. About the size of my thumbnail, the males can change color, this one a beautiful blue. I read the paragraph below and discover it's deadly, the venom killing up to a hundred people. The tribesman use their poison on arrow tips. The Poison Arrow Frog. I shudder, and the first bit of doubt about our plan creeps into my mind. Where am I taking us?

It is early morning, the taxi drivers chanting out prices to weary travelers. Leaving the terminal, I quickly ducked past them with my mom, and found a seat at a large fountain in front of the Manaus airport. The tiled cement cool and smooth. The threat of rain is implied in the sky, the dark clouds looming. We aren't the only ones enjoying the last of the sunshine, a family seated close to us. We are all swatting at the mosquitos, my mom spraying herself down with repellent. One lands on my arm and I squash it, but not before he has managed to extract a small amount of blood. The spot stings. I hear Sergio's voice rising, shouting at one of the drivers. I catch a few words in English, "Ferry Building." Then the word "no," over and over again, followed by a string of obscenities. He is so angry and it's obvious why they call him Sarge in the kitchens. I've never seen him like this and it's the tiniest bit scary. My mom is trying to start a conversation with one of the children closest to us, but *her* mom is shielding her. My parents traveled extensively through the western part of South America. Chile, and little bits of Peru. They grew to love the people there. She never mastered the Spanish language though, and is completely adrift in Portuguese.

"I think she's telling you to leave the kid alone Mom," I say, since she doesn't seem to be getting the hint from the grumbling, and icy stare down she's receiving.

"No, she thinks I'm going to steal her child," she whispers to me. "I don't need to speak the language to understand."

"I doubt she thinks that Mom," I say, trying hard not to roll my eyes, "Maybe she's anti-social."

"You don't think so, huh?" she looks past me, staring into the distance, "you haven't seen anything yet. You've always traveled to comfortable destinations, touristy places. Cities who hide their poverty behind the sale of cheap knick knacks, and an old beggar woman on the sidewalk."

"I've seen my fair share of poverty, it hasn't always been comfortable travel for Sergio and me. We've had our own adventures, been off the beaten path. Besides, I know most of the developed countries see America as the butt of a joke, a country to make fun of. While the rest of them. . .well if they don't want to be us, they want to hate us, right?"

She laughs with me, "You're right, but there's also the people who don't hate us, they fear us too. I have a feeling we're heading to one of those places."

"Are you having second thoughts about coming?" I ask her.

She turns her whole body toward me, leaning forward. "No, I have wanted to know my father my entire life. If I can't know him, than I want to know his family. Who they were, why they left us. There's also some, unknown force, pulling us to Manacapuru. I can feel it. I can feel that we need to be there."

She has expressed my own feelings so exactly that I can only nod dumbly and look back over to Sergio, his arguing reaching a fever pitch. I'm thinking about intervening when I see him break into a wide smile. The driver clutches at his hand and they grip shoulders like old buddies, laughing into each other. He calls out to my mom and I, waving us over.

I shrug my shoulders, "I think Sergio's ready for us."

We cross the street and head straight for the cab. The driver has a cell phone out, flipping through photos of his children. His arm draped casually over Sergio's shoulders. They are laughing now, the driver pantomiming an oversized belly. Holding up four fingers. He opens the back door of the cab as we approach, and I nearly step through the hole in the floorboards. When we begin moving, I can see the street rolling underneath us. The seat belts have been cut out, the ragged ends hanging. I drop my head on the seat rest, and settle in for the long ride to the ferry building.

The airport is as opposite from the port as you can get, and we'll have to drive right through the center of town. We had an argument about this on the plane, a flight attendant finally intervening. Sergio wanted to stay here a night, get some clothes, have a proper nights sleep. My mom and I thought it'd be best to find a boat immediately, we can only hide our trip from our family for so long before they will suspect. As it is, we haven't been able to call them yet, the phone number giving us away. Better to find our answers as quick as possible, better to keep moving.

One of the flight attendants had a copy of the ferry schedule and knowledge of Manacapuru. When she learned I was a fellow flight attendant, Nina was even more helpful, handing me a scrap of paper with a hotel's address and a name, Eli. "He and his wife own a resort outside of Manacapuru," she told us. "His son Matt runs their store nearby. I grew up with Matt, and we went to high school in Idaho together. He returned home to be with his parents, and I ended up working here. The resort isn't in Manacapuru exactly, but they will help you find what you're looking for." It was a total relief, I hadn't thought about where we would stay, and even Sergio visibly relaxed after talking to her. It decided us, we would try and get to Manacapuru as soon as possible.

It is freezing in the cab. Tired of wearing one of my mom's pantsuits, I switched my jacket and shell for a tourist T-shirt in Manaus. At 2 for 3 dollars it was a steal, but also incredibly thin. I ended up layering them on top of each other so my bra wouldn't show through. Sergio is in a pair of my cousin's slacks and a button up. Both are a little long on him, the sleeves are rolled up to his bicep. He sits in the front of the taxi, still chattering in rapid fire Spanish, trying to avoid knocking over the large monument to the Virgin Mary on the dashboard. I desperately want to roll the windows down, but don't think it would go over so well.

"Why do people from warm climates always have to have their AC on full blast? It's like the arctic in here, we should be wearing sweaters in this temperature." I whisper to my mom. She is studying her guide, scribbling notations in the margins. I stopped reading on the plane, the emphasis on tourism and not survival. Judging by this cab ride I'm wondering if they might be the same thing.

"It's like the people in cold climates who turn their heaters up into the eighties and it's sweltering wherever you go. Look at this Lara," she says, pointing into the book. "Manuas means Mother of the Gods. The tourists come here to see the meeting of the waters. There's a stretch where the Rio Solimões and Rio Negro meet, continuing next to each other for almost nine miles before merging." There's a note of genuine awe in her voice. "How amazing."

She looks to me for a response, but I don't find it amazing at all. I'm feeling nauseous, and I'm anxious to stop moving. "Does it say where the Amazon rainforest is? This is nothing but a giant city," I wave half heartedly toward the window, whining. "I can't even see any trees, let alone a forest."

My mom looks up from her book, removing her reading glasses. "We're all tired Honey, it's been an exhausting two," she counts her fingers. "No, three days? Oh, I don't even know how many days, but we're almost there. I'm sure we'll be able to take a few breaths when we arrive at this Eli's place." She places a hand on my arm, "until then let's try and keep our spirits up." She gives me a small smile that reduces me to a puddle of guilt, at the same time as making me feel like a three year old kid. It's a talent I'm sure all mothers possess.

"Okay Mom," I say, before turning to stare out the window. She returns to her book, and I watch the buildings creep by.

The city is not so different from a dozen other places I've been in Mexico. I see a few billboards in English which make me smile. It's always funny to see American movie stars advertising things like gum in other countries. It makes them seem much more like real people. "Humanizes them," my mom would say, in their glitzy gowns and bright teeth, holding a tube of toothpaste. We finally pull into a dockyard and our car is surrounded by children. Faces pressed against the glass, little hands banging against the windows. They are a filthy bunch, half dressed, some of them with mangled limbs. I think I should have pity, but I can't help but feel annoyed and disgusted.

Sergio turns around in his seat. "We have to get through the gate up here, Jose has a friend who will take us to Manacapuru- wait for him to get out first before you exit the cab. Some of these children will steal everything you have, before you're even out of the car."

"You take ferry- eleven dollars! 6 hours! You go with friend and you pay 15 dollar, but only 3 half hour! Better, you see?" The driver yells this while staring at us in the rear view mirror. He is missing all but three golden teeth in the front. He is so happy to be able to help us that it does the impossible, and cheers me up a little.

"Better! Thank you!" I yell. Sergio smiles and turns back around. My mom is staring at the children, and I start to pull out a chocolate bar, reaching for the window handle, when I feel her grip my arm.

"No! Don't open the window- it's not chocolate they want, and you'll only cause a fight."

Heat rushes to my cheeks, and I drop the chocolate. Moving my hand away from the door, I tell her, "I was just trying to help."

"I know honey, but most of these kids- you can't help them like that."

The driver is suddenly shaking his head, pointing his finger out the front window, "Crianças da rua!"

"Yes," my mom sighs, "it's the same in other places." She translates our drivers words, "Street children, addicted to shoe glue."

I stare out at them again, and this time feel real pity, to be so hungry you need to get high to forget about it. To be so young, that stealing becomes your only option. A vicious circle that could have been solved easily. I think of all the food that goes to waste in our own country and am shamed.

"There are shelters here, missions and such who try and help," my mom says as she pats my leg. "It's hard I know, but try not to think about it, we have our own troubles coming up."

The children suddenly abandon us as a tour bus pulls into the lot. Bigger fish to fry. We pull right out on to a makeshift dock, feet in front of the brown murky water.

"That's our boat?" I whisper to my mom. It's a ramshackle affair, and I can't help the skepticism about its seaworthiness. I guess it might be called a house boat, and the bottom is more or less shaped like a ship. White paint is peeling from the wood surfaces, the name Rosita 3 barely legible on the front. Car tires hang from the colorful ropes, swinging down the side hooks. I watch the boat collide with its neighbor, and understand the purpose of the rubber tire barrier. A house sits precariously atop, the large windows open to the elements, a blue tarp tied above each of them.

A man who could be our drivers twin leans against this contraption. A woman, who must be his wife, is hidden behind him and trying to wrangle a gaggle of children into the house. Their heads and limbs hanging out the windows, obviously excited about the upcoming journey. He breaks into a smile as Jose emerges from the cab, and I see that he is missing all of his teeth. Easy way to tell them apart. Sergio follows him out and I see a lot more hand shaking and hugging. I feel a sense of gratitude toward my husband. How could my mom and I do this alone?

The boat is faster than it looks; we easily pass most of the larger vessels in the water. I'm sitting in the very back on a low bench, my feet propped up on the fence guarding us from the engine. Literally, a fence. The chain links cutting into my ankles. The engine makes a loud ticking noise in place of the usual roaring sound, reminding me of a large annoying cricket. I'm trying not to let it bother me while I watch the wave of water fan out behind us.

My hair is tucked into a bright yellow ball cap, *Brasilia!* written across my chest, a canvas tote slung over my shoulder. "All I need is a big camera around my neck, and some zinc oxide smeared on my nose," I whisper to myself. I've never felt more like a tourist.

"Lunch!" Sergio says, appearing at my side.

"Oh good, I'm starving. I didn't want to break into our emergency stash of Cheetos."

"Better than Cheetos," he responds, before handing me a plate. I almost drop it when I see a fish eyeing me beneath the fried batter. A side of boiled mush and a warm can of something called Schin accompanies it.

These rations must have been pulled off the roof of our houseboat. Bags of grain and crates of pumpkins, competing for space with large red barrels. I look behind me through the house, more than a dozen hammocks strung across the small space. I see my mom is already digging in, talking to Jose's twin, Gustavo. It turns out he speaks fairly good English and is enjoying his role as tour guide. His wife is passing food to the children, who are all munching happily, swinging from their individual seats.

I take another glance at my plate.

"I'm not sure I can eat this," I tell him.

"Why not?" he asks me, around a mouth full of food.

"It's staring at me."

"The head is the best part."

"For what?"

"For eating, stop being such a wuss. You've eaten worse."

"I don't think I have."

127

"What about the restaurant in New York? With the bugs on the menu?"

"They were completely unrecognizable as bugs. They could have been chicken nuggets."

He rolls his eyes, and breaks the head off in one swift motion, throwing it overboard before anyone can notice.

"Thank you," I say, before picking at the fish, dipping it in the mush before bringing it to my mouth. Sergio nodding encouragingly.

"This is delicious, what is the mushy white stuff?" I ask him.

"Yucca, and I think he's mixed it with a potato and some garlic. It is good, I told you." He smiles and I know he's teasing me. He is right; he knows my palate better than I do.

I take a swig of the Schin and am relieved to find it's also good and fruity, if a little too warm. I move to sit closer to him, and he wraps an arm around my shoulders. I munch on my fish while staring out at the horizon. Dark clouds are fully formed there, some covering the sun. A thunderstorm on its way, flashes of electricity in the distance. We can't see the shore from here, the river is impossibly big. Its bushy outline only perceptible because of my awareness. Gustavo assures us we'll outrun the storm. Sergio gives my shoulders a squeeze. We could almost be on vacation, the troubles at home behind us. If only what was ahead of us, didn't worry me more.

Chapter Twelve

There is no warning when we're suddenly confronted by the jungle. One minute we're in open water, the brown below us, the cloudy blue above. On and on and on. The next minute a tree appears, solitary, out of place in the surrounding water. We pass two more and I lean over the boat railing, searching for their trunks. The murky depths conceal them from view. A shoreline is ahead of us, indistinct masses in the distance, trees gradually taking shape around us. A macaw flies overhead, a burst of red and yellow. Then the noise! So much noise I can't even hear myself think a rational thought. Like a hundred people talking, screaming, at once. My mom and Sergio rush to the front of the boat, calling out the names of different animals they see- searching for hidden tribesmen in the shadows. Gustavo yelling out one's they don't know. My head is throbbing and I try to rub the pain away, ignoring the request to join them, I feel sick again and decide to lay down. My face is on fire, and I think I may have a fever. I root around in my canvas bag until I find our earplugs, shoving them in my ear canals. I remove two Tylenols as well, and swallow them down with my last gulp of soda. The earplugs only muffle the noise, but it's enough, and I try to nap.

I feel nauseous as soon as I wake up. My head is in Sergio's lap, and I clutch at him before beginning to dry heave. Someone shoves a bucket in my face before I'm retching, my lunch churning in my stomach. I choke on the chunks burning my throat. When it's over I'm exhausted, my mom rubbing my back, Sergio whispering soothing words into my ear. We are already at the dock, arms lifting me from the boat and jumping back. Our friend, Gustavo, unloading us as quickly as possible, the threat of Malaria making his actions speedy. I am shoved into the back of a truck, where I start dry heaving again. My body shivering uncontrollably. So cold. I am so cold. There is nothing left in my stomach, but I am still sick. Propped up against Sergio, I can hear his barking commands. I close my eyes against the dizziness, and suddenly there is nothing but darkness.

Monkeys. I hear the screeching of far-off monkeys, my eyes blinking open. I sit straight up in bed before a wave of queasiness hits and I roll back down. Closing my eyes and breathing through my nose slowly. Absorbing the sounds around me. I blink my eyes open again when I hear a rustling noise to my left. A woman is here. No, not a woman, an angel. Beautiful blonde tresses fall down her back, she is at least my mother's age, without a hint of gray. Her blue eyes shining, her white skin even paler than my Scandinavian coloring. High cheekbones, sharp petite nose, everything in such perfect proportion. I think she may be a hallucination and so I reach out to touch her. I'm so sure she's a dream, that when my fingers touch warm skin I flinch, embarrassed. She laughs, a chord of music issuing from her windpipe.

"Have a cracker," she says, reaching into a box. "Are you feeling better?" Her English is perfect with a slight, what I think is, German, accent. For once in my life, I am at a complete loss for words. She hands me a melba cracker, something I normally hate, but I take it to be polite. Bland as I remember, I'm glad it stays in my stomach. I reach for another and she hands me a bottle of ice cold water. I take a long swig, sigh, and lay back in the bed. My throat still burns a little.

"Where's my husband?" I ask, my voice is scratchy and weak.

"He and your mother are asleep in the next room. I'm told your mother snores and she didn't want to disturb you. The doctor didn't want Sergio near you until they could figure out what you have. We don't think it's malaria. Your fever was gone by the time the doctor arrived. Maybe a stomach bug? I've had everything this jungle could offer, so I convinced your husband I would watch over you. He is fearfully worried. I should probably go rouse him, to let him know you're awake." She makes a motion to leave, but I grip her arm, holding her in place.

"How long has he been sleeping?" I ask her.

"A few hours," she replies hesitant. "I would rather let him sleep, but he was insistent."

I think about this, the both of them always so protective of me.

"Don't wake him, let them both sleep. I'll be okay." I let go of her arm, and she relaxes back into the chair. There is a large window next to the bed looking out to a dense forest. . .jungle. I'm startled when I see the form of an iguana on the ledge, he completely blends into the landscape behind him.

"Tell me please, I don't remember, am I in Maracapuru?" I squint at her, "and, who are you?"

She laughs again, and the musical tone is even more pronounced. "I am Matt's mother, Elisabeth."

She peers at me carefully, "You remember who Matt is?"

I nod in assent, before picking at my eyelashes, clearing the crustiness. Matt is one of the people we were supposed to find. He is supposed to help us.

"You'll meet Matt a little later, he always loves the American tourists." She smiles widely, "I own this hotel, and we're located right outside of Manacapuru."

"We made it," I say, under my breath. I turn to her, and ask a little louder. "Did my mom tell you why we're here?"

Her brow pinches together. "No one has said anything of importance. Sergio handed us a scrap of paper with Nina's scrawl on it, told us she'd recommended you coming here. We sent for a doctor right away, and then had to practically force Sergio and your mother into showers and bed. They were obviously exhausted." She pauses to hand me another cracker.

"I am curious though, how did you arrive into Manacapuru with no reservations, and no luggage? Not the typical tourists we get here, in the luxury boats and tour groups."

There is a throbbing in my temple and I don't know how much I should tell her. My back is sore, and I think I must have slept funny. I can't meet her eyes. She is so kind and beautiful, and my instinct tells me she can be trusted to keep our secret. My mom hasn't said anything though, and maybe I should take my cue from her. Keep the secrets until we know more about this place. I take a bite of the cracker and drink some water to cover the awkwardness.

"It's okay," she says, placing the crackers on a nightstand next to me, "you don't have to tell me. I understand secrets, better than most I would think." A deep tenor fills the air around us as she laughs bitterly to herself. "Anyway, try and sleep. Please don't leave this room until your husband or mother come for you. The doctor should be in again a little later to check on you."

She drifts across the room and gives me a small smile before closing the door. I hear a lock click into place. I munch on another cracker, grateful to have something in my stomach. I am still nauseous and achey, but otherwise fine. I think about sleeping, but it is so noisy here, I wonder how anyone could fall asleep to this. Those white noise machines a joke in comparison. I suddenly have to pee, urgently, and jump out of bed. The movement brings on another wave of nausea and I grasp the table next to me to let it pass. Out of bed I realize how sticky the air is, my dirty clothes clinging to my body. I fumble to the bathroom and relieve myself. There is a huge jetted tub next to the toilet and I turn the taps, letting out a stream of lukewarm water. I drop my clothes and slip into it, grateful for the little bottles of soap and shampoo lining the edge. The water may not be refreshing, but the jets soothe my sore body. I lounge longer than I normally would, until my skin is so wrinkled it's painful.

Wrapping a fluffy towel around myself, I realize I haven't considered what I'm going to wear. I have no clean clothes, or any clothes at all for that matter. I poke at the T-shirt I dropped on the floor and a dirt clod releases from the collar. The pants from my mother's suit are even more disgusting off my body. My underwear a total loss. I pad out to the room and contemplate fashioning something out of the curtains, when there's a loud rap on my door. I look down at myself and tighten the towel across my chest. I think it must be the doctor, and of the four people who could be at my door, I don't think I mind any of them seeing me undressed. The doctor is sure to have seen worse. Another knock on the door. I switch the lock and swing it open.

It is not the doctor. It is not Sergio, my mom, or Elisabeth.

It is a man I have never seen before. He is tall and handsome in a rugged way. Blonde hair falls over one of his deep blue eyes. We stare at each other for a brief second before his gaze strays down to my towel. I jump back to slam the door shut again, but he has the decency to look embarrassed and avert his eyes.

"Ummm...Miss? There's a robe in the closet behind you." He sounds so sheepish, my embarrassment disappears and I want to giggle at his discomfort. He glances back over at me before shielding his eyes with a hand.

"Sorry, I thought Sergio. . .maybe I should come back later?" He mumbles.

A snort of laughter escapes from my nose, and a woman appears behind him. Dark skin, dark eyes, and her hair thrown up in a ponytail. She has a bag in her hand, a stethoscope slung over her neck. Taking in the appearance of us both, she raises an eyebrow at the man, who I'm sure now, must be Matt.

"Am I interrupting something?" she asks him teasingly. I can't help the smile spreading across my face. It's all so ridiculous that I start really laughing. Straight from the belly laughing.

A blush creeps up his neck, and still averting his eyes, he turns away from me.

"I'll come back later," he says before rushing down the hall. Running away from us both.

The doctor gives me a warm smile, and holds out her hand. "I'm Emily," she says.

I have to wipe at my eyes, the tears squeezing their way out. My towel has slipped a little, and I hold it in place with one hand, reaching for her with the other.

"Lara," I reply, taking her hand and giving it a good shake. "Come on in."

"You seem to be feeling better." She walks in and takes a seat at a small table near the window, arranging her things. I use the minute to grab the robe out of my closet, sliding it on over my towel and sitting in the chair opposite her.

She clears her throat, "I thought it might be a stomach bug. Not enough water, dehydration. Your mother told me you guys were traveling at a pretty frantic pace. Most tourists are lucky if they can leave the Amazon unscathed."

She pokes a thermometer under my tongue and slides a cuff over my arm to check my vitals. "Blood pressure, a little high maybe," she mutters, "still a slight fever." Listening to my heart, she asks about my symptoms, and is fairly satisfied with my answers.

"I'd like to take a blood sample if you don't mind?" she asks.

I don't mind, and it takes her a few minutes to get a clean needle out and pull some blood from me. Packing everything back into her case, she advises me on what to eat. Tells me to drink plenty of fluids while I'm here.

"I'm sure you're fine. Take it easy for a few days, Elisabeth runs a fantastic resort here, so try to rest. I'll let you know the results soon." With that she stands up and shakes my hand again, letting herself out the door. I sit for a few minutes, staring out the window, watching the birds. There are hundreds of them in the trees. Tiny things strung out across the branches, and great giant ones in the air. Their color the only thing brightening the every shade of green. A butterfly races past my window, her black and white wings fluttering frantically. The iguana has decided to move on, he has really disappeared from my ledge this time. I stand up to peer out the window, and realize it's a sliding glass door. Reaching for the handle a face pops out in front of mine. I let out a short scream before catching myself. It's Sergio. With shaking hands I unlatch the lock and he easily slides it open, laughing hysterically.

"You gave me a fright," he says, "I wasn't expecting you to be up."

"I gave you a fright!" I playfully punch him in the arm, trying to push him away. He pulls me into a hug, "You scared me to death!" I tell him, before he gives me a long kiss on the mouth. I melt into his kiss, not wanting it to stop. I can't remember the last time we were alone. He is wearing an unfamiliar long sleeve T-shirt, and cotton pants. His hiking

134

boots add two more inches to his height, making me feel shorter than I already am. My grip tightens around his waist.

"Well, I see you're feeling better," he says, pulling away. "Did the doctor come by already?"

I sit back down in my chair, and comb my hair with my fingers. "She came by earlier and told me I needed to rest, but otherwise was fine. Dehydration was her diagnosis, or something like that. She took some blood tests to make sure."

My mom appears at the glass door, looking strange in cargo pants and a long sleeve T-shirt. Younger somehow. She hands me a pile of clothing, and a pair of hiking boots, before yanking me up from the chair and into a hug.

"Why didn't Elisabeth wake us up?" she asks, gripping my arms. "I was so worried last night."

"I told her not too, I thought you needed sleep, and I was fine. The doctor says dehydration is all. Rest and lots of fluids." The nausea is completely gone, leaving my throat sore. I'm trying to be reassuring despite the pain I'm still in. Her look tells me she's not buying it. I flip my hair forward to try and dry it with the towel.

"I'm starving," I tell them, "let me get dressed and we can talk about our game plan."

My hair is still dripping, but I pull on some underwear, and slip into the matching cargo pants my mom's bought for me.

"Well first, I think we should do what the doctor advised and rest. We can afford to spend a couple of days here." She watches me spread the bug repellant into my skin, "and we don't want to rush your recovery."

"Mom, I'm fine. Honestly. We've come so far, and we're so close. I want to find out about this Princess Julianne, and maybe we can track down the mailing address today." The Mosquito bite I received yesterday has turned into a solid lump. I resist the urge to itch it, and yank the shirt over my head, relieved it doesn't have any obvious slogans across the front this time.

Sergio interrupts us. "I know the address," he says. I have only one arm through my shirt when I freeze, staring blankly at him.

"Now don't be mad at me, I didn't let any secrets out. But while your mom was talking to Elisabeth about our rooms and everything, Matt asked me some pretty pointed questions. I avoided what I could, but I did end up asking him where we could find the address on the mailing label we have."

I look at my mom. She looks at me.

"I didn't want to say anything to Elisabeth, until we had talked," she says. "After everything that happened back in California, I don't know who we can trust."

I shake my head, "I didn't say anything either." I turn back to Sergio, and finish sliding my arm into the shirt. "So what did Matt say?"

He clears his throat. "You're going to find this hard to believe, but the address on the mailing label? It's the address for their store. The one Matt and his father own." My mom and I both sink into the bed simultaneously. "And it's right across the street from us."

We pepper him with questions, but he has nothing else to tell us. Matt assumed it was another address Nina had given us and Sergio let him believe it. The doctor had arrived almost immediately and there hadn't been any more time to talk. They had all been busy trying to take care of me, as I drifted in and out of consciousness.

"Okay, I guess the question is now, do we trust them?" I ask.

"I think we have to," my mom responds. "I don't know how else we're going to get answers, and it does look like they're the ones receiving Marion's mail."

"Not a very good reason to trust them, since everything went so well with Marion," I say sarcastically. I thrust my feet into the new hiking boots. "Okay, what do you think Sarge? I need to eat, so let's have a game plan."

I stand and test the new shoes. My toes wiggle happily, encased again in comfort. They're a little snug, but better than the pumps I've been wearing for three days.

"I'll ask him," he says, watching me. "I think we have to ask them, but it doesn't mean we have to trust them."

We walk down a flight of stairs outside of my door, and the smell of food wafts past us. I recoil as another wave of nausea hits me, and I inhale deep breaths to try and clear it. Sergio is instantly at my side. "Are you okay?" he asks me anxiously.

"I'm fine I think. I don't like the smell. It's making me. . .sick."

He looks confused, "you usually love the smell of bacon."

My mom is looking at me curiously, "I think the doctors right, you need your rest. Let's eat some breakfast anyway, you'll probably feel better once something is in your stomach."

I follow them quietly, and concentrate on counting breaths rather than my recoiling stomach. The dining room is filled with tables, windows opening out to the jungle beyond. It's quite a vista. I fill a plate with eggs and fruit, following Sergio to a seat near an open window. We watch a bird perched on a magnolia bush, eating its bulbous fruit. The creamy flowers beautiful against the green waxy backdrop. A familiar figure joins us, the man from this morning. He grabs a chair and brings it over to our table, shaking Sergio's hand. Introducing himself to my mom, he is pointedly trying not to look at me, when he holds out a hand for me to shake.

"Nice to meet you," he says. "I'm Matt."

"I figured," I smirk at him. "And it's so good to see you again. . .fully clothed," I add, giggling a little.

He turns a bright pink.

Sergio's eyebrows arch in surprise. "You've met already?"

Matt holds both hands up in front of himself, stumbling a step back. "Your Misses answered the door, and umm, she was in a towel! I didn't mean to look, but, umm, well. . ." He stutters, as Sergio bursts into laughter.

"You answered the door in a towel, Lara? No wonder the poor payaso can't look you in the eye. It's okay dude, I know my wife's hot." He pats him on the back, wiggling his eyebrows. My mom shakes her head in a sign of disapproval.

I whisper to her, "I thought it was the doctor, Mom. I wouldn't have answered the door in a towel if I had known it was someone else. Besides, I didn't have any clean clothes."

She shakes her head again before returning to her cereal. I start peeling a banana as Matt sits down in the seat.

"What are your plans for today?" he asks. "Elisabeth wants me to serve as ya'lls tour guide, and since we're in rainy season there's not many tourists to look after. Pop can manage on his own today."

Mom and I look to Sergio. "Well we wanted to ask you about the store," he begins. "Remember how I asked you about the address yesterday?"

"Uh-huh," Matt mumbles, taking a bite of a roll he's pulled from his pocket.

"Well, ah-hem," Sergio says, clearing his throat again. He is clearly uncomfortable with his role as spokesman for our group. "We have some mail that was postmarked from your store and. . ."

He stops mid sentence when Matt's mouth drops open, and a bit of bread slips out. Glancing suspiciously at the three of us, Matt asks, "does this have something to do with Founder?"

The three of us stare at him, and no one knows what to say next. "Yes," I finally answer timidly, "it's about Founder." My brain is tingling, *we have the name of the village!*

"What do you know of it?" I ask, trying to sound off-hand.

He is watching the three of us, his gaze landing on Sergio. He gives him a long steady look before standing up. Leaning into the table he whispers, "y'all look like real nice people, but I would leave Founder alone." Loudly he says, "I'll be around a little later to show you the town." With that, he leaves the three of us to the rest of our breakfast, retreating into the kitchen.

Mom and Sergio start whispering frantically, but I sit back. Anger slowly taking control. We flew all this way, hundreds of miles, to be dismissed by him? I don't think so.

"I'll be right back," I tell them both. "Bathroom?" I mouth to my mom. She nods her head and points vaguely in the direction of the kitchen, which is exactly where I'm headed. I march across the dining room, through the doors, but stop short when I hear arguing directly inside.

"They're asking about Founder!" I hear Matt's voice. I duck behind a serving cart to my left, crouching next to a bag of potatoes.

"So?" a man's voice asks. "We've had others come before. Marion has always been careful with the information she sends out to the other Patrons. They have to know they can't really visit the Colony, and maybe they can explain why the mail has stopped."

"This is different," Matt says. "They're not like the other weirdo's. The ones who visited before. Sergio for instance, he's not even branco! We've never had someone who wasn't white. I don't think they know what Founder really is."

There's a long pause. "We have to be careful with how much information we give them. You know we get paid a lot of money to keep their secrets. It's how we manage your schooling, the bribes we need to keep this place afloat. One wrong step and we could lose everything Matt." I have to strain to hear his next words. "I'll warn your mother."

A door slams loudly, and I jump upright. Too quickly, Matt is directly in front of me.

"So what is Founder really?" I ask him.

He looks flummoxed. "How long were you back there?" he asks, looking around to see if anyone else is going to pop out of the potatoes.

"Long enough," I tell him, placing my hands on my hips. "Long enough to know you have the answers to my questions."

"You heard my Father," he says. "I shouldn't say anything, and you should leave Founder alone. I only know enough to tell you it's not a place you want to mess with."

"I'm not going to leave it alone," I tell him. "My house was burned to the ground, my Mom's house trashed, and we were lucky not to be killed in a high speed car chase. Not to mention flying hundreds of miles to get some answers." I walk right up to him and point my finger directly in his face. "You have those answers. So start talking."

"You can be kind of scary," he grins at me. I drop my hand, and raise an eyebrow at him.

"I'll tell you what," I say, flashing to the conversation with his dad. "You give me information, and I can tell you why the mail has stopped."

"A deal?" he asks, wrinkling his nose, considering it. "I don't know."

I place my hands back on my hips, tapping my foot against the tile floor.

He follows my movements with his eyes before breaking into a grin. "I guess I can tell you what I know, but I've gotta warn you, it's not much. Elisabeth's who you need to talk too, and good luck getting a straight answer out of her." He looks around the kitchen, before moving toward the dining room door. "Just remember what you promised," he brushes his hair back with one of his hands. "Now let's go get that husband and mother of yours."

Chapter Thirteen

"It starts with three princesses," he begins. We are sitting on a dock overlooking a small bay. Children swimming in the water. Their bodies like fish, slipping around each other. I snort, and try not to laugh.

"Princesses?" I ask skeptically. "What is this? A fairy tale?" My mom gives me *that* look and I blush, suddenly quiet.

Matt shakes his head before continuing. "Like I said, three princesses." He shrugs. "That's what they're called anyway, the first of the three Aryan princesses. Blond hair, blue eyes, pale skin, they call them the requirements."

"Everyone has them," he says quietly, almost to himself. Sergio clears his throat and it startles him back to the present.

"What!? Oh yeah, three princesses," he says, "and ten men for them. To impregnate them." He glances over at me, expecting me to be shocked I guess, but when there's no reaction he continues. "So these Princesses get pregnant and have babies. Lots and lots of babies who fit the requirements. They manage to survive in the jungle, which is a total feat in itself, and have more babies. Until they can establish a whole colony, called Founder." His hands make a little flourish in the air. "The end."

"Wait?! What do you mean the end?" I ask, indignantly.

"The end. That's the story of Founder, it's a colony in the Amazon filled with white people. They're super secretive, and live like your Amish, no electricity and all that jazz. Sometimes a few of them will come here to pick up their mail and groceries. That's it, the big secret." He folds his arms in front of him and leans back, a smug smile on his face. "I told you I didn't know much."

Sergio is on the same page as me, his face bunched up and annoyed.

"I don't believe you," Sergio says, "There's more to this. Lara told you our house burned down. If it was just about a colony of white people in the jungle, why would there be people trying to kill us? It makes no sense." One of the children suddenly jumps too close to the dock. Sergio blocks the water from hitting the rest of us by turning his body against the spray. His shirt immediately dripping. He pulls it away from his body to wave it dry, and I start to giggle at him. Matt yells in rapid Portuguese at the bobbing head that reappears, and the boy swims back to his friends, laughing.

Sergio's hair is slightly wet, and he slicks it back with his free hand. "I didn't believe in any of this until now," he says to Matt. "You say there's a colony of people in the jungle? That no one has ever seen? I want to see them."

"I want to see them too," my mom says, her feet dangling over the water. "This isn't about the colony to me, this is about my family. My aunt was involved in this, maybe my father. I want to know why."

"I don't think I should say anything else." Matt stares at the three of us, and we glare back at him. "Really. My dad would be mad." Three pairs of angry eyes, boring into him. He lets out a long breath of air.

"Okay, the rest of this, well it's what you would call. . .speculation. I know my mom left the colony to marry my dad," he explains. "Elisabeth is actually my stepmother, and my mom's sister. My mom died when I was born, and Elisabeth started coming here a lot. Like I said, two of them come, every month, to collect their mail. She became one of the two, every month. She used to bring me presents and stuff. When I was five she disappeared and my dad was furious. I remember he would have these rages at the men who still arrived every month, and when they didn't do anything, my dad threatened to bring the whole colony down. Months went by, and around the time I turned six, she came back. Alone."

I interrupt him, "What do you mean alone?"

"One minute she wasn't here, and the next morning she was. No one else to pick up the mail or anything. Dad told me she would be living with us from now on. I was thrilled of course, and didn't even think to ask him why. When I was about ten I got up the courage, but. . ." A glance at us, "You haven't heard her laugh, it's the most beautiful sound in the world." His face has a faraway look, "she told me I was silly. That she chose to leave Founder and be with us. I accepted it then, but it never explained where she was the year before. Why she never visited. When I asked her recently, she told me I'm remembering it wrong, that she never stopped coming." His eyes harden, "she has a way of talking, a way of making you think you're wrong." His face is defiant, anger flashing across his features. "I know I'm not." He pounds his fist into the opposite hand.

"I really haven't thought about it much," he continues. "Until a few days ago." He pulls a knee into his chest, fiddling with a ring on his thumb. "When they arrived to collect their mail."

My eyes open wide in astonishment, as my mom holds her hand up to interrupt him. "Wait a minute," she says. "They were here a few days ago? We just missed them?"

"Yeah, they left the day before you arrived. There hasn't been mail for them in months, and my dad was beginning to get worried." His hands go still and he gives me a pointed look. "Is still worried."

I nod at him. He'll get his information.

He juts his chin out, "there's always been two of them, just two of them, and always men. Almost always the same men; at least since Elisabeth arrived. Then last week, three people arrive, and one of them was a girl."

I narrow my eyes at him, "So they changed it up a little, sent a girl, what's the big deal?" I cross my arms in front of my chest, "I don't get it."

"No, you don't get it. These people, they all look exactly the same, and they're like seriously serious. They collect their mail, buy their groceries, and leave. Sometimes they go to the internet cafe down the street to watch youtube and be updated on current events," he shrugs his shoulders, "but that's it." He watches one of the children take a dive off the pier, her brown skin glistening. "Then last week this girl arrives, and she's totally different."

"You mean she's a girl?" Sergio asks, laughing a little.

"Yeah laugh, but that's not what I mean. First off she's a morena, a brunette, with brown eyes, and skin as dark as mine!" He holds up his arm to make a point, and I raise my eyebrows, crinkling my nose. He's not nearly as dark as Sergio, more like a deep tan.

"You're missing the point," he says, huffing. "You would get it if you knew them." He looks off into the distance and goes quiet.

"Is there something else?" My mom prompts him.

"You're going to think I'm crazy," he says.

"This whole thing is crazy!" I tell him. "This whole thing!" I yell, startling the kids. One of the girls is eyeing me warily.

"Right," he chuckles, noticing the girl. She is talking to a friend now, circling her ear with a finger. "Well this girl, her name was Marta, the same name as my mom. I didn't think anything of it at first, because they all have these generic, old-fashioned names. Then I caught her alone at breakfast, and she asked me something."

"What did she ask you?"

His face flushes a familiar pink. "I was trying to pump her for information about the colony, about why she was here. I thought it might have something to do with Elisabeth. Then Marta asked me about her mother and it suddenly hit me I knew exactly who her mother was. She reminded me of her, and someone else. Then, the way they acted after she left. . .well, that confirmed it."

"Confirmed what?" I ask.

"Marta is my sister."

"What?!" All three of us shout at him in unison.

"Half sister actually," he says. "Elisabeth is her mother, and I'm sure my father is her father. They have the exact same eyes, and we both have his skin tone. There have been a lot of whispered conversations between my parents since she left, and Elisabeth hasn't been the same. I think she hasn't seen her since she was a baby."

We fall silent, digesting this. My mom breaks the silence first. "How terrible." She stares at me. "That couldn't have been a choice." She glares at Matt, "You said they could choose to leave, but I can't believe she would have made that choice."

144

"I don't know," Matt says, bowing his head. "I don't know what choices they have. I don't know that what they've told me is even true."

"I promised you information," I say, and he perks up. "We're not sure how our Aunt Marion is connected, but I overheard your dad, and I believe Marion was their Patron, right?"

He nods his head, "Yeah, she's the main Patron. Collecting donations and sending them packages filled with medicines and stuff. Things they need to survive. Things we need to survive too. Hush money you could call it, and this resort for other Patrons to visit."

"Other Patrons?" my mother asks.

He shrugs, "I don't know much about the other Patrons, just that they're strange. They're not allowed to visit the colony, but they think this is some sort of Holy Ground. They do a lot of chanting."

I give him a smirk. "Okay," I breathe out, "so this will be something of a shock to your parents, but Marion is dead. She was in a home for a little while, and she died a few days ago. That's why your packages have stopped."

His mouth drops open in shock, digesting this.

"We have to find my dad. Now." He jumps up and rushes off, leaving us to follow him. I groan loudly when I stand up, my joints stiff from sitting in the awkward position. My mom slips me some crackers as my stomach growls loudly. I smile at her, "You're such a Mom. What else do you have in there?" I pretend to peek in her bag, and she swipes at my head. "Baby wipes and antiseptic?" I duck her arm, laughing.

I lean heavily on her as we walk up the path. She hands me another cracker, demanding that I eat it. "I don't want you sick again," she says.

Sergio hears us and drops back, taking my hand. "Are you feeling sick?" he asks.

"No, I'm fine," I say, giving him a smile. "I'm hungry for lunch, that's all."

"We're almost there, mi amor," he says reassuringly.

We walk through the resort entrance and into the dining room, our feet tapping against the shining tile floor. There is a low mumbling from the few stragglers who are left. The remnants of lunch service on the tables we pass. Sergio pulls one of the wooden chairs out for me, and I slump into it. There doesn't seem to be a buffet in the afternoon, and a waitress appears with our menus. I move to pluck mine from the table, when Matt joins us again. His father and Elisabeth flanking him. They sit with us and look around nervously, waving the waitress off after she drops our drinks on the table.

"I'm Eli," Matt's father says, reaching his hand out to shake ours, "we haven't formally met."

Not one of us makes a move to shake his hand, and it hangs there in the air, until he decides to tuck it back under the table.

"We need to know what happened back at your home, with Marion," Eli says. Elisabeth tenses at his side.

My mom looks sternly at them both. "Are we being honest with each other now? Maybe we should start with information on Marta?"

Elisabeth is visibly hurt by my mom's remark, her face crumpling. Eli scowls, "You have no idea what you're talking about. You have no idea how dangerous this situation is."

"Why don't you tell us then?" Sergio speaks up, putting a hand on my mom's arm before she can speak again.

"If Marion is dead, they'll be coming soon. They'll need to replace her, and they won't do it without a visit."

"Who are we talking about?" Sergio asks.

"The Patrons for them all," Elisabeth says. "Hasn't Matt told you the story? The ten men? They didn't all stay in the colony. They fathered the children, built the houses, and as soon as the children were old enough to fend for themselves, seven of them left."

"Where did they go?" I ask her.

"They built more colonies, fathered more children, built an unstoppable force to the cause. It's hard to explain their thinking, that the pale skin, blue eyes, and light hair make you somehow smarter, or stronger than others. That everyone

146

else is cursed. The point is, Founder is one of their colonies." Elisabeth pauses. "I've been in contact with some of the other resort owners. They've visited here to see how we're doing, how large our colony is. It's mainly to gloat about the strength of their own numbers. We've been lucky, Marion has been our single Patron since the beginning. She's never visited, never genuinely cared how Founder was being run, or how we were doing. She's never been involved in the politics. It's allowed us to fly under the radar, break some of the rules, keep our Untouchables."

"Your what?" Sergio asks. Even Matt appears shocked by the term. I can tell he's never heard this part of the story.

"Untouchables," Elisabeth replies. She brushes some hair back from Eli's eyes, kissing him on the cheek. "The ones who aren't born with the correct genetic formula for blonde hair, blue eyes, and white skin."

"Like Marta," Matt says.

Elisabeth looks pained again, but she continues, "yes, like Marta, our daughter." She takes Eli's hand, "I had to leave them behind. It was the only deal I could make to be spared my life. I knew she would be fine there, and I thought, maybe some day. . ."

My mom is the only one who catches the mistake. "Them?" she asks, "you have other children there?"

Elisabeth's head drops as she nods her head. "Two more," she replies, "a prince and a princess." She says the next part so softly, we can barely hear her. "You see, I was the wife of the Führer."

We are shocked by this announcement. Even Matt is looking at them in disbelief, seeing his stepmother in a new light. Eli interrupts the silence.

"This has nothing to do with what is important right now. We have to decide our next step. Did Marion leave any resources for us to pull from?"

My mom shakes her head. "Everything was burned or seized. I assume by the same Patrons you're talking about."

"We'll be getting a message soon, I'm sure of it," Eli says to Elisabeth, hushed. "They know our Colony can't survive without a Patron for long, and they're already running drastically low on food and supplies."

"The hair dye and contacts," Elisabeth whispers to him.

"I still have some at the store from the last time," he says to her softly. "The problem is Founder, the mail run was only last week, someone has to warn them."

"Warn who?" Sergio asks loudly.

This question jars Eli, he looks up at us as if he has forgotten we are here. He looks as if he has said too much. Elisabeth stands, pulls him along with her. "We'll send the waitress over with lunch." She gives a look to Matt who jumps up as well. They back away quickly from our table and head for the kitchen. The three of them can't get away fast enough.

A waitress scurries over and drops a bounty of sandwiches and fried plantains in front of us, refreshes all our waters.

"They're going to Founder," my mom states.

"They are," I respond, "but what can we do about it?"

Chapter Fourteen

We discuss ideas the rest of the afternoon, but none of us can come up with a viable plan. The "What if's", and "How about's," seem endless. It all comes to one conclusion, we can't get to Founder, if we don't know where Founder is. There's also the Patrons to worry about now. Would it be better if we just returned home? Gave our new information to the police? Sergio shakes his head to this, the whole thing sounds ridiculous to him. They're not going to believe us with no real evidence. We have to continue our journey to Founder, find the evidence of a White Supremacist camp, and get home- before the Patrons can arrive.

My mom is the first one to mention helping them. She's still thinking of Marta, wondering how she reconcile's her life, with what she knows to be true.

"I think we could fix this," my mom says. "Without having to expose them to the outside world." She is folding the few t-shirts and cargo pants we've managed to acquire. The two canvas bags open at the end of my bed. I'm pacing near the window, trying to loosen my tightened joint muscles. Sergio sits solemnly in the single chair, the computer out in front of him. He is clicking through web pages at a frantic pace.

"Are you listening to yourself Mom!" I exclaim. "These people burned our house down!"

"Not them specifically Lara," she says. "I think we should help them. We could give them options, without forcing our own beliefs on them."

"Why shouldn't we expose them though? If what they're doing is wrong?" I ask.

"The problem is," she says, "they don't think so."

"That's fine Mom, but what happens when we tell the Untouchables? What's to stop them from exposing themselves?" I ask, flinging my arms out in exasperation.

"That's a bridge we can cross when we get there." Her hands rest on her hips, her mouth tight. I recognize defeat, but can't resist the sarcastic reply.

"*If* we get there."

We have changed positions in the resort often, wandering all over the grounds. I catch glimpses of Matt scurrying about, sometimes his arms loaded with packages, but he doesn't stop to talk, and runs quickly in the other direction of us. We don't see the rest of his family at all. My mom keeps me fed all day, but I still begin feeling nauseous again during dinner and decide to return to my room. The ache in my back has returned with more intensity, my shoulders stinging. Sergio is feeling antsy and I convince him to go on a walk into town with my mom. She's been bugging us both that she needs to get a few more things. I beg her to find Tylenol before I settle in for a lengthy rest, my head propped up on a pillow, my eyes wide open. My mind won't shut down, the problems too insistent, calling for attention.

Steal a boat? How can we steal one, when none of us know how to operate one. We'd have to hire one, and ask around if anyone else has information about a hidden colony in the jungle. Even in my brain the idea sounds stupid. We could always take the shot in the dark approach, tour around the Amazon and hope we spot something. I glance out my glass door. Four bright eyes stare at me through the trees, reiterating the idea that this isn't a place we want to be lost in. Sergio suggested hiring a helicopter. They're plentiful around here, and we could try and spot something from the air. We just don't know what direction we should be heading in, and the expense may be too much. My head throbbing again, I switch my thoughts over to home. Wonder how the rest of our family is doing. If they're still safe. I pull my cell phone from my purse to check the time. *I have service here!* I contemplate calling my Aunt Tina, to see if she's had her baby. Cousin number 41. I know my mom is worried about her. I also haven't checked into work, and I'm sure they're wondering how I'm doing with the fire and everything. The cell phone rests in my hand, there are too many phone calls to make. I don't know where to begin and so I don't call anybody. I am on the edge of sleep when a knock on my glass door startles me. I groggily roll over to my side and see Matt blowing his mouth wide on the window. His tongue licking the glass. Something only a teenage boy would find funny.

Sliding the door open, I motion him in.

"What are you doing here stranger?" I meant it to come out teasingly, but it sounds forced, more like the accusation it should be.

He wipes at his mouth and looks apologetic. "Where's Sergio and Sylvia?" he asks.

"They've gone into town to get supplies," I reply.

He seems to understand my implication, that we're going to try and find Founder, even without their help.

"You know, I'm not like my parents. They've lived their whole life here, or around here. They don't know any different. I did most of my schooling in Idaho. A Patron sponsored me, expected me to become educated in their way of life. I think it had the opposite effect they intended." I cross my arms in front of my chest.

"Sometimes the more you push someone towards something, the more they push back," I say.

He begins walking the floor, flipping his hair out of his eyes occasionally. "Oh, I wasn't obvious about it. I played along with them for the most part. It helped my parents clearly didn't believe in *the cause*. I mean, my mother is married to an Untouchable." He spits out the last part, disgusted with the word. "I thought the colony in the jungle here, well I thought it was a cult. Not even a cult, more like those Polygamous families you see near the Arizona border. Harmless and misguided, you know?"

He stops pacing to have a seat at my table. Thrusting his feet forward and leaning back on the two legs.

"Do you want my forgiveness or something? Permission to go? I don't understand what you're asking," I say, confused about why he's here. In my room. Disturbing my sleep.

"Well, no, not exactly," he says, "I know you all want to go. I understand why, at least I think I do, and I'm here to invite you along with me."

I am shocked by this completely unexpected move. I collapse on the bed as he explains his plan.

We will have to check out of the hotel tomorrow. Pretend to be leaving for home. His parents will be relieved, they're afraid we may make trouble here in Manacapuru for them, they're sure no one will believe our story in the States. We will hire a boat to take us back to Manaus in the afternoon. Matt leaves alone, in the early morning. He will watch for us on the river and meet us. "You have until two," he says. A large bribe to our captain should keep him quiet. Matt warns me the trip will be dangerous. It's two days on the river and we go right through tribal territory. He only has approximate coordinates, from fishing trips he's been on with his Father. His mother assures him the tribesman will not harm a blonde head, they have a truce with the Colony. Sergio will have to stay hidden most of the trip, and it's not a large boat. We're lucky it's rainy season or we would be in for an awfully long hike, the tributary we need begins disappearing in June. There's also Pirates along the river. "They'll leave us alone, ol' drinking buddies of my Pops," he says. He'll bring money with him just in case.

"But why would you risk it?" I ask him, still not quite believing we have a way to Founder. "Why would you risk taking us?"

He stretches his arms above his head, interlacing his fingers behind his neck. "I thought you of all people would understand," he says. "From what I hear, you're the one who convinced everyone to hop on a plane. Why'd you do it? You couldn't have thought this was safe. I think Sergio and Sylvia would have done anything that you asked of them."

"Even follow me to Brazil," I whisper to myself. Wondering if he could be right.

He smiles in satisfaction. "So the question remains, why are you here?"

I don't answer him right away, thinking through the last few days. Trying to balance how much of my decision was based in anger, and how much was based in plain curiosity.

"I don't like to not know," I tell him. "I don't like everyone making decisions for me, and I hate the people who burned my house down. I want answers so badly, I'm willing to risk everything to get them."

He nods in approval, "even if it means being a little reckless?" he asks.

"My life has always been safe, I've always stayed on the straight and narrow. I think I can afford to be a little reckless now."

He stretches his arms again and his chair drops forward.

"I understand if you decide not to go with me," he says seriously. "I'm sure I'll be accepted in the Colony with very little trouble." He stands up and gives me an exaggerated wink. "I can't promise I'm not going to *make* some trouble though."

He slides out the door, leaving me with me with my own thoughts.

Marta

➤→

Chapter Fifteen

The boat ride back to Founder is uneventful, no one speaking the two days it takes to get home, the river quiet. My resolve to leave Manacapuru weakens the longer we are on the water. Returning to the Colony, to my old life, to the new lies I'll have to tell. I'm glad to have this time on the boat, this time to think over all the things Henrik has told me. This time to think over what's really out there.

Shortly after we leave the port I discover a puppy concealed under a canvas flap, Julianne's pet. I mean to hate the dog, but I can't help but love her. Someone has to take care of it, Henrik wrinkling his nose up at the job and Jacob ignoring us both. As much as I long to ignore her as well, the little yaps tug at the core of my resolve. She is as much a prisoner on this boat as I am. A white ball of fluff, only slightly larger than a dwarf monkey, I let her out of the cage and care for her. Pamper her, she is too cute not to adore, running all over the deck of the boat- barking at the boys. When she curls up next to me in sleep, her warm little body is such a comfort. I know it can only be temporary, there is no stopping the boat to rest this time. Henrik is clearly anxious to get home.

My Uncle Dale is the only one on the beach when we arrive. Henrik leaves immediately to tell the Führer the bad news about the mail. Jacob runs off as well, to find his friends, or give orders to someone. The supplies abandoned, I shoulder the backpack with its contraband and pull the puppy up in my arms. I slide off the back of the boat, and walk down the beach until the puppy wriggles its way free of my arms. Rooted in place, I watch her play in the water until my Uncle Dale approaches tentatively.

"I'm glad to see you," he says, shuffling his feet. I don't turn to him, watching the sun rise on the horizon. The two feet of air between us might as well be two hundred. The awkwardness is tangible.

"Were you expecting me to come back?" I ask.

"I'm not sure what I expected. I know you weigh duty more heavily than I do. So I thought you'd return, but I couldn't be certain." He moves to block my view of the water. "I know it's a lot to ask of you, to continue to live like you do, when you know there's an escape. I think about escaping every day." I see him clearly, his eyebrows pinched, brow furrowed. His gaze is uncomfortable and I stare at my feet, a beetle burying itself in the sand there. I don't need to know why he stays here, why he doesn't leave. I want to know why he didn't say anything. Why he couldn't tell me the truth. The accusations won't form themselves on my tongue, and I can only will him to go away.

"I would love to live a real life out there," he continues, gesturing to the river. It is calm, reflecting the new rays of sunlight. "We're the exceptions, Marta. Most of the citizens, they're happier here, even if they don't know it." He grips my arms, and I am forced to look at him. Forced to recognize the determination in his eyes. "Even the Untouchables."

I shake my head and look away, I don't know if I believe him.

"You know it too, or else you wouldn't be back here. We keep the secrets to protect everybody from the outside world. It's not much to give up one life, to protect so many others."

He pulls me into a quick hug, patting me on the back. A small, pitying smile on his face, before turning away and sprinting for the undergrowth.

I call out to the puppy, scoop her up when she rushes into my arms. I won't be able to show this much affection to her again, so I nuzzle into her fur, kissing her on the nose. I allow myself a few tears before placing her carefully in my pack. I leave a vent at the top where she can stick her head out, and reach for one of the walking sticks hanging from my Uncle Dale's hut. I brush the tears away roughly with the back of my hand. I tug at the weeds in the undergrowth, pull at the long straws growing here. We used them as whistles when I was younger, holding them between our palms and blowing sharply. There is something soothing in yanking them out of the ground. Uprooting them from where they belong, and then discarding them to the breeze. I follow my uncle's footsteps in the sand, and start running as soon as I see the path through the jungle.

There is nothing like a good run to clear my head, wipe away my emotions. I concentrate on placing my feet on the dirt path, watching for the deep ruts and vines. I pump my arms in an easy rhythm, feel the breath flow in my nose, through my lungs, out my mouth. Noises above, in front, and behind me- a chorus which keeps my mind occupied in song.

I am to the first wooden pathway before I know it, this one leading directly to Jul's huts. I don't even bother speaking with the guard at her door, and walk through without issue. I pull the puppy from my bag as Jul enters her front room, and squeals with delight. The puppy tries to squirm away from her, a whine in its throat. Jul has a firm grip, and doesn't let her go until the Führer's wife, Heidi, appears. Julianne places the dog on the floor and she runs for Heidi's ankles, nipping at them. When her nose hits one of the little bells, she jumps back startled, hiding behind a box. Heidi coaxes her out, tells Julianne she will bathe the dog. She asks if we need anything, but Julianne dismisses her with a wave of her hand. Her momentary distraction with the puppy over, she begins talking. Asking me about the trip, where the mail is, telling me about her latest clothing disaster, moving on to each subject without even bothering to wait for an answer. She suddenly notices I'm not even trying to answer. Looking confused, she glances behind me, her eyes scanning the empty air there.

"Mar-turd, where's Henrik?" she asks.

I wince at the nickname and make a decision. I am already doing so many things I don't want to do. I am already pretending too much. I don't have to pretend with her.

"I don't know," I respond, before walking out her door.

I'm smiling when I hear her calling after me to come back, cajoling me, and finally threatening me. I break into a run, my feet pounding on the wood, over the bridge, and to my hut.

I sense something is wrong before I open my door. There is a choking sound coming from inside, and I quickly fling the door aside. Ani is sitting in my chair. Crying. Tears and snot running lines down her bright red face. I hang my backpack from one of our hooks, and go to the sideboard to get her a gourd of water. Setting it on the table, I grab a scrap of cloth for her nose.

"Are you okay?" I ask, kneeling over her.

She starts hiccuping and can't answer for a few minutes. I hand her the water, and she drinks quickly.

"Thanks," she says, wiping her nose across the back of her hand. I give her the cloth.

"Oh." She wipes her face again with the cloth, and begins wringing it through her fingers. "I'm sorry. I'm fine."

Fresh tears squeeze themselves out of her eyes, and I give her a look which means, I know very well you are not fine.

She wipes at them before sighing.

"I didn't want you to see me like this, I didn't realize you'd be back so soon."

"We made good time," I tell her. "Is it Derrik?" I ask her softly.

"No," she looks at me, "Derrik and I have never been together. We're friends." She peers out the window, her eyes unfocused and blurry. I don't want to interrupt her musing. The tears dropping silently on her lap. Her breaths ragged.

She finally looks at me, her face firm. "Marta, I'm pregnant."

There is a moment where I can only blink at her, before my legs give out, and I collapse on the floor in a heap. When I've finally recovered myself, I crawl over to her side.

"How is it even possible?" I ask her. "We take medicines to prevent it."

"Apparently mine didn't work," she chuckles bitterly. The pain obvious in her face. I am so horrified for her.

"What are we going to do?" I ask, pulling at my braid and chewing on the end. My own problems disappear as I think through her consequences, none of them good.

"I'll try and hide it for now, until I can think of something. Marie already knows, but won't tell. For being Pure, she can be decent," she says, shrugging her shoulders and then releasing another sigh. "Even if I could keep it, would I even want too?"

Confused by this statement, I ask her, "but you said, you and Derrik? I don't understand. Who else is there?" There aren't many other Untouchable men who aren't already coupled, or even our own age. There are many more women.

"He's not Untouchable, and it wasn't by choice," she says. "You don't want to know."

I do want to know, but her eyes plead with me not to ask. I want to hear her story and so I remain silent until she begins talking slowly.

"It happened about a month ago, I was working late at Marie's." She shakes her head, "You're the only one who's never had a problem being by yourself. You can run around without fear, the rest of us. . .well, we try and stick together. I didn't have a walk home that night, and someone caught me, pulled me off a path into the trees. I tried protesting at first, telling him who I was, that I was allowed out. Then when he started, I tried screaming, but he kept going, clamped a hand over my mouth. My hands were tied, he told me he had to punish me, that I was evil. I threatened to tell, and he kicked me in the stomach. Said I could tell anyone I wanted, no one would believe me. He left laughing. He left me crying and bleeding in the under bush, and he left laughing. When it was over I couldn't come here. I limped back to Marie's, and she took care of me. Washed me up, didn't even seem surprised."

"I can't believe it," I say, my hand has involuntarily found my throat and I'm gripping it, terrified for her. "They're usually so scarcd of us, scared of the contamination from us."

"He wasn't scared, that's for sure." She reaches for my hand, "I haven't heard of this happening before, at least not to the Untouchables, and I would know Marta." She pats my hand, trying to soothe me, when I so desperately want to soothe her. "I've warned the others so they know to watch out for him."

"You know who it is?" I whisper in shock.

"Of course, it was obvious," she says, rising to her feet, pulling me up with her. "It was your brother, Jacob."

Jacob. Of course it was Jacob. I can't even be surprised.

"I have to go Marta, I have laundry duty today." She starts packing things into her satchel and slings it over her shoulder. "How was your trip?"

"Scarier than I thought it'd be," I reply numbly.

She gives me a concerned look, but doesn't comment. Instead she asks, "Do I look okay?"

I examine her ragged dress and dirty sandals carefully. Her face blotchy from crying. Her black hair is still glossy and bright. She is one of the few Untouchables blessed with blue eyes. They are sparkling from the tears.

"You look beautiful," I tell her, because no one ever says it to us, and she is.

Her cheeks grow even redder as she blushes, but instead of disagreeing with me, she hops over and kisses me lightly. "Thank you," she says, before running out the door.

I sit in the chair she has abandoned and touch her kiss with my fingertips. *What am I going to do?*

I end up do nothing all day. I sit at my desk and think about composing a letter. I realize it doesn't even matter, now that I know the truth. Am I helping anyone anyway? Mail hasn't arrived in months, our Patrons have either forgotten or abandoned us. I'm done with the farce, let Julianne compose them herself.

I lay in my hammock, my thoughts jumbled and confusing. I count the straws which line our roof. I lose count around 300 and start over again. When I'm finished I trace the lines in the walls around me. Find shapes in the cracks. Recite the alphabet in every language I know. When Ani arrives mid- afternoon I feign sleep until she leaves. Food is left out on the table, and I nibble at its edges, enough so someone will think I have eaten. I go back to my hammock and immediately dismiss the thought of attending a drill. The whole charade ridiculous. There's no war to train for. No physical threat outside of this colony I need to fight. I count the straws again, until I finally do fall asleep.

I wake before the morning, the suns rays barely piercing the night sky. The horn will be sounding soon and so I rise, quietly as I can. Stealthily I sneak through our hut and out the back, not even daring to glance at Ani's prone and sleeping figure. I make a trip to the latrine before walking into the jungle, looking for someplace to conceal myself. I settle in behind a bush, and begin picking apart a vine. Braiding the string-like tendons into a rope. I continue picking, pulling, and twisting until the steam rising from the rain shower indicates the sun is fully up. Still I wait in the jungle, listening to the leaves break around me, the cat calls of the animals to one another. I only move when the branch above me grows too heavy with water. The leaves dropping suddenly, the water drenching me. I am soaked and so I return to the hut. It's empty when I arrive, Ani attending to one of her many duties. I am not ready to face her questions about the outside world. How can I deny her the truth which she has already guessed at? Especially now, when she could use it the most.

Our hut is exactly the same as always, and I am fundamentally different. I don't want the clean dress hanging from the hook or the cracker sitting in the cloth. Standing in the middle of my room, my eyes closed, counting the rain drops, I want to break free from this nightmare. It is too damp for me to dry, and I pray for sickness. An escape from the decisions I have already made. When my legs grow too weak to stand, I lay back in my hammock, and slip into sleep once more.

It is night again when I awake from a dream which leaves me trembling. My shaking soon turns to shivering as the night grows cooler around me. I try and curl into myself, pulling my dress around my legs. Ani's even snores fill the darkness. She has replaced the mosquito nets around us. I don't know how long I'll be able to avoid her, when we occupy the same space. A mosquito flies lazily around my net, before getting caught in its threads. It thrashes about, ensnaring itself even more, until it finally submits, and just the occasional jerk occurs. When it has been still so long I think it must be dead, I sit up and shake the net to release it. It is not dead, and it flies back through the window, into the night.

The rain has started again. I contemplate hiding in the same bushes as yesterday. The sun will be up soon. If I try to pretend sleep Ani might waken me anyway, to make sure I'm alright. I drink some water, and the pain twisting through my stomach surprises me. I thought I had become immune to the hunger. I sneak back out again and see my path from yesterday has already been erased. The broken branches grown over, I find a different tree to conceal myself in and decide to climb. I barely make it above shoulder height before I am winded. The tree trunk slippery and covered in stickiness. I am soaking wet already, and so I sit on a thick vine, uncomfortable and shivering. More shapes appear around me as the sun rises, and I decide I will not be able to stay out as long today. My nose dripping down my face, there is nothing dry to wipe it with. I am so weak with hunger I catch myself on the edge of unconsciousness twice, narrowly missing tumbling to the forest floor. When I hear the horn sound I am grateful, Ani will be leaving our hut soon and I can hide in there. I count my breaths to steady my nerves and keep myself awake. Can anyone human be truly comfortable in these trees? I have lived here my whole life, and the jungle still frightens me with its energy. Its aggression. I pick at an orchid near me, in half bloom and lovely.

A monkey suddenly swings within inches and startles me. My fingers wrap around the vine, but it is too slick to hold on to. I topple out of the tree, my dress catching on a limb, ripping the cloth. I land in a thick fern, a sharp pain scratched down the length of my arm as I shake myself loose. Wincing, I touch it gingerly. My fingers are covered in warm red wetness. I have never been good with blood, my vision blurring. I limp back through the jungle and towards our hut. I make it to the latrine where I can pause to breathe. Pulling air though my mouth in large gulps. I look down and notice a pool of blood forming around my feet. My leg is also scratched, the pain of my arm concealing this wound. A trail of bloody footprints follows me from the jungle. Blackness starts to lick at the edges of my eyesight, and I take a few more steps forward. I make it through the back door of our hut before falling to my knees on the floor. I collapse on my stomach, vaguely aware Ani is still here, before I am completely gone.

I wake up confused. Voices whispering. I blink my eyes rapidly, trying to adjust to the light. I am laying on the floor, a hammock slung above me. My fingers search the ground and there is fabric underneath me. My head pounds, and there is a sharp pain running up the side of my leg. My arm is encased in cloth and tender. I remember falling, stumbling back here. I remember I do not want to see Ani, but that she is here somewhere. I hear her speaking.

"It must have been schrecklich, if she is hiding from me. The outside world must be worse than we thought," she says.

Derrik is here, his voice answering her. "I'm telling you the war is over, it has to be. No supplies for four months now. Something is going on and they're not telling us. I bet she has answers."

"Why would she come back Derrik? Honestly. Don't you bother her when she wakes up either. She's clearly been through enough. I already have to report to her Uncle Dale as soon as she's conscious. He was here this afternoon looking for her."

I snap my eyes closed and groan inwardly. What could he possibly want from me now? Haven't I already given them everything?

"Well I don't care what you say Ani, something is going on here and I intend to find out what!" Derrik pounds a fist against a wall, and the hammock above me shakes slightly.

"Don't you think if the war was over, they'd be celebrating!" Ani is trying to keep quiet but her voice is annoyed, angry at him. "Instead they're as nervous as we are!"

"Maybe because the war is over and they didn't win? Have you ever thought of the possibility they could lose? Or they have lost and we're all hidden here like scared children?"

"You've been spending too much time with Julianne's pet," she hisses at him, "Martin."

"I won't be scared anymore Ani," he responds, "I'm tired of living like a slave, in fear and always cowering to their stupid superiority."

This is too close to the truth for me to lay here comfortably. I make a deep guttural sound of pain, which brings Ani running to my side. I hear Derrik stomp out.

She places some clothing behind my shoulders to prop me up, coaxing me to drink her hot tea and broth. While I'm sipping she explains everything that has happened since I've been out. It has been two days since I fell out of the tree. Four since I last spoke with her. The supplies from our Patron have completely run out and the Pure are finally beginning to take notice. Life hasn't been as comfortable for them and they're taking more interest in the amount of food our gardens produce, how much meat is being brought in from the jungle, the fish that have been caught. There hasn't been much left during meal times for the Untouchables to eat, and they have been venturing further into the jungle to find food. Drills have been cancelled twice now, unstructured time the Untouchables have taken full advantage of. Stripping the trees of their mangos and bananas, Untouchables have always known how to find food in the jungle.

"The Pure have also been in the jungle." Ani whispers to me, replacing the bandage on my leg. "They've been trying to learn to hunt." Their pampered lifestyle has left them ill prepared for the dangers there. Military training and strength exercises are nothing against the silent killers in the trees. The insects, the snake bites, the poisonous frogs. Scratches and bruises from the vines and trees. Some have not returned. Marie and Ani have had their hands full, because even those who have made it back, have not all survived their injuries. I feel a deep sense of shame for taking her away from her duties when my own injuries are self inflicted. Wallowing in my own pity, instead of doing something to help the colony.

When I have drained the last of the broth, I venture to use my voice and say two words to her. "I'm sorry." The tears leaking out of my eyes and running down my cheeks.

"I'm so very, very sorry." She wraps her arms around me and tries to shush me, but I can't be comforted. I can't tell her why I'm sorry, or for what, and so I sit in her arms and whisper the words over and over, until she's crying too. "I'm sorry."

Chapter Sixteen

I sleep through until the next morning, a visitor's voice pulling me from unconsciousness. I smile involuntarily, it's Henrik. He sounds angry and immediately the smile disappears. I turn to find his face through my netting. He is glaring at Ani, who is awake and packing her medical supplies. She mumbles a quick apology, to no one in particular, before scurrying out the door. Henrik rubs his hands together before sitting in my chair. Looking straight at me. This triggers a twinge of annoyance. How easily the Pure walk into our spaces and take charge. Even my Henrik. This is Ani's home, and my home too. He acts as if it were his. I use the hammock to pull myself into a sitting position, move the net aside so I can see him. He doesn't notice my expression.

"Your father is angry with you," he says. "Infuriated."

I roll my eyes and stand up, testing my legs. "Why am I not surprised?" I ask him.

"It's not a joke, Marta," he says. "I explained the expectations of returning to the colony. He's not happy with what's going on. The Pure are fighting for food, the last of the medications. They've turned on Jul, and now she can't even leave her hut without a guard."

"Why should I care, Henrik?" My nostrils flare at him.

"Jacob has been organizing a group to raid the Untouchable barracks," he says gently. "A lot of the anger is focused on them. Why aren't they starving? Why do they still have medicines to keep the bugs away? I said you would have to befriend him, make him an ally. Instead you've been in hiding for days."

His remark about Jacob burns me. He wouldn't say these things if he knew who Jacob was.

"I won't befriend him, impossible now," I say firmly.

Henrik's eyes soften when he looks at me. "You know about him," he states.

I am dumbfounded. "*You* know about him."

Henrik nods guiltily. "For a while now. There's nothing we can do about it- the Führer has spoken to him. Some of the guards have carefully complained about it. But he's Royalty Marta." He looks out my window, "and he is trying to procreate. Just in a different way."

"Trying to Procreate?" I don't even try to keep my voice down. "Innocent girls Henrik! Do you understand? Innocent girls who are being abused for no reason! That's not trying to procreate!" I am shaking with fury at him, at the Führer, and most of all at Jacob. Henrik puts his hands out in a gesture of defeat.

"Marta, what am I supposed to do? He can't be punished, it's impossible. I'm trying to make the best of it."

I shake my head in disbelief. He reaches for me and I shudder in revulsion. "You are not the man I thought you were," I tell him, backing away from his touch.

His face hardens. "Even if you can't befriend Jacob, you'll have to make an alliance with him. For the good of the whole colony."

I stare at him. "How are the problems of the Pure my concern? I can't control that there is no mail! No supplies! Do you want me to steal food from the Untouchables? Steal medicines they've carefully rationed, because you're own Princess hasn't been as careful? You want me to make nice with Jacob so he can abuse my friends? I won't do that!" I march over and lean into him, practically yell in his face. "I'll keep pretending there's a war. I'll keep pretending we're some sort of inferior race. But I won't pretend this."

I turn on my heel and stomp over to my sideboard. My hands are shaking and I grip the shelf to steady myself. Try not to cry with fury.

"Then there will be a war, Marta," he says quietly. He stands up and walks to my door. "A war that would be impossible for *your friends* to win."

He says over his shoulder as he steps down, loudly. "We're meeting this afternoon, at your uncle's. You'll need to be there."

I lay in my hammock through lunch. Count the straws on my roof again. Ani stopped in after Henrik left, and I explained about the meeting with the Führer. I don't know if he's ever visited my uncle's hut. He's certainly never asked to meet with me before. I expected Ani to pester me with questions, but she was quiet, told me she'd be back later. I should have left already, but I don't have the strength to go. I wonder what will happen if I don't show up. Ani appears at my side suddenly, and it's her appearance which finally rouses me. She's pulling at my good arm.

"Get up, get up! They'll be waiting for you Marta! You have to get going!"

I know no one will be waiting for me. The Führer will definitely be late, expecting the rest of us to wait on him. It would be a sign of too much respect for the rest of us, if he were to be on time to his own meeting. We are always waiting on him. I close my eyes, let him wait on me for once.

Ani won't let me feign sleep though, she continues pulling on me, until I'm forced to stand. "C'mon, you're already in so much trouble." She snatches my sandals from the corner, hooks them around her arm. She pushes me out the door, and continues pushing me across the bridge, into the jungle. I try stopping a few times but the firmer I plant my bare feet, the more she pulls on my arm, until I am being half dragged through the jungle. Eventually I break into a run alongside her, turning it into a race. We are both laughing when we hit the beach line. I collapse on a rock panting, and she hands me my shoes.

"I'll wait here," she says. I stand up and waver in front of her. My legs are tired from the run and I'm not ready to face this. She gives me a shove toward the sand. Because I know it is dangerous for her to go any farther, and because I know she will, I continue forward. Stumbling across the rocks. The river has risen dramatically since I was here last, almost reaching the ladder of my uncle's hut. The canoe is already tethered, so he can leave at will. I grip the first rung and take a deep breath. There is a thundering yell above me as I start climbing. Ani was right, the Führer has been left waiting.

"Where is she?!" I hear him shout.

No one answers the Führer, afraid of his wrath I'm sure. My head peeks over the side, his back to me, his finger in my Uncle Dale's face. I've never realized how small a man he is, since I've never had the opportunity to stand near enough to him. If not for his substantial size, he wouldn't be a physical threat at all. I have spent my entire life afraid of this man. That mantle of fear drops now. I step forward. "I'm here."

He turns, his eyes trained on me, irate. His face a deep red. "Why are you late?" he says it quietly and I recognize the dangerous note in his tone.

"I took a nap. Overslept," I say, shrugging my shoulders. I begin to make my way to an empty chair when he grabs for me. I have anticipated the attack, and swing my body away from him. I pivot on my foot and brace myself to strike back if necessary. He is put off balance, tripping over his robe and leaning heavily against the wall. The Führer rights himself and turns again, eyes alight. I am in a fight position.

"You will not touch me." I say forcefully. "Unless you want the entire Untouchable camp to know what is going on." I smirk when I realize something else, "and you can not kill me. Unless you want a martyr. So it looks like you'll need to sit down, and say whatever it is you dragged me out here to say."

We stare at each other, until Jacob jumps up from a corner. "Let me kill her," he whispers loudly. "Let me do it."

A rage like I have never known sweeps over me and I have to clench my fingers together. I could kill them both now. I know I could, Jacob has never taken his training seriously, and the Führer is slow and awkward. Would my Uncle Dale or Henrik intervene? My eyes dart back and forth between them before settling on Jacob. My disgust with him replaces my anger. My features must make this obvious because a slow smile spreads across his face. He realizes I must know about Ani, and mouths, "you're next."

I control myself. I don't know how I do, because I am shaking so badly. A phrase from one of the videos I watched in Manacapuru comes back to me, and I have a sudden mad desire to laugh. "Bring it," I threaten. "Bring it on."

I take one step toward them before my Uncle Dale jumps between us.

"Sit," he barks at me. "Sit," he commands my father. I've never seen the Führer take an order, but he sits heavily in his old throne chair. I sit across from him, and Jacob takes his position back in the corner.

Now that we're sitting my uncle doesn't seem to know where to begin. He looks to the Führer.

"John, you decided to let her know the secrets. You decided you needed an ally in the Untouchable encampment. Now that she knows, you can't expect to control her. You forget about the truth." The Führer is silent as my Uncle Dale turns to me, "Marta, you decided to return. You decided to ally with them, to keep your friends safe. You knew what that entailed."

He looks between the two of us.

"I did," I speak up, "before I knew about Jacob. No one bothered to tell me those truths." I glare at Jacob in the corner, who smiles at me.

"What's happened now?" The Führer turns to look at Jacob, angry. The smile disappears from his face under his fathers glare, but it is Henrik who speaks first.

"Marta found out he abused her friend," Henrik pauses, "an Untouchable."

I have dropped the grenade, Henrik ignited it, and the Führer explodes in anger. There is a wooden walking staff near his seat and he grabs it, beating Jacob around the head and shoulders. Yelling indistinguishable words at him. Never about the abuse, never about the girls, but about pride and honor. Keeping the blood line Pure and free of contamination. The Führer tires quickly, the swings of his arm missing their mark. Jacob's lip is left bleeding, yellow and green markings brandished across his face.

"Do I need to get you a whore?" the Führer taunts, "will she keep you in line?" He asks, before straightening his clothing, brushing what hairs are left, back. He sits heavily in his chair. "You may be my son," he says, "but I can still arrange your disappearance from this colony."

"It won't happen again," Jacob whispers from the corner. I try not to look at him.

The Führer begins speaking lowly to Henrik. Now that it has quieted somewhat I hear a voice echoing outside.

"Does anyone else hear her?" I ask them. Henrik shoots me a look. I'm interrupting the Führer, but my father hasn't noticed my rudeness, or has chosen to overlook it. He keeps talking quietly.

My uncle stares at me quizzically.

The voice is louder. I'm sure someone is crying for help. I cock my head to the side, but it isn't coming from behind us- where I left Ani. It sounds as if it is in front of the hut, on the water. The yell is louder and I make out the single word. "Help!"

I stand up suddenly. The Führer can't help but notice my action and is instantly angry at me.

"What are you doing? Sit down immediately!" he commands me.

I ignore him and walk to the hut opening. "A boat," I say, absently.

Everyone goes silent behind me. "A boat!" I yell this time and point.

"Yes," my Uncle Dale says. "There's fishing boats along the river occasionally, but they never dock here."

"Not on the river," I assert. A blonde head is jumping over the side of an aluminum boat. A girl is with him, she is screaming. Two words. "Help, Sergio."

"They need help," I say. I wonder at my calmness. There has been no reaction behind me.

"What do you mean they need help?" My uncle says, finally by my side. He is looking down my arm to where I am pointing.

"My goodness," he responds. "There is a boat." We watch as a dark head runs across the beach to join them. *Ani*, I think. It's Ani. This puts me in motion. Climbing down the ladder frantically. My legs can't move as fast as my mind is willing them too. The others are pushing my Uncle Dale aside above me. He forces his way between them, climbing down after me. I am running across the beach toward the

174

boat. I hear his steps in synch with my own, a few feet behind me. Another high pitched scream for help. Something has clearly gone wrong in that boat.

The blonde man is gesturing dramatically as Ani shouts instructions. She is in medical mode, searching through the knapsack at her hip. She pulls herself up and over the side of the boat.

I am close enough to recognize Matt, from Manacapuru. He jumps easily in behind her, and she throws a bundle in his arms. Fabric. He begins shredding it into long strips, blood dripping down the side of his face. My attention focuses on the screaming girl, and I notice another blonde woman, older. She has her arms locked around the girls waist, keeping her away from Ani. The girl is in hysterics, tears running freely down both their faces.

My Uncle Dale has passed me, he reaches the boat first. Easily swinging his legs up, and catapulting inside. I arrive next, but there is no room in the boat for me. There is an Untouchable man lying on the floor. An arrow protruding from his chest.

He is obviously dead.

Chapter Seventeen

Ani is leaning into the chest of the dead man, her fingers on his neck. She briefly closes her eyes before speaking to my Uncle Dale, "there's nothing we can do." Tears continue to slide down the older woman's face. The younger woman is already curled into a ball on the floor of the boat, rocking back and forth. I want to reach in and comfort her, but her eyes scare me. Pupils overlarge and twitching.

"It must be from one of the tribal Untouchables. They haven't been seen around here in decades though," Ani remarks, pulling at the arrow, breaking it off at the shaft. "How did it happen?" she asks, directing her quesiton toward Matt. Blood is dripping from his chin and on to his shoulder.

"It was this morning, out of the blue. There was no warning at all. An arrow lodged in Sergio's gut before I could even react. I thought we were dead, but there was nothing else. Not even a rustling from the trees. We talked about turning around," he shoots a glance at the crying girl, who is blubbering while she continues to rock. "More than once." The older woman leans down and begins trying to console her. "I knew we were close though, and I knew we could get help here."

He looks between Ani and my Uncle Dale. It's obvious he doesn't know what else to say in front of her, and my uncle saves him. "Why don't we leave," he glances down at the body, "Sergio? Here for a minute. Get these woman up to my hut, where we can talk." He looks over to me, nods towards Ani.

She has finished looking over the body, and is now cleaning Matt's head wound. "It looks worse than it is," he tells her. He gestures at the crying girl, and we understand. His injuries were caused by her. He moves Ani's hand away. "But thank you."

She blushes, flicking her hair over her shoulder, before turning from him and jumping out of the boat next to me.

I take her arm and direct her a few steps away. The girl on the boat begins a fresh round of screams when Matt begins talking to her. The woman is her mother. She is refusing to leave the body. Words like "husband, nothing we can do, resting" drifting in the air. Comprehension is dawning on Ani's face. I have to get her away from here.

"Ani, Jacob is here," I say, and I know it's cruel, but it focuses her attention immediately on me.

"Where?" she asks.

"My Uncle Dale's hut," I tell her. "Please go back to the Colony. I promise I'll tell you everything when I get there."

She nods her head and turns to leave.

"Ani, one more thing." When she looks back at me, for the first time I realize the difference between us. There is so much trust in her glance that I choke on the next words. "Please don't say anything about this to the others."

Nodding again, she does a quick stretch, before running for the jungle. I watch her disappear until I hear Henrik's voice. "What's going on?" he asks me. I notice the Führer and Jacob haven't condescended to join us. Their curiosity not outweighing their pride.

"I know as much as you do," I say, "but my Uncle Dale wants everyone to go back to the hut."

"The Führer wants that as well," he responds. I want to make a cutting remark, but Henrik has already turned away from me. Another scream has ripped through the air and distracted him. He focuses on my uncle, who is standing with Matt and talking furiously. The woman has wrapped herself around the body of her husband. Henrik joins the conversation with my uncle, and makes a motion for me to join them. I raise an eyebrow at him. I don't feel like listening to them, and their plans. Instead I walk to the boat and climb in. The woman's screams have turned into low choking sobs. Her mother has pulled her from the body and into a hug.

I don't know what to say, and so I stand still, until the moment becomes unbearable. My question welling up until it can't be held in.

"Was this her husband?" I ask.

The mother's eyes are red from crying, but I see they are a bright blue. Her hair is short and blonde, graying at the edges. No one in the colony cuts their hair this short, but it suits her. She has a pokey sort of face, and it gives the illusion of roundness. She is wearing a pair of man's pants, and a man's shirt. A beautiful ring on her finger, sparkling. I'm concentrating on her jewelry when she speaks.

"Yes," she states. "This was her husband, Sergio. I'm Sylvia, and this is Lara." She hugs the crying girl tighter. "I would think you are probably Marta."

I'm taken aback and open my mouth to say something when noises cut through the air. A tune, like music.

Lara pushes away from her mother, her expression disbelieving. "My phone!" she cries. She pulls up a bag next to her and starts digging through it, handing the contents to Sylvia.

"You couldn't possibly have reception Lara?!" Sylvia says incredibly.

"I did in Manacapuru! I just didn't call anyone there." She holds up a small device and begins pulling it apart. Frantically pressing at the buttons, snot dripping from her nose. Sylvia grabs the bag and begins replacing the contents. She pulls another bag off the floor and hands them both over to me. I take them instinctively.

Lara is pressing something on the device, yelling nonsensical words at it. She holds it in the air and does a dance, moving it this way and that. Checking it over and over again. Poking it a few times. Her face crumples. "It's only my alarm," she says, a fresh wave of tears overflowing from her eyes. Shoving the device in her pants, her hands drop to her side and she collapses on the floor. Transfixed by her husband, she reaches for his hand and holds it to her face. The tears continuing to fall. Sylvia squeezes her shoulders, massaging them with her hands.

"I thought there might be a way to get help," Lara says. "My phone." She shakes her head, "I thought there was still a chance to get him out of here. I just can't leave him here Mom."

"We have to go," she responds. "The faster we can do our business here, the faster we can get Sergio back to Manacapuru, and home."

Lara looks up at her mother, her forehead scrunched together in pain. "I can't believe he's gone," she says. "I won't believe this is real."

"We have each other Lara, you'll be okay. I know it's hard, the ache will never disappear entirely, but some day, you'll be okay. I promise," Sylvia says.

"Oh Mom, it's like Dad all over again. Then it's so much worse, because Sergio was mine. I think the pain can get better, but that knowledge makes it hurt even more." They hug each other again. Lara's body shuddering. Sylvia turns her face to me expectedly.

My mouth has been hanging open and I suddenly feel intrusive. Such a private moment shared in front of me.

"Where do we go now?" Sylvia asks me.

I point in the direction of my Uncle Dale's hut, and Sylvia helps Lara clamber over the side of the boat. She doesn't want to leave her husband and Sylvia whispers frantically to her, reassuring her we'll stay within sight of the boat. They both take their bags from me, and we join Henrik to tromp across the sand.

Lara leans heavily against her mother and they fall behind, whispering quietly. My Uncle Dale and Henrik race ahead of us, arguing. Matt is left somewhere in the middle of the two groups, and naturally falls into step with me.

"Hey Marta," he says shyly.

"Hey Matt," I echo him, although I don't know what *Hey* means. Obviously some sort of greeting. I have so many questions for him, but my mind is blank. Henrik and my uncle have reached the hut and are calling out to the Führer and Jacob. There is not enough room inside for all of us, so they will have to join us on the beach. I watch the Führer's large backside protrude from the doorway. He looks comical trying to climb down a ladder he can't see, because of his enormous stomach. Jacob appears next and is much faster. He accidentally steps on one of the Führer's hands. It produces a yelp of pain, the Führer slapping at Jacob's foot with his free hand. Jacob bounds back up and the Führer releases the ladder with his fingers. He's obviously forgotten he's not holding on to anything, and his arms circle the air for a minute before he crashes down heavily on his backside.

"Oh my goodness!" A shout from behind me, Sylvia suddenly rushing past. The rest of us don't move. Jacob is back in the hut, probably hiding. Henrik and my uncle avert their gaze, pretend not to have witnessed the spectacle. I follow their lead and find myself staring straight into Matt's deep blue eyes. They dance in merriment, but thankfully he hasn't laughed out loud.

"Before we get there," he says. "I want to tell you something, away from everyone else." Lara has slouched past us, joining her mother in helping the Führer to his feet. I know he is annoyed with them both, but is trying not to show it. Waving them off of him.

"What is it?" I ask Matt.

"Your mother," he says. "I know your mother's name is. . ."

Another shout from Henrik, interrupting us. I smile because he remembered. Did he find information for me? He returns my smile, and begins to finish his sentence, when Henrik calls my name. He looks upset at us both. "I'm coming," I yell to him.

"Elisabeth," I whisper to Matt, "my mother's name was Elisabeth."

Henrik's voice again.   "Any time now," he yells impatiently.

I shrug apologetically at Matt, "later," I mouth before halfheartedly jogging toward my Uncle Dale and Henrik.

We gather in a loose circle. Jacob has appeared, and is sitting as far away from his father and me as he possibly can. Lara is sitting beside her mother on a rock, her attention still on the boat, a frown etched into her face. Henrik and my uncle prefer to stand on either side of the Führer, who is sitting on a makeshift bench. I lounge next to a tree, kick my feet in front of me.

Unexpectedly Sylvia stands and speaks first, not aware of procedure here.

"You're wondering what we're doing here, and I'd like to begin our story by introducing ourselves." She gestures to herself and to Lara, "I'm Sylvia and this is my daughter Lara. Her husband Sergio was killed by some natives on our boat ride over here. We were warned by Elisabeth and her son Matt," she gestures to Matt, "that this may happen. We have some important information to give you. We don't want to disturb your colony here, but we do have some questions we would like answered."

I'm the only one watching Lara while Sylvia gives her speech, her head bowed low, her face covered by her hands. She glances up briefly at her mom to roll her eyes, before looking back down at the ground. I wonder what it means, what her mother said that annoys her so much.

"The first thing you should know," the Führer says, "is no one speaks without permission from me."

Sylvia looks abashed and makes a motion to sit back down, when Lara jumps to her feet.

"I don't need permission to speak," Lara says angrily. Sylvia tries to shush her. "No Mom, this isn't how this is going to be. Sergio dead." She waves her hand in the air, tears leaking down her face again. "I'm not going to be shushed and bossed by this old white guy." She points her finger at him. "I don't care if it is rude, you don't talk to my Mom that way. She was trying to be polite, something you seem to know very little about." She places a hand on her stomach, and breathes in deeply.

The Führer's face turns an ugly shade of purple. "No one talks to me that way!" He yells. Standing up he makes a familiar motion, to order his guards to strike, before realizing there are no guards here. Henrik doesn't move, and his face betrays him. He is trying to figure out how much weight he has against these two woman. He is remembering the rules are different outside our world.

The Führer takes a few steps in the direction of the two women, pointing his finger back at them. "If you expect any help from us," he says, "any information, you will obey our rules here!" He crinkles his nose as if smelling something foul. "The first rule is, no one speaks without permission!"

He puffs his chest out, pulling himself up to his full height, breathing heavily.

Sylvia has taken a protective step in front of Lara who holds up both her hands tauntingly, "Ohhh, you're so scary. Is this guy for real?" She asks us, pointing at the Führer, appealing to us. "This is some kid of joke right? This guy is your leader? Come on Mom, let's go, this is ridiculous." She tries pulling on her mom's hand, but Sylvia gives her a hard look.

"Lara! Sit down." Sylvia whispers loudly, her eyes boring into her daughter, before turning back to the Führer. "I'm sorry for my daughter's behavior, like I said, her husband was killed. She's not really herself."

The Führer nods in her direction. "I understand," he says, "but if we're going to have any type of discussion, you will need to get her under control."

A loud "humph," ushers from Lara's mouth, and Sylvia turns again to look at her. Wanting her to be quiet.

"Führer, right?" Matt asks. The Führer nods his head. "Alright, we're wasting time. We have some information about the mail, why it has stopped."

"Why didn't you give us the information when we were in town? Or waited until we came next month?" Henrik asks. "Then this," he searches for a word, "tragedy, might not have occurred." I glance at Jacob who is curling his nose up. I know he doesn't see an Untouchables death as much of a tragedy.

"We didn't have the luxury of time," Sylvia says, eyes still on Lara. "The Patrons might be here soon."

It's as if lightning has struck straight through the Führer and my Uncle Dale. They look through each other and I am forced to acknowledge them as siblings, brothers. They are of the same mind when my uncle turns to Sylvia, inching closer to her. He touches her arm gently. "We need to talk to you," he says. "Privately." He glances around at the group.

I stand up and walk to the center of the grouping, my back straight and strong. Their eyes watch my movements, and I am careful to keep my hands gripped at my sides. I'm tired of this. "No more secrets," I tell them. It's the second time I've issued a command today, and it's the first one I believe is right. "We all have something worth losing here. I won't be left out of this anymore." I stomp my foot angrily. Lara steps in front of her mother, taking my hand. We are such opposites. She is pale everywhere, even her eyes a light gray blue, so beautiful. "No more secrets," she says, squeezing my hand, a tear rolling down her face.

There is no command, but everyone returns to their seat, an unspoken cue.

"Who wants to start?" I ask, looking from person to person. They each avert their eyes, no one willing to spill their secrets first. My gaze finally lands on Matt, who half smiles at me. I give him a puzzled look and he stands up, pointing at himself.

"Me first?" he asks redundantly. "I seem to know the most about what's going on anyway, and I already have some information I've been wanting to tell Marta." Henrik moves to shush him, but Matt holds up an arm. "Stop," he says, looking at me. "Marta, I'm your brother. We share the same father, and our mothers are sisters. My mother died and Elisabeth raised me as her own son. She's alive Marta, alive and missing you. You never had a chance to meet our father Eli. They would have been here to tell you themselves, if they weren't so afraid of. . ." He glances at the Führer and doesn't finish the sentence.

"I think I knew," I tell him. "I mean, not about my mother of course, but that we were siblings. That we were somehow related." I shoot him a smile, knowing we will talk later.

"Who cares?" Jacob yells from the corner. The bruises are beginning to darken around his face. "I'm not going to sit here and listen to old news about Marta and our mother. What about the Patrons?"

"I was getting to them," Matt says. He glances at Sylvia, before turning back to the rest of us. "Your Patron Marion, is dead. She died a little over a week ago. We're expecting visitors soon and they'll probably want to visit the colony. It's procedural, so the new Patron gets to know the needs of her charges, reassure the colony of the ongoing war, and whatever else."

"I could guess as much," says my Uncle Dale. "But what it doesn't explain is the appearance of these two woman," he gestures to Sylvia and Lara. "And their friend."

Lara jumps up again. "He wasn't a friend you pompous. . ."

Sylvia manages to get a hold of her before Lara gets too far, whispering quietly in her ear. Lara has begun crying again. Her body slackens at her mother's words, and she places her fist in her mouth.

"I was trying to be delicate," my Uncle Dale says, his forehead furrowed. "We don't inter-marry here."

Lara looks out to the boat, away from the rest of us. Lost in her own world, still gnawing on her hand.

"I believe you may have information about my father, John," Sylvia says. He was Marion's nephew and I know nothing about him."

My Uncle Dale and the Führer turn to each other and seem to be having a conversation with their eyes. A cloud passes overhead and obscures us in darkness for a few minutes. A sign it will be raining again soon.

"It will be raining again soon," Matt repeats my thoughts aloud. A glance at the sky, a nod to my uncle, and the Führer rises to his feet.

"We'll have to talk more about this later. I need to return to the colony. Matt, you are welcome to join us. You will share quarters with Henrik, where you will pretend to be a visitor from another colony. Henrik will be with you and I expect him to be your mouthpiece. You are not to answer any question without his approval." He turns to Sylvia, "We would like the three of you to leave as soon as possible." He points to my uncle, "Dale will take care of you and your daughter. He will help you wrap the body, and prepare the boat. He will also answer any questions you might have. He has food and water here, so there will be no need to go into the village." The threat in his voice implied, Sylvia bobs her head briefly at him.

"Marta." I have never heard him say my name before. "Marta, I am not your father, but I am still the Führer. Henrik has explained to you the consequences of your actions. I expect you to work things out with my son. Now." He sends a withering look in Jacob's direction, before snapping his fingers at Henrik.

They begin walking toward the jungle path, Matt fast on their heels.

They are out view instantly, my uncle approaching Lara and her mother, "we'll need to hurry before it rains. I'll have to find accommodations for you in one of my spare rooms." He rushes toward the boat before either of them can say a word. Sylvia pulls Lara to her feet and they follow him down the beach silently.

Jacob and I sit, glaring at each other. I drop my eyes first and begin unraveling a string from my dress. An exhaustion has overtaken me, my bandaged arm is aching. I think about the walk back to my hut. It will be raining and I'll have to run. I wrap the string tightly around my index finger, around and around, tighter and tighter. The tip of my finger is turning blue when I pull the end. It unravels quickly, my finger back to its normal color immediately. Better get this over with.

"I think we both know, an alliance will never be made between us," Jacob speaks first.

Well that's a relief. At least we don't have to play games with each other.

"And the Untouchables will never win a war between us."

Maybe not.

"So I don't see that there is anything for us to talk about."

Honestly? Nothing?

He stands, and takes a menacing step towards me. When I don't react he gives me a wink. "Don't worry about your friend," he says. "I never go back for seconds."

He begins running before I can even get to my feet, furious. So angry I can't control the tears that fill my eyes. So angry I think the trees are moving, until I realize that I am shaking involuntarily. I feel a hand on my shoulder and my arm flies up to protect myself, but I am blocked by her other arm. Sylvia is here, by my side. She pulls me into a hug and I sink into her. Let the tears flow down my nose, soaking her shirt. She holds me tighter and I feel her chin rest on the top of my head, her lips brushing my hair.

"It's okay," she whispers, rubbing my back.

I take a deep breath and for the first time today, I feel like it might be.

I pull myself together and she steps back to examine me. Her eyes don't seem to miss a detail, and I wonder briefly if she's going to be reporting back to Elisabeth. My mother. Realization sets in, she has spoken to my mother.

"What's she like?" I whisper.

"She misses you," she says. "I think she would do almost anything to get you back." Sylvia averts her eyes, looking slightly uncomfortable. "Unfortunately, she thinks duty to the colony is more important than being a mother to you." She examines the growing clouds above us, thunder rumbling near.

"We have that in common," I tell her. She looks surprised by this statement, and searches my face. Her eyes puzzled. *Could this be the truth?* I read it in her gaze as if she has spoken it aloud.

"It's the truth," I say. "I believe the Colony is better the way that it is. I don't think we would make it out there. In the real world. I think it would destroy us, and we can't survive without the funding."

She places a hand on her forehead, shielding her eyes to glance back at where my Uncle Dale and Lara are standing by the boat.

"Do you think she'll be. . ." I try and form a question, but I don't know what word to use. Will she be fine, or healthy, or adequate? They all seem like inadequate expressions. Sylvia's own eyes watery and grim.

She shakes her head, her short hair flying loose from the bandanna she has wrapped there. "I'm more afraid of when she's back home, when she realizes what's gone, and what's left to live for. I'm more afraid for her future." She pauses to turn back to me. "Until then, well, she'll stay busy. Here, she has the adrenaline of the thing to keep her going. We have lots of work to do, regardless of what Dale, John, and," her eyes narrow, "Marta, may think."

I feel my mouth drop open, and my eyes flick to the ground, searching for a response.

"Marta, we have so much to share with you, and I don't think there will be nearly enough time."

A raindrop touches my cheek, as if to reinforce her statement. I examine her face, a hundred tiny wrinkles around her eyes and mouth. The wisdom reflected back to me in her blue eyes.

"We'll be in the colony tomorrow. We'll try and talk then," she says, before walking away from me and back to the boat.

I stay frozen in my spot, before another raindrop lands squarely on my nose. I stagger toward the trees, concentrating on her statement instead of my feet. Coming to the colony tomorrow? When the Führer so expressly forbid it? These women are so strange, doing whatever they want, saying whatever they please. No thought about the repercussions.

Is this what freedom is? I trip on one of the rocks, my actions without purpose. They won't be there tomorrow, my Uncle Dale will see to it. If they were to disobey a direct order from the Führer, especially in front of the whole colony. I shiver thinking about it, my body absorbing the rapidly cooling air. I jump back to my feet and focus. The trees quiver, the rain smacking against the canopy. I climb over one of the thick vines, heavy with moss, before beginning my run down the clear cut path. If that's freedom, then I don't want it.

Chapter Eighteen

The howling begins and even though I can't see the sun on the jungle floor, I know it is disappearing. I pick up my pace, sprinting through the trees, the monkey's chorus keeping me company, telling me the time. When they stop it will be nightfall, in all likelihood raining, and I will be lost without a path to follow. I hit the junction where I have to split off from the wooden pathway. The nicer path leads to the Pure encampment, and I have to follow a rough trail to the bridge. It is getting difficult to make out the broken branches, muddy footprints, and small strips of cloth which mark the way. The tinkling of a stream on my left alerts me that I'm almost home. I can see the bridge ahead of me, and I slow into a jog before coming to an abrupt halt. What am I going to tell Ani?

The lamp is on when I enter, it was too much to hope she would be asleep. She is brushing her hair with a comb, wetting the long strands in a bucket at her feet. She gives me a broad smile when I stomp in, shaking the mud from my toes.

"What are you doing?" I ask her, pulling off my sandals.

"Washing my hair," she says, and a beat later, "I want to look good for Matt."

I freeze. "Why?" I ask incredulously.

She rotates her body to face me, the end of a long strand of hair held up by her comb, dripping on the floor. "Didn't you see?" she asks, the excitement barely contained in her voice. "The girl was married to an Untouchable, Marta! *An Untouchable!*" Her face is filled with wonder. "I never truly believed Derrik could be right, about the war being over and everything. I would say those things to shock you, but Marta! He is right!" Her face glowing, before realizing I haven't confirmed her theories. I haven't said anything at all. Her mouth twitches, a seed of doubt planted.

"He is right. . . isn't he?" she asks.

I sit in my chair and lean over. My head in both hands.

"Ani," I say to the floorboards, "We can't tell anyone. Not a single person, Untouchable or Pure. Do you understand?" I peek through my fingers to watch her reaction.

Confusion crosses her face, replaced by hurt.

"But why Marta? Why can't we say anything? This is good news for us. Isn't it?"

Why does the truth have to hurt so much?

"Ani, I've been out there. The war isn't over, and the people outside of this jungle are scary. You saw what they did to her husband. That could be us Ani! If we left here- that could be us!" I am scaring her with my intensity, her eyes clouding over with tears. Her hair is dripping on the floor, a puddle forming at her feet.

"So the war isn't over?" she asks again.

I want to scream. She doesn't understand!

"Yes, THE war is over, but it doesn't mean there aren't others out there that wouldn't like to see us dead, see us massacred. We are safer here, you have to believe me." My voice cracks. "You have to trust me."

She wraps her hair expertly in a cloth before leaning over to pick up the bucket. The water has left lines of wet down her back, brightening the colors of the fabric. She heaves the bucket outside and I hear the water sloshing out, slapping the ground. She returns with it empty, hanging it from the roof. "I do believe you," she says, "I believe you think you know what's best for us." Her index finger is pointed at me, "I think you need to understand though, I'm going to have to think about what's best for me." Unconsciously she rubs at her belly, staring out the window. "Staying here might not be it."

I peer out the window with her, watch the birds take flight in the night, squawking to each other. "Ruf der Liebe," she says under her breath. *The call of love.*

I blink rapidly. "You have to stay here," I tell her anxiously, "you have no other choice."

She pushes away from the window, and pulls the shade closed forcefully. "That's where you're wrong Marta," she says, climbing into her hammock, "that's exactly what they have brought us. Choice."

I stare at her backside while numbly rinsing my feet. I blow out the lamp and lay down in my own hammock. My mind consumed by what Ani has said. Choice. I think about the choices I've made, and the choices I'll have to make, until eventually I harmonize the two and find sleep.

I reach for something in my dreams, something out of reach, something beyond. It is never clear what I'm straining to find, only that I need it. I urgently, desperately need it. I wake up confused and upset. The Untouchable who brings our cracker and clean laundry is usually a silent creature. There is a rustling near my head that is unfamiliar. An impatient shuffling of feet.

I turn over to see Derrik staring at me, inches from my face. I muffle a scream of shock, waking Ani with her own yelp.

What is he doing in our hut? The memories wash over me, the reason he might be here. Ani is faster than I am and has already jumped out of her hammock.

"So you've heard?" she asks him.

"It's true? There's a visitor from another colony here?" he asks intently.

"Where did you hear that from?" I ask him, bleary eyed and still a little befuddled. I'm trying to pull myself free of the netting that has wrapped itself around my feet in the night. I must have forgotten to zip it closed.

He won't answer me at first, doubt lining his forehead, distrust in his eyes. He shoots a glance at Ani who nods her head.

"Martin told me. He was with the Princess last night and returned with the news. Another Pure? Visiting? What does he want?" His questions fire at my brain in quick succession, and my head instantly aches again. I sit up and try to remember what I'm supposed to tell him, when there's a knock at our door. Another visitor? Knocking? Ani raises a single eyebrow at me, no one knocks on an Untouchable door, there is no privacy for us.

"Come in?" I say flummoxed, before realizing there is only one person who it could be.

"Surprise!" Matt says, as he bustles through the door. "Henrik told me where ya'll lived. I've seen these huts from the river but never got to tour one before. They're kind of cool. Like camping or something."

"Camping or something," I echo. My face has gone blank, devoid of expression. Derrik is staring at Matt, his mouth hanging wide open. Ani is frantically pulling her hair out of the cloth, smiling maniacally at him.

"I'm Matt," he says, reaching a hand out to Derrik. Derrik stares at it, hanging in front of him. He looks to me, he doesn't know what to do. We don't shake hands here, especially with a Pure. They're usually afraid of even brushing up against us. *Is this man fooling with him? Is this some sort of game?* His face begins turning a dark shade of purple, the anger slowly building beneath his surface. I realize I have to nip this in the bud. Now.

"Matt?" I ask, "Can I speak with you outside for a minute?"

He drops his hand, shrugging his shoulders. He glances sideways at Ani, whispering, "Hello," to her. She blushes before mouthing, "How are you doing?"

I pull at his arm before he can answer, making him follow me to the back enclosure. It begins raining heavily and we stand under the overhang, welcome the relief it always brings to the stifling humidity.

I look him straight in the eye, "What kind of game do you think you're playing?" I ask him. "Where is Henrik? Why aren't you with him? You heard the Führer."

"Oh! Is that it?" he says, laughing. "I don't think this is a game, Marta. Henrik was easy enough to ditch, not really that smart is he?"

I give him a heated look and he puts both hands in front of him.

"Whoa! I guess I touched on a sore spot, sorry. Just so you know though," he puts a hand on my shoulder, "we're taking this very seriously." He starts to laugh again.

We?

Voices drift out over the pounding rain from inside the hut. They are distant, as if my ears are blocking the sound. Protecting me from the coming danger. I turn slowly around and pull the shade from the window. Sylvia is sitting on my chair, laughing, wringing her hair out. Lara swinging in the hammock, a faraway expression on her face. She is covered in a canvas cloth, still gripping an umbrella. Ani is pouring them both cups of water.

No, I think. *No,no,no,no.*

The scene is playing out in front of me in slow motion. My eyes refusing to focus. Derrik leaving through the front door, excited. Matt joins them and Ani begins twirling her hair between her fingers. Smiling shyly at him. Sylvia plucks my album from the table, the one of our ancestors. The story of our beginnings, the three Princesses. She flicks through the pages, examining each photograph carefully. Stopping to ask Ani a question. Ani looks confused, she doesn't know the history as well as I do. Lara is pale behind the redness of her cheeks. Rocking back and forth. Occasionally moving her mouth, to interrupt or interject Matt's story.

I move back into the room, gripping the side of the doorway. My world is crashing down around me, and no one seems to notice.

Chapter Nineteen

Our hut becomes a meeting place, and there is not enough room to host all the people who try and flow in. I find myself asking over and over again, "Why isn't anyone at drill? Or breakfast? Who is doing the laundry, tending the gardens, doling out the medicines?" There is no breakfast cracker this morning, no one bringing us a clean dress, refilling our water gourds. Everyone ignores me and my questions. The crowd pushing against the walls of our hut, until I am finally physically and emotionally, pushed outside. I watch through the window, Matt the center of attention, talking excitedly. The disbelief on their faces, followed by amazement, and finally acceptance. I recognize Martin near Ani. She is standing as close as possible to Matt, soaking in every word. He is performing for her, and seeking her approval.

Martin's face is dispassionate, almost solemn. Julianne's pet. He glances up, meeting my gaze. I can't look away fast enough, embarrassed by his naked stare.

Remembering the last time I saw him.

I step away from the window and recognize Lara is here, sitting on a container under the eaves. She has a hand held out to the rain and is watching a monkey perform acrobats in the tree.

"It was getting a little crowded in there," she says, glancing back at me over her shoulder.

"A little," I say sarcastically. I move to sit next to her and notice her eyes, which are red and puffy. She's been crying. I'm uncomfortable this close to her, when she's so obviously in pain.

"Why did you have to do this?" I ask. "Why couldn't you have left everything alone?" I pick at the leather strap of my sandal. "I'm afraid of what will happen now."

She draws her hand back and wipes it on her pants. Pulling her knees into her chest.

"You can't allow fear to make your choices," she says. I hear her whisper something to herself.

"I'm sorry?" I ask, not quite hearing the last part.

She smiles sadly, before pulling the cloth around her neck up and rubbing at her eyes. "It's nothing, I was doing a mantra, an affirmation. It's something my Aunt Kathryn does once in a while. I find it helps me to remember myself, my purpose. It helps me stay positive even when it's the most difficult."

I continue to pick at my sandals, and notice her shoes for the first time.

"What are you wearing on your feet?" I ask.

"They're called hiking boots. They're killing me, you usually have to wear them in for a bit. I think my shoe size may have changed, or your sizes are funny here. My feet feel unusually fat."

It seems like a lot of material encased around her foot, and I touch the ropes which hold her shoe together. They remind me of the ones we use to cinch our food bags closed.

"You could pick up some sandals from one of the Untouchables who make them. Try asking Derrik."

"I will," she says. "Thanks." She continues looking into the trees, the monkey has disappeared and is replaced by a macaw. The red and blue wings vibrant against the green backdrop. "This place is so beautiful," she says smacking her arm, "if you can get past the bugs." I reach back and hand her a tube of ointment from one of our supply boxes, and show her how to smear it into her arms.

"This stuff smells awful," she says.

I laugh. "It's effective though, one of our Shaman's secrets. You could also wear longer sleeves- that helps as well. Most of us have been rubbing this stuff in for so long it's naturally become our smell. We don't have to bother with it as much anymore."

She wrinkles her nose, but spreads it in. "We have repellent but it doesn't seem to be doing anything."

"So what was your mantra?" I like the word, the way it rolls off my tongue. I say it out loud again, rolling my r's. "Lara's mantra."

Her eyes focus into the distance and a tear escapes down her cheek, "Sergio used to do that. Roll his r's to make me laugh. The way he said my name."

I bite my lip, and mumble, "I'm sorry Lara, I had no idea."

"Of course you didn't," she says. "It's okay." A small pitiful smile at me. "It's a quote. My mantra today. *I will not fail because I did not try.*"

She stares at me intently. "What would you do Marta?" she asks sincerely. Her gaze becomes probing, but I can't look away from her eyes. So focused. "A women named Eleanor Roosevelt once asked that. What would you attempt to do, if you knew you would not fail?"

I know what I would do. I would save Ani, I would save her baby. I would punish Jacob. I would allow Elise a fair fight, the chance to feel really powerful. I would get married to whomever I wanted. I would have babies and raise them in a place where they were equal. My list is so long it's several minutes before I can think logically again.

I shake the thoughts out of my head. *Ridiculous.* "I have to accept failure," I say. "The things I want, impossible dreams in the world we live in."

"Marta," she says seriously. "We never have to accept failure. Nothing is ever impossible. That's one of the greatest truths of the world we live in." She stands up groaning. "I'm sorry, I'm not feeling well all the sudden. I need to find my mom, but let me leave you with something else to think about," she stretches her arms above her head. "Maybe this can be your mantra for today."

She thinks for a few seconds, composing her thoughts. "Fear," she grins at me, "is nothing but silence speaking."

She pats me on the head distractedly. "It's a Lara original," she says, before wandering back into the fray of my hut.

I sit thinking for a long time. I list the things I have been afraid of for so long, I can't even remember them. The list has changed since returning from Manacapuru. The outside world becoming much more frightening. The colony becoming much less so. I'm not afraid of the Führer, but I'm afraid of the consequences of disobeying the Führer.

A rustling to my left alerts me to two people whispering cautiously. Derrik and Martin. I tuck my feet into my body, disguising myself behind the container Lara has vacated. I can only hear snatches of Derrik's side, his voice high pitched and wobbly. "Session tonight. Do you think we can? How many people will we need?" *What is that about?* Martin looks angry, he is gesturing wildly. I wonder what it would be like to have to spend so much time with my sister.

What am I thinking? I already know. They move away from my hut as another Untouchable man joins them.

I uncurl my body and stand up, peeking at the scene unfolding through my window.

The crowds have diminished slightly, Ani waving everyone out and ushering Lara back into my hammock. *Is she sick?* Peevish and pale she lays back into the hammock, swinging her legs up. I don't think Sylvia is too concerned, and she hands her a pill. Lara makes a face, her cheeks red and eyebrows drawn together. I recognize the expression. I conceal a laugh with my hand. Despite everything, I think I like Lara. The way she speaks her mind all the time, regardless of what the rest of us might think. Ani gives her a cup of water, and she takes a long drink. I feel a stab of pain at this simple gesture of friendship. Envious at how easily they have all fit into our world, how easily they have been accepted, even though they're Pure. Matt is still busy talking, a group of the younger children gathered around him now. I recognize some of them from my reading lessons. Elise spots me through the window and waves. I wiggle my fingers at her, but she's already turned back to Matt. My stomach clenches and I realize I've forgotten to eat. I tap on the window frame and motion to Ani. She looks over at me and I mouth, "I'll be back later." She nods in my direction but doesn't move from her position by Lara's side. I watch for another minute before turning away from them, heading out into the rain.

I wonder if my uncle is in the colony, or if he's hiding in his own hut. If I were him, I'd be hiding, and we're enough alike I think that must be where he is. I'm running in his direction when my stomach gives another growl. I decide to detour through the fruit trees, and follow the stream. There is no one here today, and I am confused before I remember the Untouchables do most of the labor. *Why wouldn't the Pure still try and harvest? Are they so afraid of getting their hands dirty?* I pull a mango from the tree and bite into it, the juice dribbling down my chin. I sigh in pleasure before running again, picking a path over the wet rocks, trying to find a shallow area to cross over.

I've never ventured this way before, and so I am surprised when I come across a well worn tree braced above the water. Its trunk is smooth, a natural bridge that's easy for me to cross. I'm carefully stepping from the tree trunk to a mossy rock when a voice in the shadows nearly upends me. I balance precariously for a moment on one foot, before thrusting my hips forward and landing on solid ground. I dive for a bush before anyone can see me.

Too late.

"Marta?" my uncle's voice. "We know you're there."

I stand up, wiping the grass and mud from my hands on my dress. My face burns with embarrassment, I must have looked ridiculous. Standing up I notice there is a clearing on this side of the water. It is surrounded by a barrier of braided mats and sticks. A fence. A hut is off to the side, outside the fence on my far left. There is a path branching off from its entrance, towards the Pure Colony. My Uncle Dale is here, along with Henrik, and they are propped up on an old tree that is cut into a rough bench. I notice there are more benches, around the inside of the circle. Some of the bench trees have growth on them, small plants sprouting from the trunks. The fence has begun crumbling in spots, the jungle overwhelming it. This place has been abandoned for a long time. It must have been used for training exercises, long ago. *But why is it so far from the center of the colony?* I look over at my Uncle Dale and Henrik. My uncle radiates calm, his shoulders back and relaxed. Henrik is a ball of nervous energy, tapping his foot erratically. I walk over to the both of them.

"So where are they?" Henrik asks, before I've even reached them.

I'm not surprised he should assume I know where they are. If Henrik and my uncle are here, there's only one place they could have gone, one other person they would trust.

"They're at my hut. Ani is caring for them." I say this deceptively, looking down at my hands.

They don't notice anything amiss in my behavior. "I thought as much," my uncle says. My carefully chosen words seem to infuriate Henrik.

"I can't believe they'd do that? After everything we've done for Matt and his family? To come here and blatantly disobey a direct order from the Führer." His face is disgusted. "I have to go back and tell him." He stands up, but my uncle grabs his arm to stop him.

"Henrik, you can't. I think there can still be a peaceful resolution to this. There won't be if you tell John."

"I don't think we have much time," I tell them both, thinking of Derrik and Martin's conversation in the shadows.

They pick up my meaning immediately, but misinterpret it. "You've heard something? About an uprising? I don't think Jacob means it," Henrik says.

"Not Jacob," I respond.

They both look at me, and amusement crosses Henrik's face. "The Untouchables wouldn't try anything, at least not immediately. They're way too outnumbered, it would be stupid of them."

There it is again, the Pure superiority. Even coming from Henrik who has spent so much time away from here. We will never be considered equals here, no matter what the others might think. I can only imagine what a peaceful resolution means to my Uncle Dale.

I hear my name and my head shoots up, I haven't been following the thread of conversation.

"Yes?"

"Okay great," my uncle says. "We'll meet here right after Session tonight. I'll light the lamps."

"Wait, what?" I ask, confused.

Henrik rolls his eyes at me, and annoyance twinges at me again. What is wrong with me, I've never felt this irritated with him before.

"We're meeting back here after Session. You need to bring Lara and her mother, I'll bring Matt. If there's to be a peaceful resolution, we'll have to discuss it after the Führer makes his speech.

"There's a Session tonight?" I ask. I vaguely remember someone else mentioning this to me, but can't remember who.

"Marta, where have you been? Of course there's a Session tonight, the Führer has to formally welcome our visitor." Henrik looks at me as if he can't believe I'm so stupid, and suddenly I'm angry.

"What are you going to do with Matt before then?" I ask him, my voice smug. "He's been busy educating the Untouchables all morning." I instantly clap my hand over my mouth. I hadn't meant to say so much.

"He's been doing what?" Henrik yells, enraged. He takes a threatening step toward me, his features contorted with anger. "Tell me exactly what they've been saying."

The damage is already done now, I want to say. I back up a few paces, "I don't know." I tell him in a small voice. "I decided to try and find Uncle as soon as I realized what was going on." My Uncle Dale is rubbing his eyes. "It may be too late," he says.

"It's not," Henrik answers, "there's still time before Session. Time for the Führer to know, and make some veiled threats in the Untouchable's direction. They wouldn't attempt anything immediately, they wouldn't be capable of it."

My uncle looks at us both. "We'll need to get our visitors out of here. Immediately, before they're in any more danger. When the Führer knows this information, their lives will be in jeopardy. They can hide in the hut here, until we can meet them." His eyes are trained on me. "Do you understand Marta?"

"After Session?" I ask.

He nods once.

"We'll be here."

Chapter Twenty

I thought it would be easy, to get Lara, Sylvia, and Matt to come with me. To hide. I thought they would understand the real danger they were putting themselves, and us, in.

That didn't turn out to be the case.

I raced back from the meeting with Henrik and my Uncle Dale. I knew Henrik had a longer run than I did, and it would only be a matter of hours before the Führer sent his guards. When I got back to the hut I was relieved to find only the five us here. Lara asleep in the hammock. Matt jumping up from his seat, a look of concern on his face. I try to whisper as quietly as possible. Try to tell them what has happened, what Henrik is planning on doing. Breathless and panting I try to make them see how desperate our situation is.

Sylvia is the first to react.

"I guess I'm going to have to wake up Lara," she says. "She got a good hour nap in at least." She leans over and feels her forehead, brushing some loose strands away from her face.

"Yes, please," I cry. "Wake her up so we can get moving."

Ani stays rooted to her spot, watching us all carefully.

Matt looks at me in confusion. "What do you mean get moving, Marta? We're not going anywhere." To prove his point he sits back down in the chair, picking up a pen of mine and beginning to examine it. "I've never seen writing utensils like this," he says. "A fountain pen I think they're called?"

What is he talking about?! I want to yell, but I just stare at them all. Dumbfounded and silent.

"Yes," Sylvia answers him, "we used them when I was younger. When people cared more about quality products. We've become such a disposable society now. It's despicable." She shakes her head in displeasure before gently nudging Lara awake.

Lara's eyes flutter briefly. She is mumbling Sergio's name. Something about five more minutes, her hand trying to brush her mother aside. Sylvia nudges her harder and she suddenly wakes fully. She sits up and luckily Sylvia has a good grip on her arm so she doesn't tumble out of the hammock. Lara blinks rapidly, absorbing her surroundings. Her eyes wide with discernment, and then replaced by raw fear, bloodshot and rimmed in red. Her mother envelops her in a hug before the sobs begin racking her body.

"I was dreaming of him," she says, choking on the words. "I was dreaming of him." Ani brings her a cup of water as the hiccups begin. "Sleep is hard," she says, taking a sip of the water, "because he's so alive in my dreams. So vibrant." She gives the cup to Sylvia, "Oh Mom!" she cries before hiding her head in Sylvia's chest. I hand Sylvia a scrap of cloth, and Lara uses it to blow her nose loudly. "I don't want to wake back to reality."

I'm still staring blankly at them all, tapping my foot impatiently. Breathing heavily through my nose. I'm trying to feel compassion for Lara, for her situation, but we need to get moving. *Now.*

"I don't mean to interrupt, but I don't think you understand me. The Führer will know you're here by now. He will know you're in the Untouchable encampment." Everyone is finally giving me their full attention. "He will not be happy about it. In fact he will be more than angry. His punishments can be humiliating. He may spare your life, but he won't spare you from the Pure, he won't spare you from anything they may inflict upon you."

"I think I need another Tylenol," Lara says, rubbing her forehead. "I have a migraine coming on."

I throw my hands up in the air, and a noise of frustration escapes, but she doesn't seem to have heard me. My last sentence appears to have had the desired effect on Sylvia though, worry flickering across her features.

"Lara, I need to tell you something," Sylvia says, handing her a pill, "something important. I want to give you the chance to decide what to do. I'm almost positive, although it would have been nice to have the doctor's blood results before we left Manacapuru."

"What?" Lara asks, curious. She reaches a hand out and rests it on Sylvia's arm. "What is it Mom?"

"I think you're pregnant," Sylvia announces bluntly.

Lara is visibly stunned, and I feel a sense of relief. Then guilt at my relief. *Pregnant!* Surely they will leave now. For the sake of her baby.

"I can take you back Lara," Matt says suddenly. "If that's what you want. I'll take you and Sergio back." He looks down at his hands, "we know you don't want to be here as badly as us. Sylvia and I have already discussed it. She will stay here, and I can take you home."

Lara nods her head, bewildered. Her face rapidly losing color.

"I need to think," she says, vaguely. "I need to think."

"There isn't time," I burst out, surprising them all. Even Lara turns to look at me. "There isn't time to think," I say again, firmly. "We need to go." I'm so angry at them all, still rooted in their spots. Unmoving.

"Marta," Sylvia reaches for me. "Marta, let's go talk." She makes a motion to grab my arm and I shrink from her. She looks hurt but drops her arm. Moving to the back entrance she pauses there, waiting for me to decide.

"You're really not going with me?" I ask them, looking around the room. Ani has hidden herself in a corner, her eyes wide and watching.

"Marta," Sylvia says again, "let's talk." Her tone is also firm and I yield. Moving past her in the direction of the back enclosure. She follows me out and I'm too jumpy to sit. Pacing back and forth. Sylvia stands near the door, watching me patiently. She pulls a banana from the eaves, and begins eating it slowly, giving me time to think.

"I don't understand why you don't want to leave!" I say, breaking the silence between us.

She sighs, throwing the banana peel into the compost bin. "I know you're frustrated with us Marta. I'm sure you think we're doing this to aggravate you." She throws her arms up in a mock gesture, and I explode.

"I don't think that at all!" I yell. "I think you're all dumm!" I feel so relieved to have it out in the open that I continue. "I think you're stupid for coming here. For risking your lives, to ruin ours. I hate all of you, I hate your smugness, your superiority. That you somehow think you know better than us what's good for the colony." I realize I'm not only yelling at her, I'm yelling at the Pure too. The one's who have put us in this situation in the first place. I yell out to the trees, as loud as my voice can carry, my double meaning clear. "I hate you!"

I collapse on the patio, exhausted now. "I hate you," I whisper again.

"Where to begin," she says under her breath. She sits close to me, and I don't recoil from her touch. Emotionally exhausted by my declaration.

"You don't hate us," she says.

"Yes I do," I say, the petulant note in my voice clear.

"Marta," she smiles at me, "you hate the situation we're putting you in. You hate that we're making you confront truths which everyone here has been too blind to see, and lie's they've been too scared to fight against."

I thrust out my lower lip, she's right, but I don't want to admit it.

"What if they want to leave?" I ask her. "The Untouchables? What if they want to leave here? They aren't educated about the outside world. They could never survive out there."

Her blue eyes quiver in confusion. "What have they been telling you Marta?"

"I saw the images," I tell her, annoyed. "I saw the images on that computer!"

The muscles in her face relax as she contemplates what I've said. "Of course the world can seem scary in that context," she says, "but you're not accounting for all the goodness out there too. If they want to leave, well, we can help them, we can figure it out. They won't be alone out there."

"But Henrik said. . ." I try and remember what arguments he used, but my mind is empty.

"Don't you think they should be given that choice?"

Choices again. It all comes down to the right of choice. Am I doing the right thing by shielding them from their choices? I think I am.

"I don't understand why it's so bad here," I argue. "Why it's so bad to make people do what you think is right. If they don't know any better, how is it wrong?"

She looks at me grimly for a long time. Assessing my words, I can tell by her silence I have fallen in her estimation, and I am suddenly ashamed of myself.

"That's not a question for me to answer for you," she finally says. "That is a question you need to answer for yourself. I want you to look inside yourself. Were you honestly happier in ignorance? Were you truly happier before you were given the choice to leave?"

I bow my head, and whisper to the floorboards. "How are we supposed to achieve it though? How are we supposed to change everyone's minds? We will never be considered equals here."

Lara responds from behind us, and I jump in my seat, startled.

"It is not always possible to change everyone's mind- it will take time. But Marta," she says, "you can do something about it- you can change your mind. You can change your actions. It only takes one person. You think you're doing the right thing. You think you're helping them by keeping silent. Remember what we talked about earlier, remember my mantra. Silence is nothing but fear talking. Make your choice, live in fear. But do not expect us to do the same."

She turns to Sylvia, shaking her head. "I'm staying," she states. "Matt has gone to warn the others."

A glance filled with meaning passes between them before they both turn together and walk back into the hut. Leaving me alone with my thoughts.

I pull a banana from the bunch. Shove it quickly down my throat before sitting down. It has begun to rain again, and I listen to the noises enveloping me in the familiar. The melody of a thousand different birds, the soft patter of the water hitting the leaves. It ends quickly, the sun breaking through the clouds. The fog lifting from the forest floor, making the jungle appear dangerous, eerie.

Could we really make them see us as equals?

A loud bang interrupts my thoughts and I jump to my feet. Six guards have entered our hut. Thomas is here, but Henrik is not among them. He is barking orders, and the largest guard roughly grabs Lara by the arm. His blonde hair is bright, his blue eyes fierce. There is a large mole on his neck. I leap back into my hut and reach for him, trying to pull Lara away.

"Be careful," I yell before grabbing his arm, "she's pregnant."

He only glares at me for a second before backhanding my face. The force of his hit sends me flailing across the room, and I fall heavily into my desk.

"Don't you ever touch me," he says. "Now I have to disinfect my arm," he grumbles to the man next to him.

Thomas helps me to my feet, whispering in my ear. "It has to be this way Marta."

He stands up straight. "The Führer doesn't want anyone harmed," he says, glaring at the guard.

"At least not yet," one of the men leers at Lara. Sylvia's eyes flash with anger, but she remains silent. Restrained between two of her own guards.

"James," Thomas says, "why don't you hold on to the girl."

Henrik's older brother steps forward, gently taking Lara by the arm and pulling her to the back of the grouping. She doesn't resist him.

"Where's the boy?" Thomas asks Sylvia.

"Gone," she states.

"We don't know where," Ani squeaks from her corner.

"No one asked you to speak," the guard with the mole barks. He makes a motion toward her, but Thomas intervenes, placing a hand on his shoulder. Ani hasn't moved, staring rigidly at them both.

"We'll find him later," Thomas says quietly. He marches from the room, pushing the guard ahead of him. The rest of the guards pull Sylvia and Lara along behind them.

I watch as they march out. Taste the blood in my mouth, a tooth loose in the back. I wonder if I'll ever see Sylvia and Lara again.

Chapter Twenty-one

The hut feels empty with only the two of us. I grab a piece of cloth from the floor to soak up the blood, cradling my face in my hand. I pull myself to my feet and straighten up. Ani and I standing here, staring at one another. The accusations unspoken between us. We have lived and worked beside each other for so many years. I know her better than anyone, and she thought she knew me. I take a step forward as she takes one back, evading me. Does she think I'm going to touch her?

Our uneasy dance has made the silence even more heavy, the empty air between us growing into an impossible chasm. What is the next step? Is there still a chance to save them?

She turns away from me and opens her mouth to speak, but I'm afraid to hear it. I fumble for the door, and without a word to Ani, I flee.

I head straight for the meeting place. I have to know if my Uncle Dale is here, if he is waiting for me. I need direction, someone to tell me what to do. I run hard, tripping over roots and low hanging vines. The huts closest to us are occupied, a group of Untouchables gathered here. They yell out to me and I ignore them. Pump my legs harder, move my arms in an unrelenting beat. Spit the blood from my mouth, push my way through the ferns and brush. Slip on the mossy rocks. I reach the crossing quickly and sprint over the log, jump the rocks hastily, unconcerned about falling. I am at the bench and my uncle is sitting here, his head in his hands. Hunched over, defeated.

"Marta," he says. *"Oh, Marta."*

I'm panting with the exertion and I don't know what to say. I sit next to him, breathing heavily.

Minutes pass, the consequences spinning my head. I wring the bloody cloth in my hands. "Is it that bad?" I ask him. "Is there nothing we can do?"

He wearily straightens his back. Sitting upright. "I guess there's always hope for us. I've never seen the Führer so angry. He was insensible Marta, beyond reason. I think there's no hope for our visitors. We did all we could for them, warned them. You tried to get them to run?"

I nod my head.

I think through my conversation with them, and consider telling my uncle. It seems like an invasion of privacy for some reason. There hasn't been many secrets between us, and I'm uncomfortable withholding the information. My next question comes out before thinking,

"What are we going to do next?" I ask.

"I don't know Marta," he says. "I really don't know. I have to go back soon, Session will be starting, and they'll notice if I'm missing."

He bows his head again, "I guess I have to act the part, again."

I reach for his hand and give it a squeeze. "It will all work out," I tell him, trying to steal some of Lara and Sylvia's confidence. "Some how, it will all work out."

He doesn't miss the change in my tone, and he looks up into my face. Assessing the knowledge there.

"You know something," he says. "You know something you're not telling me." For the first time I really see the resemblance to his brother and it scares me. A chill running through my core.

"Tell me," he says. His eyes have turned icy, and he grips my wrist. "Tell me what you know."

My wrist hurts, and I know my eyes are filled with fear and pain. I'm about to give up and tell him, when he releases me suddenly. Shakes his head. "I'm sorry Marta, I'm feeling so desperate. Of course you don't know anything."

This is almost worse, and shame washes over me. If there really is no hope for them, what's the harm in telling him my suspicions?

"I think they have a plan," I say tentatively. I can almost see the the shadows under his eyes darken, his eyebrows lifting.

"A plan?" He asks, "a plan for what exactly?"

"For education," I say. A picture of my uncle taking my primer fills my head, and another shudder cuts through me. I push the thoughts aside, I'm already spilling my secrets.

There's no use in stopping now.

"Education?"

"They think we should be given choices," I tell him. My cheek is throbbing, my wrist in pain. "But they don't think we should leave necessarily." I want to make this clear to him somehow. I try and think about what they've left unsaid.

"They think the Untouchables, and the Pure, should know what's going on outside this colony. So they can make their own choices."

I rub my wrist, a bruise is forming. A monkey lets out a squeal near the makeshift bridge, scaring a flock of birds into flight.

"Why now?" he asks, but I don't answer. "Right before the Patrons are to arrive," he says to himself. "We could at least have tried to pretend until they had left, the Untouchables could have remained subordinate, or best of all, hidden. How are we to survive if we're cut off from their resources?"

"I don't know," I tell him. "I doubt they're concerned."

"Of course they're not," he says contemptuously. "They have their own lives to return too. They aren't completely dependent on others."

He is angry, and so I admit something to him. "I don't think they plan on returning home."

His eyes narrow, "what do you mean?"

"I get the idea they're here to stay," and as soon as I say it out loud, I realize it's true.

He stands up, shaking his head. "I need to talk to them, and with Session about to begin, I don't know. . ." His words melt into the background of sounds.

"Thomas had them," I tell him. "I'm going to sit here a while, I want to think."

He nods his head, before running down the path toward the Pure encampment.

The sun is beginning to go down, the howling monkeys beginning their chorus. I'm only allowed a few minutes of silence before a dark head appears next to me. Elise again.

"What are you doing here little monkey?" I ask her, completely taken by surprise.

She laughs, delighted to have scared me.

"I followed you from your hut. I knew you didn't see me, you run fast!"

I laugh at her assessment. "It comes from years of practice," I tell her, patting the seat next to me. She sits, crossing her legs and tucking them underneath her.

"Why do you look so sad?" she asks me. "Everyone else back in the barracks- they're so happy!"

I smile at her. "I know," I tell her. "But I'm afraid of what will happen if we have to fight the Pure. I'm afraid the Untouchables will lose."

She giggles and I look at her confused. *I didn't say anything funny.*

She notices my expression, and leans over to kiss me on the cheek.

"You forgot what I said," she says teasingly, hitting my arm. In that gesture she is decades older than her years. Wiser. Fragile secrets float in the air between us.

"What advice of yours did I forget?" I try and ask lightly.

She doesn't notice any change in the tone of my question. "It's all about surprise!" She says happily.

I snap my fingers as it all clicks into place, Derrik and Martin whispering, Matts sudden departure, this little girls advice. I stand up in a daze, when the truth shatters my consciousness. I try to take a wobbly step toward the path my uncle disappeared down.

"Where are you going?" Elise asks, worried now. My mind sharpens, clearer than it has been in days. I breathe deeply before answering an octave lower than normal.

"I have to check on my sister," I tell her.

She jumps up to hug me, her little arms wrapped around me tight.

"I don't think that's a good idea." Her hug has the opposite affect she intended. She looks concerned for me, at my safety. Now I am determined to go.

"I have to," I tell her, removing her arms. "Don't follow me." I give her a look of warning and she shakes her head in assent. She heads back to the log bridge, her little feet skipping across the rocks.

I walk slowly toward the Pure encampment, unfamiliar with this path. It is overgrown and crumbling, the boards rotting away under my feet. Doubts fill my mind, and I stop to turn back, again and again. Darkness is complete when I finally reach the boundary. I feel the foreboding of something amiss. The camp is too quiet, Session should be over. There should be more people on the paths, more celebrating. *All this worry, it might be for no reason at all.* Maybe I should try and find Sylvia and Lara instead. I brush these thoughts aside, my Uncle Dale will try and protect them. Now that he knows what he's up against. I continue in my original direction. My feet leading me on the path to Julianne's hut.

Her door has been flung open, there are no guards here. I approach cautiously, a glimmer of light catching my attention. Something sparkling at my toes. I lean down and roll a bead between my fingers. Glancing at the doorway, I notice the netting has been torn down. Hundreds of beads lying on the steps, and embedded in the dirt around me. I brush them off the step with my hand, and shiver when I realize they're wet. I rub the substance on my dress. There is no light here to see what it is, so I climb the steps, peer into the dimly lit darkness of her hut.

Julianne is huddled in a far corner, amid an absolute disaster. The hut has been stripped. One of her electric flashlights is hanging from the ceiling, blinking in and out. The walls are bare, bits of magazine and newspaper drift around the room, each step sending more of them flying. The things left, are in shreds, porcelain and glass shards intermixed with long strips of fabric and bits of feathers. I finish gazing around the room and study Julianne. I almost don't recognize her, the hair shaved from her head in patches.

Her eyes are smeared in what looks like black paint, running long lines down the contours of her face. The color on her lips is smudged, and in the same moment I realize it's not lipstick smeared across her mouth. It's blood, pouring freely from a scratch on her cheek. I squint, tracing the lines carved into her. A word etched into her skin. I follow the path of the blood until I notice the s*omething* in her hand. She is gripping a ball of fur. In the next flash of light I realize it's covered in blood, the small puppy from Manacapuru. My heart sinks. I watch her drop the remains of the dog, and scoot away from it. I avert my eyes and try not to vomit.

I want to ask what has happened but I'm afraid I already know. The idea which sprouted with Elise's words, confirmed. It has begun. The rebellion my uncle and the Führer wanted me so badly to stop- the rebellion Sylvia and Lara wanted so badly to ignite. It has begun without me.

I'm compelled to focus on her again, her clothes in tatters. There is blood dribbling down one of her legs.

Humiliation, not physical pain, their primary motivation.

"Who did this to you?" I whisper.

"Martin," she replies, "Martin did this to me." It explains the empty book spines spread across the floor- the pages floating in the air around us. I step closer to her and she shields her body from me, moving her knees into her chest. Curling into a ball. I want to help her and I don't know how. My heart filling with pity.

"What can I do?" I ask, "is there anything I can do?" I can't help the compassion in my voice, my absolute sorrow for her situation. *No one deserves this.*

"Leave me alone," comes the hoarse whisper from behind her arms.

I stand still, I can't leave her alone like this. Who could help her? *Marie*, I think. Shaman Marie could help her.

"I don't think you should be alone right now," I say quietly, trying to be soothing. "I'll go and get Marie." I make a move to leave when her head whips up, snarling at me, baring her teeth.

"How would you know what I need?" she screams. She tries to stand, but her legs won't support her weight. She crashes back to the floor, and shakily raises herself on all fours. Her eyes trained on me.

"You're the one that's dirt. Trash!" She hurls a book spine in my direction. "This should be you!" she screams. "An Untouchable." She spits, a wad of blood and mucus. "You leave me alone!" Her tone has become savage, and she makes a motion to get up before landing roughly on her knees again. "You leave me alone!" she yells again. Each word hits me like a knife to the stomach. I back slowly out of the entrance. I am past the door when her real screams begin. The low guttural sounds of an animal in pain, coming from inside the hut.

I begin to run.

Lara

§

Chapter Twenty-two

My mom and I are dragged through the Colony so quickly that I barely glimpse at the other huts before being deposited in a large canvas tent, completely unlike anything else we've seen in the encampment. My guard James doesn't say a word to me the whole walk over, but his silence doesn't stop me from pestering him with questions. Most of the guards don't move past the stations spread out in a circle around the tent. I think James is honestly relieved to be rid of me, but he doesn't skitter outside with the rest of them. Choosing to stand with Thomas near the door. A lavish buffet is set up in this room, and my mouth begins watering at the sight of roasted chicken and familiar vegetables.

"Baby carrots!" I murmur to my mom. I almost reach out to grab one of the biscuits, before remembering where I am.

We sit side by side on a padded bench. Embroidered fabric and linens hang down the walls. I think about Marta's sparse accommodations. No wonder the Pure are so fanatical about keeping this colony secret, if they all live in such comfort. I could almost be comfortable here.

The tapestry on the wall next to us is especially vibrant and I turn to examine it closer. The unusual design is created by hundreds of tiny swastikas. Bile rises in my throat as I face forward again, uneasy now, my appetite gone.

"It's hard to believe we're in the middle of the jungle," I say under my breath.

"The palace," my mom whispers, disgust in her voice.

"Oh," I respond. *That would explain our surroundings.*

Thomas and James remind me of sentinels, the way they stand at the doorway, eyes forward, watching an opening into another room behind us.

I whisper this to my mom who replies, "a sentinel is also the indicator of a disease."

I can't help the escaping snort, and I see her try to cover her own smile. "Appropriate comparison, don't you think?" I tell her. James has his eyebrows raised at the pair of us.

A tinkling sound fills the air, and my mom and I turn at once to watch a woman enter from the next room. Henrik appearing behind her. There's a row of tiny bells wrapped around her ankle. She has the longest hair I've ever seen, trailing behind her on the floor, like a robe of corn silk. A lacy undergarment accentuates her curves. Her eyes are a deep blue, and empty of emotion. I think she must be the most beautiful woman I've ever seen, until I notice the bruise on her cheek. It's faded a little, but not quite concealed by the rouging she's applied. There's a fresh cut on her forehead, tinged in yellow and green. She's carrying a guitar like instrument and heads past us for the door.

James and Thomas both bow to her briefly as she exits.

"The Führer is furious." Thomas says, once he's sure she is out earshot. "A direct order, he thought you understood, he thought you were leaving."

"We never agreed to those terms," my mom replies.

Henrik steps into the center of the room, furious. "The Patrons are expected, Matt told us as much. If you can't agree to leave, you will have to act the part here. The Untouchables will be forced into line. I don't care if they have to pretend, we can't lose the Patron's financing." He is turning blue in the face.

My mom shakes her head. "You don't seem to understand, it's not about pretending, or subterfuge for us. It's about basic human decency. It's about allowing everyone the same freedoms which you," she points at the pair of them, "enjoy. We don't plan on leaving until we feel this has been accomplished."

"And you think we can survive without the money from our Patrons?" Thomas asks.

"I don't see why not," I tell them, "the Untouchables live simply enough and seem to be doing fine."

"Even they are dependent on some outside resources," Henrik snarls.

"Henrik?" James asks softly, "Aren't you expected at Session?"

"I'm leaving now," he says, sending an icy stare around the room before marching out.

"I don't think we should argue," my mom says, after Henrik has left. "There's no telling when the Patrons are even going to visit here. They may visit with Elisabeth and Eli, and move on. We may still be able to take their money."

"And who cares if the money is for the right cause, if the cause is right?" I ask them annoyed.

Thomas looks to James, who shrugs his shoulders. "The Führer doesn't know what to do with you now. It would be easier to dispose of you, but unfortunately he has no idea if you've told other's of your plans. If someone outside this colony knows you're here."

I seize on the idea immediately.

"We left specific instructions with my aunt. We have three more days before we'll be reported missing." I tell him.

A smile spreads across Thomas' face. "How funny," he says. "Matt told us you had five more days, and you left instructions with his mother."

I groan inwardly and look at my mom. I fell for such an easy trick. My mom remains stone faced.

"Maybe Matt left instructions for his mother," she says. "We wouldn't know. Elisabeth wasn't aware we were coming. We left our instructions with relatives, as Lara stated."

Thomas clearly doesn't believe us, and gives a loud, "humph," before sitting down.

"She's good," he tells James. "When the Führer questions you, I would stick with Matt's story. He was very convincing."

"What?" I'm sure I look as confused as I feel.

James and Thomas exchange a knowing look. "If there's going to be a rebellion," James says. "We want it to go as peacefully as possible." He gestures to Thomas. "Thomas has been going to the village for decades, he's a good friend of Eli and Elisabeth."

"James and I have spoken about this at length. We have always been careful to protect the Untouchables from trouble. Both of us would prefer for things in the colony to remain the same. Since that's not going to happen, and given our choices, we'd prefer to ally ourselves with you."

My mom and I look at each other in disbelief. "Elisabeth led us to believe we would have no allies in the Pure camp," I tell them.

"I'm sure she had no idea what you were walking into, had no idea who she could trust anymore. It's been a long time since we helped her escape."

"We?" my mom asks.

"Thomas, Dale and myself. We smuggled her out over ten years ago," James says. "The Führer had no idea she was still alive, until you arrived with Matt. We put ourselves at great risk telling you this. She stayed hidden when the parties retrieved the mail, they only ever dealt with Matt and his father, Eli."

I suddenly wish Matt was here with us. He would be able to decipher this, help to put the pieces of truth together.

My mom has apparently decided to believe them. "What are we up against?" she asks. "Honestly?"

Thomas begins rubbing his head. A loud horn explodes with noise right outside.

"Session," James says.

"There's not enough time," Thomas sighs. "We need a plan."

I wonder how we're going to explain this to Marta and the rest of them. *Our new allies.*

"We have a. . ." My mom starts to speak, but a rustling noise outside interrupts her. A loud thump, followed by a grunt of pain.

"Everyone should be at Session by now," Thomas comments. "Stay here," he commands us all, exiting through the door.

James edges closer to the exit, so he can peer outside occasionally. "You don't want to leave now do you?" James asks us both, skeptical. "We could easily escape."

My mom gives him a dubious look.

"Then we wouldn't have to go through all of this," he says wearily, peeking out the door again.

There's another loud thump outside, and a figure slumps forward through the door opening.

James barely has time to react before a large object swings straight for his head, knocking him out.

Derrik steps over the bodies, scanning the room. "Is that it?" he says. "There's only three of them?" He's looks around the corner.

"We only knew of the two," I tell him, "and they were our allies."

He grimaces, rolling James on to his back and away from the entrance. "We have no allies. Not among the Pure."

My mom shoots me a look, *now is not the time.*

"Okay," I ask him, "what next?"

"Do you feel comfortable carrying a gun?" he asks.

It feels good to laugh out loud again, my mom and I both bursting into giggles. "Hand them over," I tell him.

He reaches out the door and whispers something to a man hidden in the shadows. We are each armed with a handgun and a long old fashioned rifle. The handgun is loaded and I tuck it into my waistband. I'm unsure how to carry the rifle and decide to keep it my hand, holding it by the long barrel.

"We're going to have to run, most of them are returning from Session by now and will be on the paths. We won't have walking sticks so you'll have follow closely behind me."

We follow a dirt path through the jungle, until my feet catch on a wooden plank leading us in the direction of the river. The gurgling noises in the distance. Despite what Derrik has said, there are no people around. We pass a few figures hunched over in the shadows, but I can't be sure they are human.

The run allows me time to think, my head throbbing. The air is so thick here, pressing into me, heavy and warm. I crinkle my nose, sticky. I never feel fully dry. Not at all like the fresh air I remember growing up on our ranch. Swallowing this air down, my lungs never satisfied.

It has been a long time since I've done any real exercise, my muscles and joints are sore. I'll have to ask my mom for more Tylenol. To ease the pain and forget the feeling of suffocation, I concentrate on the plans we made on the boat ride from Manacapuru. It feels much longer than a few days ago. We had planned on Sergio being the one to initiate the bloodless rebellion. The Sarge. He's a natural leader. *Was, was a natural leader.* I cringe at the past tense. How am I supposed to convince an entire population of people they are wrong? We knew the Untouchables would be the easiest to convince, and with Sergio, they were always our starting point. We knew he wouldn't be accepted into the Pure society. We talked about creating a power shift. Removing the control of weapons and supplies from the Pure. Once we take away their control, we remove their power. Remove the power to control, and you remove the fear of the Pure, the fear of their Führer. It would be easy after that.

I feel relieved Derrik is here, leading us over the bridge to Marta and Ani's hut. "How did it go?" my Mom whispers to him.

"Good, I think," Derrik responds. "I never saw anyone but the three guards, and I didn't hear of anyone having any trouble with the supplies, or the weapons. We're supposed to meet back at Marta's."

"And Matt?" I ask him.

"He has the boat," he reassures me, the rest of his words swallowed in the excitement of the small crowd gathered at Marta's hut. Matt had received only a little advice from his mom, his mission to inform, not to interact. He knew just enough to save his own life in case things went wrong, the one person he could trust.

We enter, and the Untouchable Martin is here with Ani. She is helping to wash blood from his hands and clothing. I reach for my mom's hand and grip it tightly, my eyes wide. *Something has gone wrong.* Why is he covered in blood?

"Their supplies are completely cut off," Martin says to Derrik, "we've even taken the gasoline for the boat. We have all the weapons, and even managed a little destruction." He grins maniacally.

"Matt said it would be bloodless," I tell him, watching the red lines run from his fingertips.

He glares at me, the years of hatred burning his eyes. I'm helping them, but I'm still Pure. I'm still one of them to him.

"It almost was," he smirks, "but I decided after all the blood they've shed on our side, a little revenge was in order." A noise escapes from his nose, half snort and half grunt.

There's a sharp pain in my stomach and I almost keel over. My mom notices and props me up.

"What blood?" She asks loudly. "What blood of yours have they shed? No one has been killed here." Her eyes are blazing as Martin continues to glower at us both.

"I've been able to listen and speak with quite a few of your number," she says, "and they all tell me they've never been seriously harmed. Matt made it clear we would only help you if this was peaceful."

"What would you know about harm?" Martin says in barely contained rage. "We don't need your help. You're all the same. You think you can order us around, like we're slaves. I won't escape one prison to be locked up in another."

Derrik and Ani are between us, and they don't seem to know which side they should be defending. We didn't account for the amount of hate there would be in the Untouchable encampment. I realize that now.

My own rage still burns brightly within me, the arrow that pierced Sergio so quickly, I didn't even realize what was happening. By the second day of sailing we had become too comfortable. There were too many other boats on the water, we grew apathetic to Elisabeth's warning. We found the tributary to their encampment easily. Eli and Elisabeth had taken Matt fishing here many times over the years, probably trying to prepare him for this eventuality. An emergency they wouldn't be able to deal with themselves. Matt had barely finished telling us we were crossing into tribal territory. Sergio helping him get through the trees that marked the shallow entrance to the new river, almost hidden among the brush. He had pushed us around the largest rock, one minute triumphant, the next slouched over the boat's bench.

My memories become hazy after. I was nonsensical, refusing to believe he could be dead in seconds.

My eyes burn now, not with tears, but for anger at this man, Martin. I know pain.

I step forward, into the center of the grouping. My legs are throbbing from the run, but I raise my head high and notice other Untouchables listening to our conversation outside. The first thing which pops into my head is so ridiculous that I almost dismiss it. Then I decide to give it a shot. It worked once before.

"I have a dream," I say softly at first. Ani straining to hear. "I have a dream," I yell at full volume, "and it's not about three Princesses."

This garners a nervous giggle from outside.

"My husband was killed yesterday. Do you understand? My husband, an Untouchable, was killed yesterday because of the color of his hair. His beautiful dark hair, and because of the color of his skin, like the cocoa he used to make me in the mornings. Dark and rich and delicious." Tears spring to my eyes at the memory and I hold my head higher, daring anyone to speak. "He was killed for the color of his eyes, his mother's eyes, brown with hints of yellow. The eyes I hope our baby will be born with."

A general exclamation of surprise is heard from outside. Apparently Ani has been discreet with her knowledge of my pregnancy. I turn to glare at each person individually. Their eyes are filled with pity, or compassion, or love. I turn to Martin last, and his are filled with fury.

"Not many of you can say you've lost someone you've loved for those same reasons," I continue, staring him down. "You've lived a hard life here, I won't take that away from you. But it has been, for the most part, safe and comfortable. You've had food to eat, you've had the companionship of each other."

I finally break away from his stare to turn to my mom, who nods at me.

"My mom and I are here to help you start a rebellion, yes, but not a war." I turn to the window, hoping the faces hidden by the brightness of this room can hear me. "We can help you, if you let us. But not like this. Not by hurting anyone else."

We all stand in silence, and I'm exhausted, not sure I can stand for another minute, when there's a ruckus at the door. All five us turn to the doorway as Marta leaps through.

Absorbing the tension in the room before asking, "What did I miss?"

Chapter Twenty-three

Martin marches out, the diluted blood dripping from his hands. Neither Ani nor Derrik make any motion to follow him. The minute his back disappears, I remove the gun from my waistband and collapse into the only chair. Ani springs into action, bringing me another Tylenol, a cup of water, a vitamin.

Derrik hastily begins explaining things to Marta, and I catch most of their conversation. Details my mom and I didn't even know, since Matt was at the center of the actual plan. Not all the Untouchables were involved, half of them attended Session in case the Führer somehow noticed the absence of all of them. They split their targets, divide and conquer being the general idea.

"Martin took charge of assigning the groups," Derrik says, after Marta explained what she had seen of Julianne. "Now I know why." He looks at me.

"We honestly weren't looking to harm anyone. We were trying to seize control of the supplies, like Matt suggested."

Yeah right, I think. I try and nod at him convincingly. "We believe you."

He squints his eyes together, confused at my tone. He turns toward my mom. "I'll rally a guard together for the bridge. We'll need to find a safe place to put the weapons," he says.

"I'll help," Marta volunteers. I raise my eyebrows at her. "It's what I want do," she says. She curls her lip in a mischievous way, "even if I might fail."

I smile with relief. If we can change Marta's mind, there's hope for the others.

Ani uncurls herself from my side, standing up straight. "If you don't need me," she says, "I'd like to go too."

"We'll be fine," I tell her.

My mom speaks up to reassure her. "We have weapons, and Lara needs to rest. I don't think your Pure will launch any retaliation tonight."

I think of Thomas and James back ˘ in the camp, hopefully they've awoken again. The confusion that must be running rampant.

"I'll station someone by the door," Derrik tells us over his shoulder, "just in case."

The three of them file out and my mom helps me move to the hammock. The room is spinning and I am so nauseous. It feels like every part of my body is sore. My stomach twists, the contents threatening to come up. I know how painful the dry heaving can be, and I command myself to focus on something else. My mom rubs my shoulder and hands me another cup of water.

"Will I always be this sick?" I ask her.

"Only for the first couple of months or so, then it should get better. . . If you're lucky." I can tell by her smile she's only teasing me, although her voice has a hint of truth to it.

I let out a long breath of air before asking my next question.

"What are we going to do about this other kind of sickness?"

"The racial sickness," she says. "I don't know, it seems easier on paper to change someone's mind, than it actually is."

"It's hard to remember what we're doing here sometimes," I tell her. "It all started out as a mission to find answers, and now we're at the center of a revolution." My voice is earnest. "I'm happy Marta has finally come around, but sometimes I wonder if she was right in the first place. That these people were better off being left alone."

My mom stares at me intently. "Marta said something to me earlier, about forcing people to do the right thing. Taking away their right to choice by requiring them only to know one way of living, one way of thought. Do you think that's fair to these people Lara? Don't you think everyone should know all of their options, all of their choices?"

"But the Pure may choose to continue in their beliefs Mom! They may choose to continue their own agenda!"

"That's their choice, Lara, but we've done what we can to give them a choice. We can't force them to accept our beliefs. We may believe we're right, but what right does that give us to force others to believe?"

I nod my head absently, contemplating what she's asked.

"It's the difference between a law and a command," I say, thinking aloud.

"Exactly," my mom says, "a dictatorship, a kingdom, allows for only one person to dictate all the rules in their own best interest. There isn't any freedom in that. If we can change their leadership, if we can teach them about true democracy. Then we have opened up a world of choices to them. A new way of thinking. Freedom, Lara, we will teach them freedom."

"We will give them the option to leave," I tell her.

"We will give them the option to leave," she asserts, "but we will also help them understand true freedom is about making good choices, not because you're forced, and not because a government or a Führer commands it. It's about making good choices because you want to."

"I think I'm beginning to understand Mom," I say, smiling. "You can bring a horse to water, but you can't force him to drink."

She laughs with me. "Especially if he's not thirsty."

I pull a fur from the floor and pull it over me, it has grown chilly in the hut.

"But at least we can provide them with the water," I say firmly.

It goes quiet as we each escape into our own thoughts, and I fall asleep. My dreams turn to nightmares. I relive every moment of Sergio's death, and each time I try to save him, I fail. I finally wake up in tears. My mom's arm is hanging from the hammock above me, reaching for me. My head hurts even more than the day before, my muscles still sore. I panic that we're alone here, asleep, before I remember Derrik was going to leave a guard with us. I have to pee urgently, but I grasp my mom's hand to reassure her.

"Lara," she wipes at my face groggily. "Are you okay?"

I try to say I'm okay, but the tears make speaking impossible.

"Oh honey," she says, pushing the mosquito netting aside, so she can climb down next to me.

I take great gulps of air, and it begins to calm me. My breathing slowing, the tears drying up.

"Mom," I say quietly, "Sometimes when I dream about going home, I think I'll see him there, that everything will be okay once we get back." I shake my head violently, "Then I realize they've taken that too."

I pump my fist firmly against my thigh. "I think I hate this place."

She doesn't attempt to say anything, pressing my hand to her mouth, giving it a kiss. It's almost worse that way, because I know what she would say, and so I answer her thoughts.

"Ani, Marta," I tell her. "I think I can see the good in them, I think I can love them. But how do you love everyone else? How do you love the people who have taken everything from you? How do you get past that?"

A loud growl issues from my stomach, a pointed, twisting pain that's more than hunger. My mom reaches to the desk behind her, scrounging through her canvas bag there. She emerges with a long sleeve of crackers, handing me one.

I hold it up, examining it. "It's so hard to eat," I tell her, "because every bite of food reminds me of him, reminds me of the times we spent together."

These words thrust me into another memory of Sergio, sharing a bowl of clam chowder on a pier in San Francisco. The sharp smell of salty air, the biting cold breeze of the bay. Seals barking in the background. The chowder warm and delicious, we were curled up on a bench watching the sun go down. The last of its rays bouncing off the water, into the clouds, purple and red. He pulled a box from his pocket and got down on his knee in front of me. A sea gull flew overhead and left him her own present in his hair. I was laughing when I said yes.

"You have to eat," she says, bringing me back to reality.

"I know I have to eat," I tell her, annoyance in my voice. "I have to support this life growing inside of me, because it's the only thing I have left of him." I take a bite of the cracker.

"But tell me Mom," I ask sincerely. "How am I supposed to move on from this? When I know it's my fault he died? My fault we're here in the first place."

"Lara!" she exclaims, "you can't think like that. We all came here willingly, none of this is your fault."

"I found the letters, Mom! I'm the one who convinced you to come!"

She shakes her head, but no amount of argument will convince me otherwise.

I remember what Matt said in Manacupura. This is my fault.

"I have to pee," I tell her, carefully sitting up. I close my eyes, let the nausea roll over me again. The pain in my joints and muscles even worse than yesterday. Maybe it's better to feel this pain, this punishment for my actions. My mom hands me another cracker and I munch it quickly before standing up and taking my shaky steps toward the back door.

The fog is curling around the trucks of the trees, the long vines disappearing into a misty darkness. I do my business as swiftly as I can and hurry back to the hut. I'm stepping inside when Derrik walks through the front door, James on his heels. There is a burst of voices coming from outside, excited, loud voices.

I freeze in place. James would not be welcome here. Not now. *Something has happened.*

My mom reaches this conclusion before I do and rushes to his side. "What has happened?" she asks urgently. "What is going on?"

Derrik is practically shaking with excitement but remains silent. He's staring at James, waiting for him to speak. *Old habits die hard.* James looks grim, but it doesn't quite conceal his own eagerness.

"The Führer," he says. "The Führer is dead."

Chapter Twenty-four

I blink rapidly in disbelief, this was never in our plans. We had planned an usurp of power of course, John could not stay in control of the colony, he was too greedy and unpredictable. We planned to introduce the democratic process, a rudimentary vote. We always assumed there would be a trial for John. Consequences yes, but consequences decided by a panel, chosen by the colony. *Not this.* I remember Matt mentioning it in jest, and wonder if he could have masterminded it. *There's no way. It was a joke.* Sarge had explained the implications, a martyr, a rallying point. We would try negotiations first.

James has taken the seat, and Derrik hovers at the door. I can see he is anxious to get out of here, now that he has delivered his news. I wish he would go, there are things I want to say to James in private. My mom and I were planning on visiting the Pure camp later today, and now our plans may have been upended. It isn't something I want to discuss in front of him.

"Derrik you don't have to stay," I tell him. "James will tell us what we need to know." He still waits in the doorway, halfway out, undecided about whether he should leave us here with James. His eyes flick to him, doubtfully.

"Really," I reassure him, "we'll be fine with James."

My words seem to do the trick, and he gives us a quick nod before leaping out the door. I don't think he even hits a step on the way down. I breathe a sigh of relief.

"Thank you," James says to me, "it will make it easier to talk with you both, without someone listening in."

"I thought so," I tell him. "Now please, we're dying to know what happened."

He sits back in the chair, stretching his legs out in front of him. "I have to begin with last night, after you both escaped," he absently rubs the back of his head.

I feel a tinge of guilt. "Well, it could have been worse," I say apologetically. "We had no idea we were going to be able to trust you, and we needed a back up plan."

"No apology?" he asks.

"I didn't hit you," I say, miffed.

"No hard feelings," he says, waving his hands in front of him. "All things considered, you most likely saved our lives by having us knocked out. There was to be some serious repercussions this morning. Our unconsciousness saving us from some mighty awkward questions."

"I do feel a little bad about the way it went down," I tell him.

"Only a little?" He chuckles, "I'm fine. Save your apologies for the old man Thomas."

"Is he okay?" my mom asks.

James shrugs his shoulders before continuing, "I'm confident he'll be fine. Barely anyone knows what happened last night. The Untouchable soldiers did their job well, only a few of us had to be knocked out, and no one missed the supplies at first. If not for what happened to Julianne, it may have been days before we noticed anything seriously amiss." He looks pointedly at us both, and I know he wants an explanation, but none is forthcoming from either of us. I look over to my mom, but her face is solemn. *I'm not about to tell him.*

He pauses another moment before clearing his throat. "Right, well Julianne was obviously. . .under some strain. Henrik was the first one to find her. He managed to move her to the Führer's hut without being seen. The Führer's wife Heidi, joined him shortly thereafter." He rubs his head again. "By then Dale, Thomas, and I were awake and attempting our explanations to the Führer. He was enraged by the news, but not without sense. He was making plans for retaliation before Heidi walked in to tell him the news." James stops the story, bowing his head briefly, saying seriously. "I've never seen anything like that kind of anger. When he saw Julianne. The fury it ignited. We were told to leave. To watch the camp, to watch his quarters, to remain silent. He would dole out his punishments in the morning, for our inadequacies, our ineptitude. Dale ran for his own hut. Henrik and I left together, but I heard the explosion of wrath after I walked out. I stayed close to his tent, listened to things breaking, the cries of pain."

My mom asks softly, "Heidi?"

He dips his head lower, holding it in his hands, "she wasn't dismissed. She was at the Session, there's no way she could have protected Julianne." He shakes his head, "she was blamed anyway. The cries were hers."

I gasp in shock. "No one did anything?" I ask him. "To help her?"

I see a tear drop land in the dust of the floor. His face concealed by his hands, his voice is filled with emotion and regret.

"You have to understand," he says. "The hut is surrounded by guards. I thought at first someone would intervene. Someone would have to put a stop to it, even without our weapons. Then when no one did, I thought about helping, but it was too late. The hut had gone silent."

I stare at my mom, a mirror of mutual horror.

"Heidi *is* recovering," he states.

I give a little exclamation of surprise, "she's still alive."

"Yes, she's still alive," he says, looking up. His eyes tired. "Which brings me to the next part of the story." He releases a long breath of air, and I recoil a little from the stench.

"I was swapped out of watch," he continues, "asleep when I heard the yells outside of my hut. I went running when I heard them, and one of the guards was at the tent and told me the news. I wanted to see for myself and pushed my way through the grouping. There were only a few people in the inner quarters, Thomas, two of the Führer's advisors, Jacob. The Führer was lying in his bed, the syringe still hanging from his arm. He was poisoned."

"How?" my mom asks.

"We're not sure, but Thomas and I have a theory, we discussed it briefly before I ran here."

"You don't think one of the Untouchables?" I ask him.

"No, not one of the Untouchables, although I think they're getting the blame right now."

239

"What?!" I exclaim. "How?"

"We think it was Heidi who killed the Führer, with help from Marie. She's our Shaman, and the only one with enough knowledge to pull it off. I know she was there last night, with Heidi, I fetched her myself. After."

"So why are the Untouchables getting the blame?" I ask him. "It's not like I can't blame Heidi, after all that's happened to her."

"Jacob," my mom says resolutely from the corner. "It's Jacob, isn't it?"

"Yes," he responds. "He's rallying for power now. He's blaming Ani, and the rest of the Untouchable encampment. He has the women under surveillance. He doesn't want any part of their story out. Thomas, my brother Henrik and I, were dismissed this morning. He has never trusted us. We're not welcome in the new regime, he made that clear. Henrik didn't take the news well."

"Has he been successful in gaining support?" my mom asks, a wobble in her voice. Obviously worried about this new development.

"Jacob has never been well liked among the Pure," he says. He briefly explains what happened to Ani, and many of the other girls in the Pure encampment. At one point I walk over to sit near my mom. I grip her hand to anchor myself, the tears flowing from us both. By the time he is finished I am shaking with anger.

"We've tried to protect them," James says apologetically. "He's royalty though, and free to do what he will."

"Not anymore," I say, my voice low.

He looks between the both of us. "There's no hope now? For pretense?"

I look steadily at my mom. Her eyes still watery and bloodshot, her nose dripping. "I think I can answer for the Untouchables, if the Patrons were to arrive today, there would be no chance of subterfuge." I feel only slightly bad for telling him this. After everything he's told us, could he expect anything different?

"They've had a taste of freedom James," my mom says. "We would never ask them to pretend anything differently." She blows her nose loudly with a cloth.

He closes his eyes briefly. "I thought as much. Thomas has run for Marta's Uncle Dale. We're hoping they return soon, Jacob has already called for a Session to be held tonight." He stares at us intently, "I need to know what your plan is. What is your next step?"

I shrug my shoulders, "we had planned to visit the Pure camp today, to try and negotiate with the Führer."

"So you think there's still hope? For some sort of truce between the two camps?" he asks.

"Of course there's hope," I tell him. "You still have something the Untouchables want- education, knowledge. We thought we could establish a committee to represent the interest of the two groups."

"Filled with members of both?" he asks.

"That's the plan at least," I tell him, "although with Jacob in power, it changes things a bit."

He nods his head. "I'd like you both to come in to camp with me today," he says. "You're still unknowns over there. Jacob hasn't mentioned any visitors, so there's only been rumors. I think you could both disguise yourselves as leaders of another colony, here on a social visit. If you don't mention anything controversial, Jacob will have no reason to object."

"He may not be in power long enough to object," I remind him.

"We can't assume anything," James says. "Dale isn't exactly well respected by the Pure community here either. He's always be seen as an outsider, rarely venturing into camp at all. Then there's my own brother to worry about. Henrik is a loyalist to his core, even if he has his moments of clarity, he may still try to rally for power."

"In that case, it may be too dangerous for us to go into the camp today," my mom says. "At least until we know Dale has some semblance of control."

"We can't back down now Mom," I say in disbelief. "We've come so far!"

"I'm not saying we should back down," she answers, "but back off. For another day at least, let Dale try and talk to him first."

"Okay, Mom," I tell her after a few moments of silence. "I think you may be right. I think we need to talk to Marta and Ani first, get them on board with everything, maybe decide who is going to take charge on this side of the water."

"Good idea," she responds. She stands up, stretching. "I'm sorry, but I have to use the latrine, if you'll excuse me for a moment. I'll be right back." She walks swiftly out the back door.

I turn to James and ask him quietly, "Before she gets back, do you have a plan to take over the Pure camp already in motion? What do you want me to do?"

He looks at me in surprise, and a rustling at the door makes us both jump. Marta has returned, her eyes shining. "Have you heard?" she says. "The news?"

She has her eyes trained on me and doesn't notice James is in the room at first. He coughs softly and she turns to him, a blush creeping across her face, until she realizes who he is. The smile plastered on her face drops. "Henrik?" she asks.

"He's safe Marta," James answers, his words full of meaning.

"The only thing you really missed," I say, as they both turn at once to face me, "is how we're going to get to the Pure camp today, without my mother knowing."

Chapter Twenty-five

Marta pushes me back into the hammock before I can say another word. She forces James out, whispering frantically in his ear. He says something to her, so low I can't hear, and she barks at him, visibly annoyed. He leaves in a huff.

"What was that about?" I ask her.

She rolls her eyes. "Nothing. I just wanted him to relay a message to his brother."

She picks up an old photo album, wrapped in thick plastic and places it in her leather sack. She notices I'm staring at her and she gives me a quizzical look.

"What?" she asks.

"You've changed," I tell her, wondering who this Henrik really is to her. She smiles at me but doesn't respond.

My mom returns from the latrine, and immediately notices my change in position. She rushes to my side, "Lara? Are you okay?"

"I'm fine Mom, a little tired again, that's all. It's the heat I think, it saps my energy."

She nods in empathy. "The seasons are reversed here, and it's never fun to be pregnant in the summer. Is there anything I can get you?"

To go with a side of guilt.

"No Mom, I'll be fine. Marta is taking care of me."

My mom begins bustling around the hut anyway, searching for things to do. Cleaning surfaces with water, picking up bits of garbage. She notices a pile of laundry in the corner and asks Marta about it.

"The Untouchables usually have laundry duty, but everything is in confusion now. The schedule off. I think everyone is doing their own." Marta does a good job of looking embarrassed. "The truth is I've never done my own laundry, I wouldn't even know how to begin, it's always been done for me."

My mom looks slightly horrified by this. Trying to conceal her shock, she begins picking up the dresses, examining them. "I guess it's a place to begin," she says. "Ani knows how to do the laundry here?"

"Yes."

"I wanted to have a talk with her, this might be the perfect opportunity."

A smile alights Marta's face. "Let me get the basket then!" she says, walking out to the back porch and bringing in a large green woven basket. My mom admires the craftsmanship before dumping the clothes in. She digs through the duffel bag purchased in Manacapuru, and adds our own dirty clothes to the pile. In her canvas sack she finds the travel soap, and a scrubbing brush.

Marta examines the soap, sniffing it, before placing it on the desk. "You can't use this," she says. "You want to be careful about smells out here. You don't want to smell unfamiliar, and the perfume will attract insects, they'll think you're food."

I begin giggling until I realize she's not joking.

"I'm serious," she tells us. "I may not do laundry, but I know about smells. It's why we don't use the fancy soaps our Patron sends us either. Julianne is the only one who dares," Marta stops in the middle of her sentence, her eyes wide. She blinks a few times, and I know she's thinking of the last time she saw Julianne. "But she doesn't usually go past the boundaries of our colony." She breathes in deeply. "Your scent can be deadly around here."

She drops a white stone in my mom's hand and gives her directions for finding Ani. "I brought some breakfast for you too," she says, "even though it's almost lunchtime now." She hands my mom a scrap of fabric sewn into a bag. It has a shoelace which cinches the whole thing closed at the top. It contains a mango and some brazil nuts.

"Thank you," my mom says, before tucking her lunch in the canvas bag she's slung across her body.

"Are you sure you're going to be okay?" she asks me again.

"I'll be fine Mom," I yawn. "Marta's going to keep me company."

Satisfied, she shoulders the laundry, and walks out the front door.

Marta pulls aside a screen at the window to watch her leave. I count to fifty slowly in my head, before leaping to my feet.

"Oh!" I yelp.

Marta looks at me over her shoulder, worried. "Are you sure you're fine?" she asks.

"Yeah, I stood up too fast. I'm a little nauseous and my legs are still sore from the run yesterday."

"Your crackers are on the table," she says, gazing out the window again. I reach for them and shove one in my mouth. Before I can swallow, a sharp pain in my stomach brings me to my knees. I spit the crackers on the floor, the bile in my stomach following. Moments later, Marta is rubbing my back, pulling the hair from my face. I continue heaving, even when there's nothing left in my stomach, until the tears are running down my face. The muscles of my neck are pinching from the strain.

The retching calms and I breathe heavily, collapsing near my mess, exhausted.

"How long have you had this rash?" she asks, staring at the back of my neck.

"I have a rash?" I ask her. "It must be a pregnancy thing."

She pinches her eyebrows together. "I haven't known many pregnant women," she says. "So I wouldn't know." Walking out the back door, she returns with a makeshift broom, pouring water on the floor and sweeping away my mess. "I'm sorry," I tell her. "I'm so useless lately."

"No," she says, "it feels good to take care of someone else."

"I know the feeling," I tell her, patting my stomach, with an exaggerated grimace.

She smiles, sweeping the rest of my vomit out the door.

I pull my thighs into my chest, rest my head on my knees.

"When my husband Sergio was shot," I tell her, "I wanted to die too. I didn't want to come here. I didn't care about the colony, or the people here, or their problems. I wanted to expose you to the world and move on." I close my eyes briefly, "let the television producers invade, sensationalizing you all." A screeching outside the window startles me before I murmur. "They'd have a field day here."

Marta has a funny expression on her face. I'm clearly speaking a different language. Shaking my head I continue, "My mom convinced me to continue on this journey. Forced me." I give a sad sort of smile. "It has helped though, helped me to move through some of the pain. Helping other people, a cause greater than myself, all that jazz."

She gives me another funny look.

"I guess you don't know what jazz is either, huh. Or television?"

"I know what a computer is," she says, proudly.

I laugh. "That's. . .something," I tell her. "Marta, I'm so happy for this baby. It prevents me from throwing myself into the wildness of your river, every single morning. My dreams are filled with Sergio, and having this little piece of him growing inside me. It keeps me going."

She looks out the window again. "Lara, *we* really need to be going."

She reaches under one of my arms, and helps me to my feet. I brush myself off, and Marta hands me my fruit and nuts. I toss the mango in the air, and try to juggle it with the nuts.

"I would kill for some Doritos," I tell her.

She cocks her head at me before racing to the back corner of the hut. Pulling a backpack down from one of the horns which protrudes from the wall. "We could definitely use this," she mumbles, and I see the glint of a gun. She slips it into her waistband before continuing to rummage through the bag. I hear the sharp crackle of cellophane.

There's no way. I drop the mango and nuts on the desk near me.

She holds the bag over her head triumphantly. "I completely forgot about these!" she says giggling. My mouth is drooling, and I can barely contain myself. I want to attack the bag, rip it from her grasp. "Wait!" she says, holding a hand up to me. "There's more!" she digs in her bag again, pulling out a glass bottle of warm Diet Coke. I almost lose it.

"I could kiss you," I tell her. "Where in the world did you get these?" She pops the bag open and the cheesy aroma assaults my nostrils. I close my eyes. It smells better than I remember.

"We have to eat these and run though," she warns me, handing over a few chips and the warm Coke. "My Uncle will be meeting us soon."

I am in Dorito ecstasy, and nod happily. I take a swig of the Coke and hand it back to her. Sigh in relief. The power of familiar food rejuvenates me.

"I think I could face anything now," I tell her.

I am normally in good physical condition, but I am no match for Marta. She notices quickly I am unable to run with her. The vines and small rocks trip me at every step, and she doesn't even seem to see them. It takes all I have to keep from breaking one of my ankles. My thighs are burning, and now that Marta's mentioned a rash, I do feel itchy. She reminds me to keep vigilant about our surroundings, warning me snakes can appear out of nowhere. I'm supposed to try and tread quietly so she can listen to the noises around us. The long stick she has given me to hold is awkward in my hand. It snags on the leaves around me, hindering my progress. I'm afraid I may trip and impale myself. She finally takes it from me, the frustration evident on her face. She whispers, "just try not to trip."

"I'm doing the best I can," I tell her crankily.

We get to the river crossing and I carefully step across. The log is mossy and slick, but I manage. The rocks are easy to hop from. I'm immediately struck by the size of the clearing, a makeshift fence surrounding a football size grass field. I want to run to the middle of it and lay down, drink in the sky above us. If only we had a ball, this would be a perfect place to play soccer. A pain in my heart as I remember, my soccer partner is gone.

We step closer and I realize James and Dale are already here, they are speaking with the man, Henrik.

When we join them they stop talking immediately. It's an uncomfortable situation, no one speaking for a few beats.

Henrik stumbles forward and offers me his hand. "I'm Henrik," he says, "we haven't been properly introduced." I shake his hand, and turn to acknowledge the others, but Henrik is already speaking again.

"I've decided to get behind Dale," he says. "As long as you can promise no more of the Pure will be harmed."

Marta steps back from him, looking as if she's been figuratively slapped. "That was Martin, acting alone Henrik. We want peace between the two encampments, not war. You know that."

"James has made good progress with the guards," Dale says, effectively ignoring both Henrik and Marta. "He has most of them on our side, and there's only a small group still loyal to Jacob."

"It's some of the younger men," James replies. "They're not guards. Well, not trained as guards. They won't be armed with anything but knives."

"Thugs mostly," Marta agrees. "I know who they are. His friends."

"Yes," Henrik responds. "We don't think they'll go quietly, so we'll have to be prepared. You'll need to stay close to me or James, Lara."

I nod, I'm not nervous. I remember Jacob from the beach, he didn't seem like much of a threat. "I will," I answer.

"You'll find the path to the Pure encampment much easier," Marta whispers. "It's wooden."

"You're coming with us?" I ask her, surprised.

"Marta goes where she wants to go," Dale says proudly. "She always has."

She brightens at his compliment, beaming.

"I wouldn't miss it," she says.

James races on without us, and when it's clear I can't run any longer, the rest of them begin walking. Marta naturally breaks off with Henrik, and they keep up a steady pace ten yards ahead of Dale and I. I'm uncomfortable being alone with him. He clearly isn't interested in talking to me, fidgeting with a large machete and focused on the wood ahead of us.

We approach a tapir in our path, and Dale puts an arm across my chest to halt my progress. He raises a finger to his lips and we stand completely still, silent. Henrik and Marta are frozen in front of us. The animal is the size of a large pig, and has a half trunk, like a disfigured elephant. He is searching the ground, his trunk erratically poking at cracks and crevices in the jungle floor. He sniffs at the wooden boards for an eternity, until I am screaming at him in my mind to move. After a few minutes more he finally does scuttle away, his steps disappearing into the noises around us. Henrik and Marta begin chatting, their words lost in the light breeze. We all begin our slow progress forward again.

"They're not dangerous usually," Dale suddenly says.

"I wasn't afraid," I tell him. "More annoyed really."

"You don't seem to be afraid of much," he smiles.

I smile to myself. "I think, when you lose everything, it's much easier to face death." I open my arms wide, "I would welcome death."

He thinks I'm joking, and snickers, "So a little tapir is nothing."

"My mom had her nose in a field guide for most of the trip here. She found the information fascinating. I begin rattling off the information she had me memorize. Most of the animals will only attack defensively, and they feed on monkeys. We need to watch for snakes and spiders, and most of the snakes will be sleeping. The bugs are the real killers out here, so bring and wear your repellents. Watch for frogs, especially the blue ones." I wince, assaulted by the brief memory of Sergio's death again. "I can even distinguish between some of the birds," I tell him, pointing up into the trees. "A toucanet."

He looks surprised.

"They're domesticated in the States," I say.

He looks confused by the term.

"They're pets," I emphasize. "People teach them tricks."

"Why?" he asks.

I shrug my shoulders. "You would have to ask them."

He's quiet for a moment. "You must really hate us."

I turn in shock. "What?"

He wipes his forehead with the rag swinging around his neck. "I grew up knowing what was going on outside of here. I've never had the same view of things my brother had. He craved the power, the money, the lifestyle. I would never command the same respect. It allowed me to hide, to pretend I didn't see what was going on. I've always thought it was hopeless to try and fight. Insurmountable. All I could hope to do was keep the ones I love safe, and I didn't always achieve that." There is a pleading, apologetic note to his voice. "I didn't think there was anything I could do."

We are at the edge of the colony now, Henrik and Marta waiting for us. I probably would have told him I hated him this morning, but he seems so pathetic, and our task ahead so impossible, that I can only be reassuring.

"We're going to do this thing, you'll see- and even if we fail, what's the worst that could happen?"

Chapter Twenty-six

People scurry all over the walkways. Women with large baskets of laundry and children tied to their hips. Men carrying machete's and dead animal carcasses. I pass a group of children playing with Lincoln Logs in a covered shelter. Chores still need to be done, children will still play, even if the whole world is changing. Dale is speaking with Marta now, and Henrik is by my side. Most of the people we pass openly gape at me. Some of them every bit as dark as any of the Untouchables. A girl about my age passes close, and her hair is much darker than mine, a dirty blonde which could easily be mistaken for brunette. *She needs highlights and a good eyebrow wax.*

"How do you tell them apart?" I whisper to Henrik.

He turns his head in surprise. "What do you mean?" he asks.

"They look just like the Untouchables to me," I respond. "How do you tell them apart?"

"The requirements," he replies simply.

"You know about hair dye, right? Contacts? I could tattoo my body in stripes, dye my hair green, and change my eye color red. I don't understand the requirements."

He shakes his head, "It's more than that, the Aryan genetic code is superior. Any variation from our requirements is viewed as a curse from God. You are literally considered sub human here. No amount of hair dye can change your genetic code."

"That's not scientifically true though," I tell him. "Our genetics for appearance have nothing to do with intelligence or strength."

"Scientists," he sneers, before releasing a short breath of air. "I realize you believe in that *theory*, but try telling anyone here," he glances around us, "and you may have trouble. Remember, most of them have been told on a regular basis for decades, that they're special because of their appearance. It won't be easy to change their mind."

We've reached the guard huts that circle the Royal tent. I somehow expected it to look different now, but the only change is in the air. Marijuana? I can't be sure, but the smell is definitely distinct.

We walk directly inside the entrance into the main room. Jacob is here, half dressed and blowing smoke through his teeth. A small crowd is with him, young Pure men causing general havoc, some of the porcelain vases we saw yesterday have been broken. The buffet service has been upended, and the spoiled food is covered in insects. There are candy wrappers and soda bottles littering the floor. A cloud of smoke is funneling out the open door.

I feel Marta stiffen behind me, and I hear her gasp. There are about a dozen girls hiding in the shadows, young girls, their ankles bleeding from the bells wrapped around them. The loose wires piercing their skin. A few are huddled in the corner closest to me, scared and scantily dressed. The sight of these girls infuriates me, and before anyone has said a word I am walking to them. I step over a man stretched out on a rug, and he grabs at my ankle. He is clearly drunk, muttering something incoherently vile. I kick him hard in the face with the heel of my boot, aiming for his nose. He cries out, and it awakens the crowd to our presence.

I continue stomping over to the girls when I hear Jacob yell, "What are you doing?"

I swivel on my foot, enraged, "What does it look like I'm doing, *moron*?"

I reach for the nearest girl and she clings to me, her fingers digging into my arm. She's twelve, tops. "Are you okay?" I ask her. "We're going to get you out of here." She is shaking, her fingers freezing cold. I search behind them for a different exit.

"No one is taking them anywhere!" Jacob screams, trying to get up. He is intoxicated and high, tripping over another body on the floor.

"You're a waste of a human being," I tell him. "You could do so much good here, and instead you wallow in your own self importance. It makes me sick." I want to spit on him for good measure, but don't want to give him the satisfaction.

I notice Marta's mouth hanging open, and she steps closer to her uncle, who is still observing the scene. Jacob tries to climb over a body, his bloodshot eyes boring into me. Trying to get to us.

The rest of the men here have begun to wake up, a few of James' guards prodding them with the long walking sticks.

Jacob notices his Uncle Dale for the first time. Calling from the floor as he continues to extricate himself from his unconscious friends. "Do you think you can take the colony from me?" he asks. "You pathetic old man."

Dale is clearly seeing his nephew for the first time. His eyes are wide with astonishment. "Where is your father Jacob? What have you done with his body?"

Jacob laughs, "As if you care, *Uncle*. I'm planning a celebration for him." He swings his arms wildly in a circle as if to indicate the celebration has already begun. He grips the shoulders of the man closest to him on the floor, who proceeds to throw up.

"The only pathetic one here is you, Jacob. You gather up your friends and leave, there are plenty of huts in the colony you can stay in."

Jacob doesn't notice the vomit, except to giggle and push the man away from him. "I'm not going anywhere," Jacob replies, grasping the longneck of a bottle. He attempts to pour the contents down his throat, but the bottle is empty. Angrily tossing it over his shoulder.

The guards begin their prodding with more earnest, forcibly ejecting some of the men out. When one of Jacob's friends is pulled up from the floor by his hair, the rest of the men scatter on their own. The hut fills with more of James' guards, most of them unfamiliar.

"I don't want to have to force you out, but I will," Dale says, making a motion to one of the beefier men that have entered. His uniform straining against his chest. The man

253

grabs Jacob by the arm and physically begins frogmarching him from the hut. Jacob starts swearing in a language I don't recognize, flailing his arms. He grips the edge of the doorway. I am trying my best to shield the girls, but he manages eye contact with me screaming, "It's not over!"

Dale looks at the girls, still shivering from fright. "I should probably mention," Dale says loudly, "if you touch any more of the girls in the colony, I will personally see you killed." Jacob's fingers finally lose their grip and his head disappears from my view.

The silence in the hut is only broken by the movement of the children, their bells jingling. I grip one of the small hands, intending to finally move them, when I notice the guard that leered at me earlier is here. Searching the girl's faces. I flinch when he steps next to me, but he only drops to a knee as one of the youngest girls races into his arms. *"Poppy!"* she screams, her little body wrapped around him.

Trembling with relief, there are tears streaming down his face. Whispering into her hair, he hugs her tightly, and lifts her from the ground easily. He mouths two words to me, *thank you*, before carrying her out the door.

I am staring dumbstruck at the place he has just abandoned when Marta is suddenly at my side, motioning the rest of the girls together. "I recognize you," she says to one. "Amalia right?" The girl bows her head. "Yes." she squeaks behind a long mane of blonde hair. Marta   smiles,   before kneeling before her, and unwrapping the bells from her ankle. "Let's get you back to your homes."

She realizes suddenly they're not appropriately attired for walking through the colony. "Do you know where your clothes are?" she asks. One of the girls grabs her hand and leads her into the back room, the rest of them following.

I turn back to Dale, "do you think it's safe to let Jacob go?"

"Someone will stay with him, watch him. He's not much of a threat," Dale states. "Not without his friends, and none of them would risk the wrath of a new Führer." He laughs lightly.

"You really think it's okay?" I ask. "After everything he's done?"

"That's something for the colony to decide," he says firmly. "After we figure out our new government."

I don't want to disagree with him here, and I'm too tired to explain the concept of prison. The effects of the Tylenol are wearing off, and I just want to nap somewhere. I hear a woman's voice outside, and let out a sigh of relief. Moments later my mom is bustling through the crowd. She marches straight up to James and slaps him across the face, before screaming at Dale.

"How dare you put my daughter in danger!"

Henrik makes a move to restrain her, but she swivels on her heel, crouching low. "You'll regret it if you touch me," she growls. If Dale was surprised by my temper, he is shocked by my mothers. He is stuttering, "I had no idea she was here without permission, I'm sorry." Henrik drops back another foot.

She glares at them both for another second before turning her full attention to me. I think I'm in danger of hearing my full name, so I hurry with my own apologies and ask if she wants to help Marta with the girls Jacob captured.

"Girls?" she asks, standing alert. "Where are they?"

I gesture to the back and her expression softens. "Is that okay with you?" she asks Dale. "I know you wanted to do the official introductions at the Session tonight."

"Someone should go with Marta," he says. "It might be better to do it this way, you'll be seen as something of a saint, returning their children to them. It might make the announcement go down easier."

My mom notices the state of the room, "this is a bit of a mess, isn't it? We'll have our work cut out for us later." I'm on the verge of collapse, when my mom notices and leads me away. I hear Dale whisper to Henrik. "What a pair of women."

I enter the back room in the middle of an argument. The children are not here, but a child is whining. Their Princess, Julianne. I collapse on the nearest bench. My mom speaks quietly to the Shaman Marie. There is another woman here, her inert figure on another bench across from me. She glances at me quickly, her face disfigured and swollen, the Führer's wife, Heidi.

"Who are you?" Julianne asks indignantly. "And shouldn't you be doing something?" She's also a mess. Her face is wrapped in cloth, but it doesn't cover the scars on her cheek. The word *Pure* etched into her face. One of her eyes is closed shut from the bruising. She's wearing a long robe, which covers her arms and legs. It doesn't conceal the trembling in her hand though, or the bruises on her feet.

I kick my feet up on the bench and roll over, my back to her. She starts squealing like a wounded pig, Marie making shushing sounds at her. I pretend it's one of the monkeys outside these walls, and close my eyes to sleep.

Unfortunately my nap doesn't last long. I wake to the aroma of food and a clenching in my stomach. My body has stiffened up again, my shoulders hurting. Julianne has fallen asleep near me, her mouth gaping open. She looks like an overgrown frog. Shaman Marie helps me to an indoor bathroom, when it's clear I'm having trouble using my legs. There is still no plumbing inside, but it's a step up from Marta's communal latrine. Marie leaves me with some water to wash, and some clothes. I notice my rash has spread across my chest and stomach. Little red dots everywhere. I must have been scratching them in my sleep.

A knock on the door alerts me to someone waiting and I pull the clothes on as quickly as I can. Wrapping my hair up into a hairband. It does feel good to be clean again.

Over dinner Dale explains his plan, my mom has been busy while I slept, most of the women already informed about the Führer's departure from this life.

"I don't know what I expected," she says, "but the reaction. . .it was joy." Her face is glowing, "unadulterated joy at the return of their children. They didn't just hate Jacob, that hate I can understand. They hated his father." She shakes her head in disbelief. "It's a miracle, but I think they're ready to hear your message," she says to Dale.

"They have always believed he would kill them, if they didn't do exactly what he said, didn't believe exactly how he believed. He was powerful, but it doesn't mean he was loved."

Henrik appears in the room. "We're ready, " he announces nervously. I understand what this means to him, to watch all of the lies unravel tonight. The lies he has spent the last few years protecting. He leads us out to an open area filled with people. I am unprepared for the sheer size of the crowd around the fire ring. Every person in uniform, drab grays and black shiny buttons. Pale round faces, at least two hundred of them, all with bright blue eyes. The colony is more than twice as large as I assumed.

"Mom," I whisper, "this is nuts. What are we doing here?"

"Shhh," she says, "it'll be fine, you'll see."

"These people are crazy-pants Mom." I match the challenging stare of a girl my own age, until I remember to look away. "I'm really not so sure about this anymore."

She doesn't even bother to shush me again, just throwing me a silencing look. No wonder the Untouchables thought this was an impossible task.

But there is no room for fear here, not now. I whisper an affirmation, and march with my mom to the side of the grouping. We are still outsiders, and will only be participating to be introduced, and to answer questions.

There is no podium, instead Dale prefers to stand on a flattened log, barely increasing his height. I see Untouchables crouched in the distance, a cough to my far right.

The meeting doesn't begin well, men and women all talking at once. Jacob is in the middle of the loudest group, encouraging his friends. "Why did we think this was going to work?" I ask my mom, who only raises a finger to her lips.

Derrik has trusted James and Henrik with two of the stolen weapons. When the mumbling becomes more audible, Henrik leaps to his feet and fires a warning shot in the air. There is suddenly the thundering sound of a hundred birds taking flight behind me, and the immediate and complete silence of two hundred people in front of me.

Dale clears his throat, "Thank you Henrik, although I'm not sure that was entirely necessary, it was effective."

"There are a couple of reasons this Session has been called tonight," he begins. There is another murmuring from the center of the group, and now James leaps to his feet. He spots the instigator Jacob, and marches right up to him. Grabbing an arm, he tugs him away. Another boy leaps up, trailing them down the path and through the trees.

Dale pretends nothing has happened, continuing his speech. "First an announcement, as most of you know the Führer was killed last night." He pauses for a moment but there is no reaction, so he moves on. "Normally the leadership would pass to his son, Jacob." The crowd is quiet, hanging on his next words.

"I do not agree with this," he says firmly. "I do not agree we need a Führer, a King, or a Leiter."

"So you're not trying to take power?" a man yells from the left. One of Jacob's minions, I think. Every eye is on Dale.

"No. You know I have never been one to want power. We will hold a vote, and elect a committee to decide the matters of the colony. A group of eight men, and women, will make the decisions. Four will be Pure. Four will be Untouchables." There is a literal explosion of sound. Pure talking angrily among themselves, the excited voices of the Untouchables. No one is unruly though, and the questions fly. About the weapons, about Pure duty, about being God's chosen people. Dale tries to answer them the best he can, and the crowd begins to calm, sweat dripping from his nose. The night has grown slightly cooler, and I'm grateful for the fires all around us. I am shivering and my mom pulls me closer to her. Dale notices, and does a quick introduction of us, explaining we are the relatives of the late Patron. This is another bomb, which requires over half an hour to diffuse. The answers awkward, from both of us. "Yes," we say, "we hope a new Patron will be chosen, but you have to become self reliant here. You can't depend on the generosity of others." This leads into the truth about the war, and Dale passes out newspapers he's collected over the last two decades.

"When I was no longer allowed to go to Manacapuru, I had Elisabeth send them to me secretly. I had to keep up on the outside world." He turns on a radio, which receives immediate approval. I suddenly remember my phone and pull it from my mom's canvas bag. The battery is still fully charged.

I flip through my videos, but my mom covers my hand. "I don't think they're ready for the concept of television yet," she says.

Most of the newspapers have been dropped, in favor of listening to the radio. Eyes shining, heads upturned.

"Maybe you're right," I tell her, dropping the phone back in her bag. "We might start a riot."

Marta suddenly arrives at our side. She crouches in the darkness behind me, whispering. "Are you ready for sleep?" she asks me. "The rest of this is going to be business, more explanations, organizing the vote. You don't need to stay."

My body is tired, almost too tired to stand and follow her. The itching in my abdomen has started again, and the food I've eaten threatens to come back up. "I don't want to go, if Dale thinks he might need us."

She glances at Dale, who is clearly enjoying his moment. The ability to give everyone in the camp such pleasure, even as he's tearing at the very fabric of their beliefs.

"He'll be fine," she says. "You must be tired."

"I think I'll stay," my mom says. "This is history unfolding for the colony, and it's my history too. I want to be here to help."

"I'll stay then," I tell them, but my words have no conviction. My head is heavy, and the ground is spinning. I don't realize what is happening, until Marta is pulling me to my feet, helping me to the bridge. We reach her hut and I trip over the steps, falling heavily into her hammock. I'm asleep before I can even pull the mosquito net around me.

Chapter Twenty-seven

Someone is calling my name, and it pulls me from sleep. There is a howling nearby, and I struggle to peer through the net that envelops me. The shape of my mom's body is hanging in the hammock above, unmoving. A rustling outside startles me into an upright position. Too quickly, the hammock swings madly and I have to be careful to balance my weight again. I let my legs hang over the side, and pull the net away so I can stand up. I grip one of the roof poles to steady myself, letting my queasiness clear. A small paper drifts to the ground, from my lap.

What is this?

I unfold the paper and recognize Marta's familiar script. Marta's *unrecognizable* script. I move to the desk and reach for my flashlight there. Shining the light directly on the paper, I notice her writing is a little easier to read than the last letter I saw. The lettering larger and less fancy. "Humph," maybe she reserves the embellishments for the official communications. I squint to read.

"Lara, I have something important you need to know. Take the path through the orchard, follow the river. You'll need to cross at the log bridge. Walk straight about a hundred meters until you get to a large outcropping, surrounded by a fence. I'll meet you in the hut there, alone. Hurry."

I recognize the directions, it's the place we met her Uncle Dale before. Why didn't she just wake me herself? We could have gone there together. She was clearly in the hut just now. I press my fingers into the bridge of my nose, pushing against the pain there. I shake my head, she must have had a hard time waking me. I was sleeping soundly. I crumple the note and shove it in my pocket. I use the flashlight to run to the latrine quickly, and rummage in our hanging feed bag to grab a few crackers to eat on the way.

Outside of our hut, Derrik is hunched over on the step. He's snoring slightly, whistling through his teeth. I roll my eyes while I step over his body, careful not to wake him.

The sun is beginning to rise as I pick my way through the jungle. I walk slowly, careful of where I'm stepping, holding the long stick vertically in front of me at arm's length. I'm much more aware of the strange sounds, now that I'm alone. Jumping at every snap of a twig, or bird squawk. Frogs occasionally leap across my path, scaring me with their momentum. The howling monkeys don't help either, their piercing cries coming from the dark depths. A flock of birds seem to alight with my every footstep, and I have the creepy feeling of my every movement being observed. There are heavy clouds above me, and I can almost taste the moisture in the air. I'm so relieved to have made it to the log bridge, until it begins to rain. I drop the stick and crawl across on all fours. By the time I reach the hut, I'm drenched. I fling open the door, and walk inside. The rain stopping almost immediately. Just my luck.

Where could Marta be? She should have beat me here, and the hut is empty as far as I can tell. I walk deeper inside, almost tripping on something. I look at my feet, and a ray of sunshine breaks through the clouds and floods the hut in light. The floor is covered in pillows.

I'm about to pick one of them up, when a creaking noise warns me to someone entering.

Finally, I think, turning toward the door. A man's shape is framed in the blinding sunshine, stepping towards me. My eyes adjust as he enters and the door slams shut behind him, a satisfied smile across his face. My feet involuntarily shuffle for the corner furthest away from the door.

I should have known.

Jacob. He looks pleased with himself. His trap worked.

He stands near the door and I stay in my corner. He has me caught, alone. He watches in satisfaction, crossing his arms, admiring his prize. I remember the story Henrik told me, and I know exactly what his plans for me are. Hot anger spreads through my chest. I am not an animal to be cornered.

I do not belong to this colony, or these people. His power comes from fear, and I refuse to be afraid of him.

"I would leave now, if I were you," I tell him, my voice more confident and strong than I even feel. His face registers surprise at my statement, and he begins to laugh.

"Maybe you're under the misguided notion you're in charge here?" he says. "I would say it's my duty to educate you." He raises an eyebrow, ogling me, licking his lips in pleasure. Would anyone hear my screams? A short hacking cough travels into the hut, and I realize someone is here, standing watch at the door. A light of hope shoots through me before realizing it's got to be one of Jacob's people.

Waiting for the leftovers.

A tiny twinge of fear takes root. I can possibly get through Jacob, but his guard too? I push the fear deeper. One thing at a time. I've never been trained in hand to hand combat, and Jacob has done little else with his life. He's got at least six inches and one-hundred pounds on me. I flip through what self defense I've gleaned from lessons with my mom, and take a defensive position.

"I'm beginning to like you," he says, as he takes in my stance. "I always like a fighter. The Untouchable was too easy, begging for me to stop. The Pure are much more fun." I don't let the comment rattle me. He takes a step forward and reaches for his sheath. I see a flash of silver as he brandishes the knife. Great, the voice in my head sarcastic, a knife.

My sarcasm reminds me of who I really am, the fear disappearing. I wonder if it will emerge later when he touches me. A shiver raccs up my spine. I need to focus. Self defense. Days of being thrown on a mat, a man in a dummy outfit coming toward me. Number one, find a weapon. Okay, a weapon. I scan the room and there is nothing here but pillows. I've never been good on my feet, so this is just something for me to trip over in flight. Concentrate Lara! Jacob takes another step closer, and my mom's voice enters my mind. "Never underestimate your own power, Lara. It's all about distraction."

Okay Mom, distraction. One look into Jacob's eyes and I realize. I have my weapon.

I lean carefully down and pick up a pillow.

"Might as well be comfortable, eh?" he smirks. He is so close now I can smell his breath. Doesn't anyone in this colony care about dental hygiene? There is no time now, I lunge toward him suddenly, pretending to trip and purposely blocking his knife with my pillow. I steady myself on one leg, and bring my knee up in a short swift motion, straight into his crotch. He lets out a yelp of pain as I scream loudly to psyche myself up. He is crouched over, his hands cradling himself. Exactly how I planned. I grab the sides of his head with both my hands, and send my thumbs straight into his eye sockets. It's a disgusting feeling, the eyeballs wet and slimy. He roars and reaches for my arms, and I fight to remain in control, hold on to his head. We struggle for a minute before I can feel his body slump, his grip slacken. I let go of his face and he collapses on the floor. A huddled mass of a man, his eyeball hanging from its socket. He has dropped the knife and I wipe my hands on my pants before reaching for it. I'm surprised the yells haven't brought the guard in. I calm my breathing and sneak over to the door, listening.

I can hear the sound of retching from far away. Taking a chance I peek through the slats, the guard is more than a hundred feet from the hut. I can see the curve of his back as he hunches over, throwing up near a tree. I have to hold my own stomach not to vomit myself. I don't even think. Jacob could awaken at any moment. The door isn't even barricaded, so I slip out and start running.

I take the first path I see, which I hope leads back to the Pure camp. I run as hard as I possibly can until I reach a familiar marker. A piece of cloth tied to a tree. My side begins cramping and I have to slow down, moving into a slow jog. I feel something dripping from my nose and I reach up to wipe it away with my hand. Blood, and I don't even have a tissue. My nose continues to bleed and I press my arm against it, hoping my sleeve will staunch the flow. It's an awkward way to run, but I'm almost to the colony. I push past a group of blonde women carrying water on their heads.

I'm surprised to see an Untouchable among them. She's not talking, but she's walking along beside them.

The outermost hut is finally in front of me and I inhale my first full breath. Bile fills my throat and I try to swallow it back down, choking on it. The terror is behind me, but I start shaking, violently. I have to slow down even more, and the guard's huts are right in front of me. The blood has soaked my arm. I always get nosebleeds when I'm nervous, but this is ridiculous. I know I can make it to the inner circle. My whole body is on fire, and I have to drop my arm. My hands have gone numb. Someone will be at the Royal Hut to help me. I know they will. The numbness spreads to my legs, and I find myself stumbling. The choking becomes worse. I can't breathe. A man steps into my view, Henrik! The name never reaches my lips though, because I trip over the feet I can no longer feel. The twill of a bird, high and sharp, calling to her mate. It's the last thing I hear before collapsing into unconsciousness.

I have the most amazing dream.

Sergio is here in front of me, and I run to him. The pain, the nausea, all the sickness, disappearing immediately. We are bathed in pale light on a beach in Hawaii. The North Shore, *my honeymoon*. I jump into his arms, and start crying. This isn't a memory though, it's a dream and so he comforts me. Holding me tight, his body warm from the late afternoon sun, he whispers, "I love you," in my ear. I touch his chest, his neck, his face, and it all feels so real. I stare into the darkness of his eyes, the yellow reflecting the last rays of the setting sun. I kiss him intently, and I never want to stop kissing this man, feeling his arms around me. Eventually we break apart, and he takes my hand to kiss it, our old familiar gesture. Holding on tight he leads me down the beach. Our feet leaving impressions in the soft sand.

We walk in silence until the sun has set, the first of the stars appearing in the twilight. It's a perfect moment, one of the hundreds we've shared as a married couple. My subconscious mind recognizes the unreality of this though, and the air around me is sometimes filled with words, echoing in my ears. Dengue Fever. . . Hemorrhaging. . . the vomiting. . .easily mistaken for pregnancy. . . fatal. . . little hope. I ignore them all, blissful for the first time since this hell began. "I never want to leave you," I tell him. "I never want to wake up."

"I wish you didn't have too," he breathes, pulling me into another embrace.

"Why?" I ask him. "Why should I wake up?" I stick my lip out like a petulant child. "They don't need me."

He smiles at my pout, watching the waves crash. "You know you're wrong mi amor," he says. "Your journey isn't over. You still have life left to live."

I shake my head, "there's no life for me now. Without you, without a baby. There's nothing left for me to live for."

He stops and pulls me in front of him, resting my chin between his hands. "It probably does feel like that," he says, "but there's so much left for you to do."

I shake myself free and settle into the sand. Trying not to feel hurt. He sits behind me and I lean into him, his arms wrapped around my chest. I dig my toes into the wet, warm dirt, the tide slowly creeping up on us. I can't be mad in this place, this perfect place.

"Lara," he murmurs into my hair, "You need to live for yourself. You need to live to help others. You'll find true joy, and gradually your ache will ease."

He hugs me tighter. "Did you think I would ever leave you?" he asks. "I'll always be waiting for you here."

I close my eyes and enjoy the moment, until I'm drifting back into the darkness.

Chapter Twenty-eight

"Ohhhhh. . .five more minutes please," I grumble as I hear "Ooh la la," hammering into my brain. I reach over to shut it off and my arm is caught on something. A sharp pain in my wrist. I blink my eyes open and they are crusted over, the light barely registering. I wipe them with my free hand, and my phone shuts off. I blink rapidly, waiting for my sight to adjust to the brightness, when I remember. I am somewhere in Brazil. I am in the Amazon jungle.

My mouth is sticky, and I try to wet my lips but there is no saliva. My hair feels unwashed and matted. I inch my body to the side and realize the sheets are stiff with dried sweat. I pat my stomach. I'm naked. I try to wrap the blanket a little tighter around myself, and notice my arms are covered in bruises, a needle inserted into my hand. There are pillows under my head, and I am laying on a soft mattress raised two or three feet in the air. I can't see the ceiling through the mosquito netting, and I try not to panic. I assume I'm in one of the Pure huts. This is much too accommodating to be an Untouchable one. I wonder how long I've been out. It feels like only minutes since I saw Sergio on the beach. I close my eyes again and try to capture the feeling of his arms around me, his lips on mine.

A noise to my right. "Mom?" I attempt to ask, but my throat is dry and it comes out raspy. "Mom!" I call again, trying for volume over technique. It works, because the person rushes to my side.

"Oh my goodness," she says. It's a voice I don't recognize. "You're awake!" she yells, before hurrying off.

Yeah I'm awake, I want to say, but there is no one to appreciate my sarcasm, and so I wait for another person to announce their arrival. Picking at the threads of the mattress underneath me. Thankfully, I don't wait long.

"Lara!" It's Ani this time, pushing back the mosquito netting, trying to get to me. I'm at the right height to stare at her belly, and I reach my hand out to her stomach, before she jerks back. She seems to understand my unspoken question.

"Oh Lara," she says, "I'm so sorry."

I don't risk speaking again, but nod my head to let her know I understand, the words I heard spoken in my dream are true. I am not pregnant. I gesture to my lips for some water.

"Of course!" she says, unhooking one of the gourds hanging from the ceiling and handing it over. I drink thirstily for a long time. I don't think I've ever felt so parched, and the water disappears in minutes. "More?" she asks. I reach out to take the next gourd from her, drinking deeply from that one as well, before feeling fully satisfied.

"How long have I been out?" I ask her softly.

"About two days," she says. "We talked about moving you several times, but it was much too risky. You slipped into Dengue shock and seemed to recover, but your body stayed in a coma. Your mom had to give you blood, and we've been trying to keep you hydrated and comfortable." She gestures around her. This is Marie's quarters, the Shaman. Someone has mostly been with you the whole time."

I notice a hammock hanging nearby.

"My mom?" I ask her.

"She's sleeping now," Ani tells me. "I'll go wake her in a minute, she was always taking the night shifts. She's been charging your dee-vice using the generator. She thought the music might wake you up, but we've had little success."

"It did. Wake me up I mean. The music I woke up too, it's my alarm at home, and the music that lets me know my mom is calling. My subconscious must have recognized it."

The woman next to her blushes. "I like that song," she says.

I give her a wide smile, "by all means, play it again!" I tell her.

They are both dancing wildly when the next song in the shuffle plays. One of my club mixes for the gym. From my bed I try to explain the application of the "booty pop," when my mom walks in, flushed still from sleep.

"I heard all the commotion," she says, rushing to my side.

"I thought I had lost you, my girl." She is physically hurting me with her embrace. My eyes overflow with tears, and I see Ani and her friend creep out of our room. Shutting the door behind them.

"What happened?" I ask her, pushing her arms away.

She settles into a seat on my bed, "you had Dengue Hemorrhagic Fever. Usually it's mild, Marie had never seen a case this bad before, and we're lucky she had a Satellite phone."

"What!?" I exclaim. "They have a phone here?"

"I was as surprised as you are, trust me." She pulls at my hair, trying to untangle some of the larger clumps.

"Apparently only Marie and the Führer knew about it. He purchased it on one of his trips, as a backup in case he ever got seriously sick. She had it hidden here."

"You got a hold of Elisabeth?" I ask her.

"Yes, Dale called her. He's been so helpful since you've been sick." Her cheeks redden slightly. "Matt had just arrived, so they were already preparing to leave. They convinced the doctor to come with them, and arrived by float plane yesterday morning. There's so much to tell you, Lara. I don't want to overwhelm you."

The last moments before unconsciousness flood back and I tell her, "No, Mom, I want know what I missed, what's happened with Jacob? I was trying to run back here, he tried too. . ."

She interrupts me. "It was clear what he was trying to do. We found the note, and Henrik was about to go looking for you. When he found Jacob, it wasn't hard to put it all together, especially after his friend confessed. Marie bandaged him up, but he will never be able to see again. Julianne too, has been forced out of the colony. She was responsible for the note. Seeing that it was delivered, seeing that you were delivered. She is staying with him out there, and Henrik is watching the pair of them."

"Henrik?" I ask, confused.

She gives me a questioning stare. "Henrik volunteered," she says. "I think he feels responsible."

"But it wasn't his fault!" I say emphatically.

"It's more than that. He's not comfortable with the changes we're making, and I think he feels a need to control something." She cocks her head ever so slightly to the side, "Julianne needs him, and so he's there. The graveyard is a good place for them." Her fingers flutter to my blanket now, smoothing the creases.

"Graveyard?" I ask.

"The big empty space," she says, "it's a graveyard. The hut they're staying in used to be for the guard posted there." I accept the gourd she offers me, taking another sip of water. Thinking over what she's said. Matt left shortly before my mom and I were taken by the guards. Eli and Elisabeth would be worried if he didn't return immediately, and we couldn't risk them coming without him. I wonder how Elisabeth is doing. This is, after all, her first home.

"Wait!" I yell. "Marta! Has she met her mother yet?"

My mom laughs at me. "Yes, but that's a story for her to tell you." My mom bows her head, "Lara, I. . ."

I know what she's going to say, and I tell her I already know. I explain my dream, I explain I'm going to be fine. I try and explain my future plans, but she interrupts me.

"I'll be staying in the colony, Lara. I've found out some things about Marion, and even my own father. Nobody really needs me in California, and you know that track home has never felt like anything other than a house. I can't leave until I know more, and I think I can find my answers here." I squeeze her hand. "There's also still so much work to do with the Pure, and they need me. Dale needs me." She blushes, and I realize my mother's found her own kind of comfort.

Tears fill my eyes, because even though I miss my Dad, I'm so happy for her, that my own sorrow buries itself a little deeper.

She wipes her own eyes, "Should I send Marta in? You have a lot to talk about."

I nod my head yes.

The next person to visit me isn't Marta.

Elisabeth bustles into the room with a blonde man I've never seen before. His grin is so familiar I know he must be a relative. The father of someone? I squint my eyes and realize, it's Eli! The surprise must register on my face because his blue eyes are twinkling.

"Quite the trick, right?" he says.

"I can't believe it!" I tell him, "you look like one of the Pure, with a dark tan."

"It fooled the Patrons," Elisabeth says, "and that's what's important."

"What?!" I adjust my position on the bed, turning on to my side. "They came already?" I ask her, incredulous.

"Yes, almost as soon as you left. I was surprised, and glad we had preparations already underway. Without your warning, I'm not sure we would have been ready for them."

They exchange a glance. "He told us about your family, asked us if they had visited." Elisabeth looks down at her hands. "We couldn't lie to them, Manacapuru isn't as large as it seems. There's plenty of people willing to share information for money. A lot of people saw you."

"So they know we're here!" I try and get out of the bed, gripping the sheet to my chest. "We have to go!"

"Hold on Lara!" Elisabeth says, helping me to lay back down. "We told them you had visited, not that you knew anything about Founder."

"Elisabeth was brilliant," Eli says proudly. "She told them you knew about the address labels, you didn't have any letters. She said there was a very nice old man boarding with us for over a year. Your aunt must have been a correspondent of his, he received mail from all over the world." Eli smiles, "*Mister* Founder was quite a popular man," he winks.

"And they accepted that?" I ask them, "they didn't think it was odd we left?"

"They ate it all up," Elisabeth says, "every word. Especially when Matt returned alone and gave us all news of the colony. It was perfect timing, he arrived just as they were planning a trip into Founder. He convinced them not to go, he was careful only to relay news to the Führer, that things were under control here."

"It's too good to be true!" I exclaim. "What about the lack of supplies? The lack of mail?"

"You doubt my ability to persuade my audience?" Matt says, peeking around the corner.

"Matt!" I try and yell, but it comes out as a croak. My throat not quite up to that kind of amplification. He moves in to gently hug me, kissing my hair.

"You smell awful," he says, plugging his nose.

"You're no rose yourself," I tell him.

His gaze flicks to my blanket and bare shoulders, before turning a bright red.

My giggle at his expense, deepens the color.

He coughs loudly, his fist covering his mouth. "Those Patrons were idiots," he says. "They even invited us to visit them! Can you believe it!" He shakes his head, "Idiots."

"So they're really gone?" I ask, reaching for Elisabeth's hand.

Elisabeth squeezes my fingers reassuringly. "For now. They'll choose a new Patron for the colony, who will want to visit. We have time to prepare ourselves though. That's important. Time to prepare the colony and ourselves," she glances at Eli, "to be self sufficient, if that's what everyone wants. It wouldn't be the first time a colony disintegrated."

I think about the other colonies that may still be out there. The ones Matt has told us about, and Elisabeth has discovered from a few direct questions. Ticking the countries off my fingers. Vietnam, Sweden, the United States, and another one south of here that's not as well hidden.

"So where's Marta?" I ask them, looking from face to face. Elisabeth's smile drops.

"She's having a hard time adjusting Lara," she says. "At first she was so happy to see us, but the last few days. . .We thought about giving her more time, more space."

"But that may have been part of the problem," Eli interjects.

"We invited her to come live with us, but she's clearly not comfortable with the idea."

I turn to Matt, "Did you ask her about our plans?"

"Well, Lara, about that. You see, I think I may stay here." He blushes a deep red again. The intention is obvious, someone else has found love here, while I've been lying in this *hospital* bed.

"Well, okay, Matt, that's fine, it changes things a little, but there's no reason she can't join us, right?" I ask him.

"Yeah. Well, actually," he says, "it's Ani, and she's pregnant."

"What?" I scream, "how is it even possible to know? You've only been here for a couple of days."

He looks confused by my question, before the innuendo dawns on him and he begins to laugh. They are all laughing so hard it's several minutes before any of them speak.

"Lara, it's not mine!" he says.

He sobers up, and I realize. Jacob. I had forgotten.

"Oh!" I exclaim. "Oh yeah. I guess I probably knew that." I don't want him to explain, and so I awkwardly ask him another question. "So what's the plan for me?"

"I think it's time you saw Marta," Elisabeth says, gesturing everyone out.

Marta enters my room with a solemn expression on her face. Her brown hair has pulled itself from its usual neat braid, and she hasn't bothered to fix it. The leather knapsack missing from her shoulder. She looks tired, and the light I saw in her last time we spoke has gone out.

"Marta, what's wrong?" I ask her.

"I don't want to tell you," she says. "My problem is so stupid, compared to the fact you almost died."

I pat the bed space next to me and she sits. Her shoulders hunched, she pulls her knees into herself, resting her chin on them.

"It can't be that stupid," I tell her. "Is it Henrik?"

She turns to me in shock. "Is it obvious?" she asks, sounding angry. "Don't I have any secrets?" The anger quickly dissolves into a puddle of tears. Her face crumpled and blotchy.

"The thing is," she continues, hiccuping, "I don't know if I even love him. Not for certain, and he won't leave Julianne's side." She bows her head dejectedly, "he's always had a soft spot for weak things like me."

"Marta!" my voice has finally returned full force. She peers at me, wide eyed. "You don't really believe you're weak. Do you?"

She shrugs halfheartedly. "I can't figure out what I'm supposed to do. The children's school is going to integrate, so they don't need my tutoring. Elisabeth is going to handle the letters now, the committee deciding what supplies the colony needs. I feel so useless, and . . .weak."

I adjust myself into a sitting position next to her and pull her into a half hug. I get a whiff of my own stench, and it isn't pretty.

"You don't have to stay here," I tell her.

"I feel like I do," Marta says. "This is my home, and Henrik is here. . ." She drifts off.

"Think of your choices," I say. "Some choices are always going to be harder than others. Henrik is making his own choices. He is choosing Julianne. He is choosing this life- this life without you." I can tell my words are hurting her, but I can't stop, her back tightening against my hug. "You can either accept it. Accept the pain and the hurt, and live with it here. Or you can be brave and open your heart to new pain, a new life. His choices don't have to be yours. You do not have to choose this life."

I squeeze her shoulders. "I have another choice for you."

Marta

➤→

Chapter Twenty-nine

I have seen planes in the sky, their distinct sound was always a signal to run for shelter. You never knew if it was the enemy attacking our colony, if we were discovered. It's silly now to think of it, Lara assuring me they were probably tourists or photographers. I am gripping the seat handles, my knuckles turning white. I try not to move while I watch the jungle and the colony, disappear beneath us. The rushing river becomes a brown line dividing the green of the forest below. We are all quiet, concentrating on the low hum of the plane's engine, sweeping us away. Away from everything that has happened. Martin is in the seat across from me, his eyes closed, his head tilted back against the pillowed backing. He is the only one in the colony who requested to go, Eli agreeing to find him work at the resort. There were others who expressed a vague interest in leaving, but in the end it was only Martin who felt comfortable climbing onboard this aircraft.

Eli promised to bring a larger boat back for the others, if they still want to go. Most of the Untouchables still harbor fears of the outside world, the terror too deeply ingrained. The Pure fear they won't find acceptance in the world they've been told about, that they would be the ones ostracized.

It has been a hard concept for them to accept.

We are leaving the colony in good hands. Sylvia and Dale are more than capable of the changes that still need to be done. Ani and Matt bringing new life into the colony. It helps that the control of information, supplies, and weaponry, still lie within the Untouchable minority. There is Pure resistance, but it's easier to swallow a bitter pill when there's so much sweet. The colony enjoying the new radios, the color television, and what Lara calls the "junk food" Eli and Elisabeth have supplied them with.

Lara has told me about some of the new things I'll experience, excited for me I suppose. She started crying when she talked about the different foods, Sylvia pulling her away from me. She had already spoken to Sergio's mother by this time, on what they call a "phone." She said it was cleansing in a way, to have someone cry with her that loved him as much as she did. Feeling the pain again and hearing it multiply.

The arrangements for Sergio's body were taken care of, he is being shipped to Mexico. Lara won't be traveling with him, she said Sergio was still with her, regardless of where his body went. I thought she might be getting sick again, making strange statements. When I tried to feel her forehead, she pushed me away laughing. Called me a "dork." She sits next to me now, still pale from her sickness, her cheeks spotted from the rash. We will have to take care of each other, since we are facing this new life alone.

My foot taps nervously against the floorboard, and she turns to me, reaching for my hand.

"We'll only be in Brazil for a little while longer," she says. "We need to get you a passport and extend my Visa."

I nod my head at her, Sylvia informed me of all the government documentation I would have to fill out. She told me of Lara's plans, to flush out the other colonies, plan other rebellions. I had every intention of joining her.

"Are you ready for this?" she asks me.

I feel the pressure of her fingertips on my hand, reassuring.

"Bring it," I respond. "Bring it on."

Acknowledgements

Indie Publishing.

Those words inspire vehement arguments on both sides of authorship. All I know for sure, is writing a book, and publishing it on any platform, requires a great deal of help. For that I'd like to thank some of the people who have put up with me over the course of writing this novel.

A big thank you to my biological sisters. They were my first readers and my sounding boards. Most especially my little sister Kimberly, who said one of the greatest things that carried me through the whole process. "I loved your book, until I really had to think about it." It changed my focus from writing, to reading, and for that I will always be grateful.

To my Twilight sisters, for their encouragement, their support, and their GNO's. Alisa, Elaine, Elisabeth, and most especially Julianne. The greatest friends a girl could ever have.

To two of my earliest beta readers, who stumbled through the grammatical mistakes and run-on sentences, to point out exactly what I could not see. Chris and Colette, I thank you.

And finally I'd like to thank my husband, who managed to survive the hell, and would love to tell you about it. I'll always be your number one fan.

Heritage, book two in the Patron Identity Series,
will be released November 2011.
Please see my website at www.lmlong.com for more
information.

Made in the USA
Charleston, SC
29 June 2011